OWL STRETCHING

OWL STRETCHING

K A Laity

IMMANION PRESS
Stafford England

Owl Stretching
By K. A. Laity
© 2012

This is a work of fiction. All the characters and events portrayed in this book are fictitious, and any resemblance to real people, or events, is purely coincidental.

Editor: Sharon Sant
Cover Art/Design by Ruby
Interior Layout/Design by Storm Constantine

Set in Palatino Linotype

IP0110

ISBN 978-1-907737-44-2

An Immanion Press Edition
8 Rowley Grove
Stafford ST17 9BJ
UK

http://www.immanion-press.com
info@immanion-press.com

Dedication

For Saint Kurt the Vonnegut, with gratitude

Acknowledgements

First and foremost thanks must go to Mildred L. Perkins, first reader and cheerleader, who was there every step of the way, refusing to let me give up or give in, even when none of it made sense; I couldn't have done it without you and that's no joke. It was a time of highs and lows—glad you could ride it out. Gracious thanks go to Mildred, Birdie Nordstrom and Susan Simko for the much-needed brain surgery they performed upon me in North Carolina with all the proper anesthetics (and thanks to Ron for the rubber room). Thanks to Storm, Sharon, Ruby and everyone at Immanion for the long and sometimes painful delivery of this child. Thanks are due also to Paul Hamilton who also allowed me to use snippets of Reticents' lyrics, even some from the cutting room floor. Thanks to Todd Mason for listening late at night. Gracious thanks to Marjorie Hope Gross, who met me at the crossroads to say, "Not that way, this," and helped me find the path again. Thanks are also offered to Crispinus, AKA Daniel Curley, who gave me an all important week in the quiet of my dream house, which just happens to belong to him, his long suffering uxor Krista and their daughter Kaitlin, because that's where I was finally able to claw my way to the end of the first draft of this story. Thanks to Gene Kannenberg Jr. for the good years (there were many) and encouragement along the way. Thanks to Stephanie Johnson, Jezebel extraordinaire and inspiration always. Thanks to my brother Robert for gourmet meals and movies of varying qualities. I raise a glass to the dead who inspire me, from Kurt Vonnegut, Jr. whose death sparked the genesis of this story, to the vastly underrated genius that was Georgette Heyer, (thank you, Stephen Fry for making me aware of her), to the sublime Christopher Marlowe, who mutters in my ears, to the inimitable Dorothy Parker, whose name I stole for Ro, and to the timeless brilliance of William Blake, ever may he shine. I am always aware of standing on the ankles of giants, not worthy yet of their shoulders. To my own guides in the spirit realms, I am ever in your debt, which I will continue to pay as best I know how. Last but far from least, thanks to my Lochee, who gives me hope and a home.

1

"There is nothing of which every person is so afraid as getting to know how enormously much she is capable of doing and becoming."
— *Søren Kierkegaard*

It was in the fourteenth year of the war that Simon woke up. It was pure luck that I was there. Not that he was asleep for the whole war. He had only been asleep for about ten years. Asleep, that childish euphemism; of course, what I meant was that he had been in a coma. Ten years in a coma—weak as a puppy, a decade out of date, a human time capsule—it was not a life you'd wish on someone lightly. Unless, I suppose, you really hated them. You'd have to hate them a lot. Ten years of visiting made that clear for me. People trimming your nails and your hair, shaving your face regularly; it was a sweet deal if you wanted six weeks off work, but ten years—well, a coma is no vacation.

You might be wondering why I kept visiting Simon over ten years, so let me tell you right away we were not in love. We were just friends. Besides, he's gay and not interested in me at all. We went to high school together, but that's no excuse either. I hate most of the people I went to high school with and I'm sure the feeling is mutual. My high school was all about making better bureaucrats. To be fair, most high schools across this great land have taken up that particular gauntlet and run with it. There's a distinct advantage these days to preparing people for an inevitable life of endless paper pushing and tedious life chained to a cubicle. Remember when that used to be just an expression?

Not me, though—I dreamed of going to Oxford. Not sure what I was going to do there, but I yearned for its medieval spires and spacious greenery in a way that my grey suburban sprawl never dreamed of invoking in my imagination. Well, imagination was one of those things both high school and the endless streets of identical houses of my home intended to drum out my head, but I was somehow stubbornly dreamy. There was that dangerous addiction to books—still a secret vice of mine, but only indulged in now when I am safely out of any disparaging view. I don't want to look like a freak, although it's hard not to do so most of the time. As the world marches east, I trip west. I think it's congenital somehow. Except no one else in my family suffers from it. Three sisters, the usual two parents (although I suppose these days two has become unusual, most kids having at least three or four) but none of them show signs of this recessive gene. My father still offers to feed me lead paint in the hopes that it will cure me, but I know he couldn't find any even if he wanted to do so. Bureaucracy took care of that, bless their pointy little heads.

Not that I could ever go to Oxford; at the time, I was just not good enough or wealthy enough, and since the Purges, of course, there is no Oxford. There are still the buildings, I suppose, but I've heard the verdant meadows and the botanic garden did not survive. Pity. It rather limits the chances to use unnecessarily grandiose terms like "verdant" in conversation. I have a postcard of Christ Church that a friend got me when she went to Oxford. She was a big Harry Potter fan at the time and I guess there was some kind of connection, maybe Dame Rowling lives there or maybe something with the films, but she went to that venerable institution of learning to take pictures of rooms that were part of a made up story about learning. Irony, eh? The world's just chock full of it.

Like Simon waking up while I was at the hospital; it was just dumb luck I suppose, but I like to think there's a little irony lurking in there somewhere. I didn't come every day; that would be crazy. Of course, there were those who thought my coming to visit a comatose individual for ten years was a bit crazy anyway. "He's been asleep how long?" I recall one itinerant lover asking with derision, "Pull the plug already!" No, that particular relationship didn't work out all that well or for very long. One of many—they did all have more or less the same response, though. What was his name? Bill? Tom? Does it matter? The many people who pass through our lives are probably no more important in the long run than the many meals we have eaten, processed and excreted. It's the remarkable ones that remain of both meals and people, as it should be, I suppose. Although the remarkably bad remain too; I'll not forget the mussels that made me vomit my guts out for hours—seafood! How long ago was that?—or the lover who asked, when told the source of my teddy bear's name, who Eugene O'Neill was. Amazing what a good projectile a book can be when thrown across the room. A vid com just doesn't have the same impact.

The few people I still spoke with over the whole of the ten year span had similarly discouraging opinions. "Give it up," my oldest sister always said, snapping closed her voluminous bag and heading off on whatever press junket she was scheduled to take, "You can't hang on forever." She knew. Her first and second husbands had been killed in the war and she never looked back. There was a little ritual. She'd invite us all over for a barbecue, firing up the gas-hog grill with the really pure stuff, throw a couple of soy burgers on, drop his photo in the fire as she shouted, "To a better world!", while motioning that we all drink up in honour of the sad man we had never known. A shot of vodka, a puff of smoke and then it was on to the burgers. "Tastes like the real thing," my mom always assured her, as she's one of those old enough to still remember with clarity. At least I assume she was talking about the meat.

My oldest sister is a journalist, which means she gets treated to lots of fancy places, fed the finest food, and for that pays the price of putting her name at the head of "reports" on the tube and the net, churned out by press agents who provide the other half of her *pas de deux*. You've seen her face, not that it matters. The news is a blur, a droning voice in our ears that tells us all is well and moving forward and this is the best of all possible worlds. Those of us who read still find that funny, but the average American, (at least in the Northern part of the continent), thinks of Voltaire as a popular singer whose operas of love and longing fill the ether between commercials. And since the arrival of the Wags five years ago, we all have more reason to believe that this is the best of all possible worlds.

Not that I was really thinking about that the day Simon woke up, although I must admit I was firmly anti-Wag five years ago, which my second oldest sister considered clear evidence of my retrograde constitution. Not that she said that, mind you. I think it was more along the lines of, "What is your terminal damage? Get with the 21!" the latter having become the most tiresome phrase in favour of the allegedly forward-looking mindset that brought us ideas like the Purges, Chronomax and the privilege of paying for water. Just because I read books does not mean I'm some kind of social conservative. It does, however, mean that I recognise when history is repeating itself; one Inquisition, after all, is very like the next one. The other lesson, one the older Voltaire would appreciate, is that nobody gives a hairy rat's ass if you do realise that history is repeating itself. People always want to believe that they are totally different from anyone who has ever lived, a notion most adherents of Hinduism would find risible, if only there weren't so few of them left. I have heard there are more Buddhists on average left behind than any other major religion, but the Purges pretty much did it for Christianity and the other Abrahamic religions, other than the odd pocket of Catholics here and there who stubbornly refuse to change and continue their weekly rituals with dogged determination. Admirable, or laughable? I cannot be much of a judge, having been an agnostic before the Purges and an agnostic after, too. There may be a god, but she's got a convoluted way of expressing divinity that may be too complex for a puny human mind, (the Wags tend to make me believe this), or else there is no god, (which is what the Wags tended to make the most devout believe).

I keep detouring from the moment of Simon waking, although it is the beginning of this story. There is a reason for my doing that, but I really should get to that day. It was a day of unremarkable things otherwise. The sky was overcast, tints of purple and red at midday, lightening to a uniform grey by afternoon, my usual visiting time. It always provided an excuse to get out of work, not that anyone missed me much. It was more the idea that I was getting away with something. I was only missing meetings, after all. Nothing ever got accomplished at these meetings that could not have been handled in a memo or an email. But I treasured the glances (not even glares) of irritation that I received from my co-workers as they headed off to the Friday afternoon meetings and I had my shackle removed so I could head off to the hospital.

Did I mention being a bureaucrat?

Somehow despite all my ironic posturing and deep reading I ended up exactly where my education wanted me to be. I work in the governor's office, that fine representative of this great state, where paperwork has been raised to an art form seldom glimpsed since the empire of Byzantium. (Did they use paper? Papyrus? I'll have to look that up.) Since the Purges we have tripled in size. Governors come and go, (well, this one has reached two terms so far), but the bureaucracy stays. Like a fat tick, it makes sure that its every move feeds that bottomless appetite for more. Electronic records must be kept in printed paper form and a more stable media, (my suggestion of stone was actually seriously considered although I submitted it as a joke—note the danger of jokes in the hands of the less than humorous). Each month all records must be uploaded to the state satellite for safety. Or at least its illusion; the Wags have called into question the safety of outer space, but the mechanical record-keeping drones seem safe enough, if superfluous. It's surprising with all this built-in redundancy that anything could ever get lost, but it does, regularly like clockwork. What a quaint old phrase! I delight in these antiquated terms that capture a bygone era, like those Franklin Mint commemorative plates that capture pop songs in imitation porcelain. What is it made of? Perhaps soy—everything else is.

I'm no ordinary 'crat either; I have a range of about five thousand meters on my shackle, which beats the hell out of the third floor folk and lower, who can barely move to the other end of the building. I can run across the street and buy coffee with impunity—well, whenever I have sufficient dinero. It takes a lot of Sacagaweas of late, so I don't often enough get some for myself, but sometimes the gov or his sycos want some and I get to go because of that free rein. Yeah, it should be the job of some lower ranking official, but the lower your rank, the shorter your range. I try not to resent the years of education spent to fetch and carry beverages, but instead assure myself that I do it with a certain panache that a less sheep-skinned colleague would not be able to muster.

The lies we tell ourselves are what make life bearable.

A great man once wrote, "Remember, happiness is egg-shaped." For a long time, I thought he was just loopy, but the words settled into the crevices of my brain and percolated for a while and finally the toast popped, so to speak. He was right. Happiness is round and fragile and things have a way of sliding off its smooth surface. It seems perfect when you've got it in your hand, but then you squeeze it a little too tight and it shatters. All at once it can never be made whole again, and what a mess has been left behind. Until you get another chicken, I suppose. Or is it ducks? I can never remember. It's all soy now anyway, but the idea of eggs is still something a five year old child can understand. Well, maybe ten year old; how long did I say the war has been going on—fourteen years?

It's not the point anyway, I was talking about happiness.

The only other patient in the ward at that moment was watching "Dexter and Sinister" on the Argent node, although the monitor had a sickly green hue that made the prospect of gazing at it too long a rather daunting prospect, unless you were already catatonic. Most of the patients here fit that description nicely. I'm not sure what was wrong with the woman in the next bed—she had been there even longer than Simon. No one came to visit her. Sometimes, just to amuse myself—or, I suppose, Simon if he were ever actually conscious as he lay there—I would talk to her as well. She was gaunt and tiny, emaciated by the illness as much as by her metabolism, but somehow that put into my mind the idea that she had been some kind of self-starving socialite, so I asked her endless questions about celebrities she might know and swanky parties she had gone to, assuming of course that she had tasted things like real caviar and avocados. I had seen a Christie's catalogue in the gov's office once with such delicacies listed, so I knew that they still existed. Well, I suppose they could be good forgeries, but you know, even that would be something.

In fact, at that very moment I had just been looking up from my book, having drifted back to its pages after Countessa Blowtung (that was the name with which I had christened the other veg) had failed to offer a suitable response to my queries on the best side of Nantucket for yachting, when Simon spoke. His voice was so soft, so tentative, that I didn't really believe it at all. I had heard it in my head so many times, I figured this was just one more of those times.

"Ro," was what he said.

It was the last thing he said before beginning the coma, too, as it happens. There I go again, circumlocutions—they come naturally to us 'crats. Never say anything directly when you can circle, sidestep, skip over or under it. But I suppose now is as good a time as any to mention that's my name. Well, it's what I go by. My whole name is a bit of a pretentious mouthful: Rothschild Amelia Aviva Parker. So Ro will do. It's what my friends call me—both of them.

So Simon said, "Ro," and I continued idly staring at the screen by the Countessa, leisurely formulating another ridiculous question to amuse the circuitous folds of my brain, when slowly the knowledge sank into my consciousness that it was not my imagination this time, that Simon really had spoken my name. It felt like a fuzzy slo-mo sequence from a vid, but I know it was more like I whipped my head around instantly, because my neck was stiff for some time afterward. I'm sure my mouth hung open indecorously, gaping and awkward, rather than the joyful moment of surprise and glowing hope that usually greets miraculous recoveries in films. I probably even drooled a bit. Who knows?

It's kind of like the arrival of the Wags. You talk to people now and they all seem to recall how calm they were, even though they realised at once that it would change their lives forever. Being the less sentimental type, I recall the screaming, the crying, people running around in the streets weeping, whooping and grabbing small children. There were at least half a dozen murder-suicides in my building alone, so I can figure a likely percentage across the city, let alone across the continent and world. I'm no math major but I can extrapolate with the best of them. The Wags seemed to be enjoying the spectacle as far as anyone could tell—not that anyone much was coolly observing them in the first few days. There was an unreality to it all that I suppose many disasters have in this era of constant media attention. We've all seen the world explode repeatedly— it fails to faze us anymore. At first, I thought it was all a hoax. I had the vid screen on but, as usual, I wasn't watching it, so it took a while to actually realise what I was hearing and that it was not another dramatic series but real events unfolding in the big city. I actually laughed when I saw my first Wag on the monitor.

Can't they do better than that, I recall thinking. It was just like this song my dad had on his phone. He is still really proud of that phone, one of the first beta iPhones. He's into that retro look, with retro music to go with it—all the greatest hits of the twentieth-century, just like his dad played for him. One I remember singing along to as a child, a naïve song about aliens, but oddly enough it was right, because they Wags have one eye and a sort of horn like projection that comes out of what seems to be their heads. Although they're not actually purple—almost a sort of indigo, but that would have too many syllables for the chorus.

And of course, they are indeed people eaters.

I suppose that's what caused most of the chaos. It's one thing to turn people's romantic notions of the peopled universe—wise, friendly aliens who heal your boo-boos and bring families together—completely inside out. It's quite another to eat their auntie. Hence, the running around on bent legs, shrieking and sobbing—not to mention mass suicides, murders and catatonic shock. No one else was thinking of a mid-twentieth century novelty song. They might have been thinking of the words of Saint Warren, but I don't think lawyers, guns or money would ever have had any effect on the Wags. Nope, just a steady supply of warm flesh. But that's the thing about us humans, we can adapt to almost anything. The bird flu carried off the birds and we adapted. We were overrun by insects and we adapted. We killed most of the animals on the planet with the pesticides, but we adapted. The Wags wanted to eat people, so we adapted. Suddenly the war took on new meaning—if we captured people, they could be fed to the Wags instead of our friends and neighbours. It was a kind of plan anyway.

Imagine trying to explain that all to someone who had fallen asleep (there I go again) during a pointless war and woke up to find a very different world and an even more desperate war. But I didn't have to think about that at first.

"Ro," Simon repeated, trying in vain to moisten his dry lips. I grabbed for the nurse's buzzer with one hand and the ever-ready sponge with the other. While I jammed the red button down with my left hand, I squeezed a little water into his mouth with my right. He didn't have to know it was part of his sponge bath, damn it. He needed water. Of course I nearly choked him at first, adding to my sense of guilt, but I got my arm behind his head and raised it and he was done choking fairly quickly. "What happened, Ro?" Simon gasped when he had finished coughing and sputtering and the slapping of the afternoon nurse's footsteps had grown audible. Myron's shift I thought automatically; their schedule had become second nature to me. "What happened?" Simon repeated as I dropped the sponge in its basin.

Would it be wrong to say I felt a surge of relief at his words, a surge that had nothing to do with my very best friend being awake again, nothing to do with ten long years of silence being broken, nothing to do even with the miraculous—we can still call it that in this age of Wags—recovery when all hope had been long lost? But a surge I did feel and I tried not to take immediate advantage of it, restrained myself from following up on his declaration of innocence, perhaps even then cannily assessing that it might only be temporary, this amnesia, that in some short time he might remember exactly what had happened, that he might not only recall but might in fact be quite unhappy about what had happened.

Unhappy—he might be livid. He might be furious. Oh, let's test my vocabulary: angry, incensed, outraged, infuriated, irate, mad. Oh I know, you won't even believe that it's my vocabulary. Any decent word processor has a thesaurus function, not that I've seen any evidence of anyone using one of late. Even my sister the journalist can't be bothered to use her perfectly good, top of the line box to insert a few individual word choices within the spewage she subsumes under her name. A well-turned-out sentence is still an object of wonder to me. Consider this: "tee hee, quod she, and clapt the window to." Well, you kind of have to know the joke that sets it up, but trust me, it's both funny and completely and economically precise. That extra syllable in the end is like eating the last lick of cold soybet off a spoon. Sweet and tasty.

But I digress, yet again. All right, yes, it was all my fault. Simon was in a coma and I was to blame and I was terrified that he had known it the whole ten years, had nursed his anger for the entire decade and would explode with fury like an incendiary bomb upon waking and finally coming to his senses. I was so guilty that I visited him as often as I could the whole time, living in despair of that day—or terror of its never arriving. How messed up is that? I would sit there with the book on my lap and contemplate for hours on end which could be worse—living the rest of my life in the suspended animation of anticipation or the horror of awakening and losing my best friend when his inevitable vitriolic attack at last came.

Instead, I received a stay of execution. After his initial query, we were all too busy with the fact of his awakening to delve too deep into the past or really even answer his question. There were all the vital requirements—pulse, blood pressure, brain scan, blood tests—none of which told the nurses and the doctors anything useful. There was nothing. Nothing gave a clue as to why he had woken up at that precise time, why not an hour later, a year earlier. Nothing. I liked to think it was the mention of yachting or Nantucket—surely Simon would have loved the classical era of New England life;I could see him in a jaunty sailor outfit on the Cape—but there was no indication that any one particular thing cause him to jar back into consciousness just then.

If I were a believing person, I'd think it was the force of my guilty sins. Fortunately, I am not, although I have to admit guilt did find a harbour in my heart, which I always imagined thumping away noisily when I recalled my culpability, because of some story I could barely recall, which I read as a child and which frightened me so badly that I could not stand living in any flat that did not have a carpeted floor because I could not bear to see bare floorboards without imagining that I would be hearing the hideous thump-thump of the buried heart of that story. Even now, it gives me the shivers. I will recall the author's name by and by, but he frightened me so much that I bury his name as deeply as that betraying organ—a metaphor that doesn't work because, of course, the heart was only shallowly dug otherwise it would not be audible. Whatever, as our president says.

"Open your mouth and shut your eyes and see what

Providence will bring you"—another famous quote, though I do not know from whom, but I see in my mind the picture of a young girl with trusting eyes and dark hair. That is the problem, you see. Thousands of stories all jumbled in my brain and no way to sort them out. If I didn't have a head like a sieve, things would be different, but there you are. Providence—or what you will—this time brought me a reprieve. Simon did not recall the events preceding his attack, and he seemed—other than absolutely weak as a baby—completely cured, and his only lingering after effects were some stiffness in extremities, poor muscle tone and a gap in his memory about ten years wide. Make that ten years and at least a few hours.

Within days he was going to be released from the hospital to return to our flat. In the intervening days, he went through a lot of physical therapy and I went through a lot of explaining. Not of the most pertinent thing, mind you, but all the other news.

News—hello, glad you're back, while you were out: the war continues, the planet was invaded, life as we know it has changed, hope you like soy, hope you don't miss your Auntie Vera too much, not to mention Uncle Chuck and cousin Dave.

My first rule was don't let him watch the vids. That would require far too much explanation. That of course did not work well. I could keep him from things while in the hospital because they only had one or two nodes that came in unscrambled and they tended to be the non-stop weepies, because who but the comatose could stomach them and someone had to be paying the bills for all that expensive equipment. I wouldn't have been surprised to see nothing but adverts for incontinence pads, sponges and rehydrating drinks of various ilks during the programs, I guess in hopes that the captive audience and their visitors would be swayed by mere repetition if nothing else. If it weren't for the public outcry, the wards would have been emptied to feed the Wags, but thanks to the need to feed propaganda, people were shamed into forgetting that food group. Once we got back to the flat, though, there was going to be regular vid access, so I wouldn't have been able to prevent anything anyway. So I had to explain the Wags a bit even before we left the ward.

That was awkward. And difficult—how do you explain something that has become such an integral part of our days but was unknown before? Well, unknown—that's too strong, right? The idea of alien life had been part of popular imagination for centuries. Really, I looked it up. Even Milton, the guy who created Satan, imagined interplanetary travel. Jules Verne, the guy who invented men on the moon—an absurd idea we all know in the last hundred years, but give him a break, it was the dark ages—he imagined meetings between our planet and travellers. Always guys—men have always had time on their hands for these kinds of imaginings. Women joined them once labour-saving devices were invented. Then we all wasted our time.

The reality, as I tried to explain to Simon, was much simpler and far weirder.

"Aliens," he said with a sense of wonder when I first began to explain. He was lifting tiny little hand weights in the physical therapy room. It was difficult for him to lift a single pound weight at first.

"They are not our friends, not that kind of aliens," I scolded. "They did not come to offer us wisdom, they did not come to save us from ourselves or even to save our planet. There was no 'klaatu barada nikto,'" I added, lapsing into an inadvertent cough. "They're just here to chow down."

"Abysmal," Simon said, his mind only half attentive, sweat beading on his brow as he struggled with the little barbells. "But, they worked it out?"

"Well, if by 'worked it out' you mean yeah, we fed them people, yeah, they (meaning the great bureaucrats of our land, long may they rejoice) worked it out." Best to be blunt, I figured. Perhaps it was a mistake.

"Jesus wept. You don't mean that?" He dropped the weight which rolled across the unsettlingly wooden floor until I jumped up to retrieve it.

"Well, at first it was just prisoners." There, that would be a way to lead up to several changes. "At first it was just death row inmates, then it got to be rapists and child murderers, and then they had to have a bit of a think."

How to convey the shock of that first day to someone who slept through it all? Here, our world changed. Not just ours, everybody's. Well, anybody who had a concept of the world, the universe, the great Milky Way and further beyond. It all changed and it changed with a horrible sight that was, naturally, broadcast across the globe in seconds. Once it's on the net, it's indelible—sort of. It's also spoofed, altered, ramped up, edited and repeated. I think that's the worst part: repeated. There's no replacing the feeling of that first sight, but it is diluted inevitably by way of the constant repetitions. Nothing stands up to repetition. It becomes banal, or it becomes a part of your skin, but it's never the first time again.

"Why are they called Wags?" Simon's mind had moved in a different direction. The horror of that first time was unknown to him, although soon we would remedy that.

"It's an approximation," I finally said, tearing myself away from my really deep thoughts. "They're really something like 'Wagacharrathaplegplegwhaharrrrrr' but—"

"Wags is easier."

"Yeah."

"So they just, what? Demanded we sacrifice virgins to fill their bellies?"

"You're such a romantic. I don't recall sexual status ever being an issue with them. And that wasn't first. First was the strafing."

"Strafing?"

"Like with lasers. They were just going around the planet shooting randomly. The moon, too. On a clear night, you can see it."

"There are clear nights now?"

"Sometimes. There's actually getting to be less pollution in the atmo because a lot of the processing plants have been closed due to the personnel shortage."

"Because people are being eaten?"

"No, because of the war. Although," I paused to think, "I suppose you could say it's the same thing."

"Why's that?" Simon was rubbing his face now, I think he was starting to hit massive information overload. Maybe I should stop. A writer—I do remember his name, Tamburlaine—once declared, "Accursed be he that first invented war." He didn't know the half of it. Explaining this war was going to be just about as difficult.

"Well, you remember why we went to war at first?"

"No," Simon said quite emphatically, dropping the weights completely. "You know me, I never cared about politics. It was all so depressing and stupid. I don't think anybody knew what they were talking about at all. And I was never going to have to serve, so I didn't try to think about it much at all."

"Well, that's one thing that's changed." His look was attentive then. "They don't let you out of the armed forces for *anything* anymore. It's the war or the Wags."

"Jesus wept. So I could be called up after all?"

"Well, I think coma patients are pretty far down on the list."

"I can hope." He didn't seem to want to know any more just then, so I let it go. It was just as well. I didn't want to have to really explain the war as it was now. A distinctly mediocre politician once said he would be glad to be judged by history. History, however, is a harsh judge. She has a tendency to narrow her eyes at you and see right into your soul—or at least the entirely self-serving intentions that crouch behind its shadow. Tamburlaine was right, but he could not have had any conception of just how bad things would get when war was no longer about ideals or real estate or macho posturing, but about feeding a real beast whose belly was never quite full enough for the battles to even pause for breath. I know, I'm mixing metaphors like a strong cocktail, but if Tamburlaine could see war today, he would add a successive layer of scorn upon those who appropriated the evil of war for even less defensible means than the usual run up to disaster.

One of the funny things about the Wags—yeah, I know, it's hard to believe there is something funny about weird creatures that don't look at all like us really, apart from maybe the eye and the sort of head thingee they have, and have taken over our planet and plunged us into a world-wide war, but trust me—one of the funny things about them is that apart from the whole people-eating, they're really easy going. You'd almost never guess that they would be the cause of such turmoil. They seem to be amused by everything, like they were teenagers on drugs. That's what made everyone panic so much at first. They were so funny, once you got past the whole space invaders motif—which almost no one believed at first anyway. We've seen better special effects in vids for decades. Honestly, the Wags looked like some kind of goofy product from Japan with their monster-size heads and roly-poly bodies. Everybody thought it was some kind of publicity stunt, and looked around to see who was filming it. We're so used to that. In fact, the first officer to go up to the first Wag ship almost seemed ready to play along with the stunt, maybe looking for some cash to retire.

I can still see him now. His partner was using her stick to keep the pressing crowds back while he walked up to the ship and tapped on the part that looked most like a door or hatch. It popped open and a Wag came out and the crowd oohed and ahhed and looked even harder for the cameras. This was some publicity stunt—it was hard to get the attention of people in this jaded market, but here they were succeeding with something surprisingly retro—flying saucers from outer space. Well, it wasn't so much a saucer in this case as a kind of overturned tea cup without a handle. Which seemed wise: something sleek and believable would have elicited nothing but yawns of boredom. I heard someone in a cubicle nearby say something to that effect, in a knowing tone of smug self-assurance. We get that a lot here. Amazing what a long tether will do for self-esteem. I would point out that my tether is even longer, yet my self-regard not as high.

The cop laid into the Wag (of course, we didn't know they were Wags then, that was to come later) with the usual "you can't park that thing here" line of guff, playing to the crowd as if he knew the cameras were rolling. Well, clearly they were or we wouldn't have been able to capture these moments in archival footage that spread across the 'net in minutes, along with stills, audio and a variety of phone shots. But they weren't the cameras of commerce that the cop thought he was posing for while he spoke, and that the crowd gathering assumed to be behind the event—they were just the cameras of record that our society has lived with for decades now, the constant surveillance that supplements the official record perched visibly on every promontory of any influential street corner.

I could never decide if the Wag was listening at first, biding his (her? There's no easy way to tell with Wags, maybe they don't have binary sexual identities anyway. Why would they? Nothing else is like us, why give them easy gender divisions? Maybe they have fifteen different genders, all as easy to spot for them as moustaches and large breasts are to us, but we're not used to looking for them in gelatinous masses. We have so much to learn. Pity we'll never get a chance to find out) time until what? A suitable size crowd had assembled? It got tired of the cop's harangue? Or just until it decided to find out how he tasted.

Because, of course, it ate him.

That was the first one we saw. When I say ate, well, that's the thing—it was more like absorbing. The Wag just kind of opened its stomach, (let's assume for the sake of argument it's something sufficiently analogous to our bodily functions), and blorped him in. It's not a mouth exactly, and it wasn't like a sort of slit to a hollow chamber. It was more like the flesh began to divide and slurp its way around the body of the cop who just froze. If it weren't for his hat lying on the ground, you'd almost believe he was never there.

No screams, no struggle—maybe that's what kept people from panicking initially. I remember we were all gathered around a single vid screen by then, watching it unfurl in the safety of a crowd, and the first reaction was disbelief.

"Did you see that?"

"Did he just disappear into that thing's stomach?"

"Oh, fetid! That's just vile!"

"What the hell is going on?"

The latter from our floor sup, who quickly noticed people not at their posts. Normally she didn't have much of a job as we were all pretty high level drones and tended to drone on in perfect autopilot mode, but she really enjoyed having to crack the whip over us when she could. Her officiousness melted, though, as she joined us around the vid to watch the aftermath.

You think of people panicking, and you think of people screaming and trampling, but it wasn't like that at first. The disappearance of the first victim was so sudden, unexpected and seemingly non-violent, (I'm sure the cop felt differently about it), that the initial reaction was disbelief. We were all waiting for the other shoe to drop, for the reveal of the trick, for the inevitable applause.

We have been trained so well.

The people who were there, not watching it, (although plenty of them were watching it through their phones anyway—why experience something when you can vid it?), but seeing it and smelling it, (I'm told the Wags are more than a tad whiffy but who knows for sure? Anyone who's been close enough to know probably isn't in a position to tell about it), they were a little quicker in the move to panic. In fact, with the next person to get eaten, absorbed, ingested, however you might want to describe it, they did begin to back away and when that didn't seem to be fast enough, there was pushing and shoving, and then shrieking and crying and screaming and running away.

None of it mattered anyway. The Wags were here, they were hungry and they weren't going anywhere while there was food to eat. They went from the streets of Manhattan to Washington, D.C. as if they had studied up on this country and knew the chain of command. While they seemed to enjoy eating, they didn't really enjoy hunting or chasing their food, so it quickly became clear that if we provided food, they would stay put and not wander abroad eating people at random.

Pity they decided to camp on the mall. It's really cut down on visits to the Smithsonian. Although the Wags aren't above posing for vids and stills. Just be careful they've just eaten— they've *all* just eaten. It's kind of hard to tell them apart. Not only can we not make many guesses about gender, (which really bugs the newsheads, I can tell you), but it's really hard to discern any kind of difference between one Wag and the next. Perhaps there are subtle things that cue another Wag—maybe they smell different—or maybe there isn't really any difference between them, like they're all part of some hive.

Imagine now trying to explain this to a friend who had been in a coma for ten years while the world—no, the universe—had changed utterly. I looked down at Simon, knowing I was going to have to take him home tomorrow and I felt despair.

It was time to go talk to my other friend.

2

I didn't have much time before Simon would be coming home, so I thought I'd better get to Harakka and find out as much as I could first. I don't know why I assumed she would be able to tell me anything, but I felt some comfort in knowing that I had somewhere to turn. Without her, I doubt I'd have been able to make it through these last ten years without losing the will to live, especially after it had taken me such a long time to regain it in the first place.

I met Harakka by accident the first time. Well, when I say accident, what I really mean is in a kind of voluntary altered state. You know—drugs. Although abstemious these days, for a time I was interested in achieving various kinds of out-of-body experiences which I was sure would lead me to some kind of enlightenment. The problem with this theory was two-fold: first, most of the drugs provided very much an in-body experience, (although they tended to affect the world around me to a surprisingly great extent), and second, they were liable to lead not so much to enlightenment as foggy nights, severe money loss, raging headaches and uncontrollable trembling.

Simon refused to join me on these escapades. He was quite happy with a wide range of recreational chemical alterations, but not the particular brands I was drifting toward. "They mess you up," he told me one morning as I lay on the carpeted floor of our flat, moaning. "And you can't dance for shit on that stuff." I probably had a witty rejoinder of some kind in the back of my head, but it came out as more moaning.

Anyway, it was a night very much like so many others when I had what seemed like a more promising ingestion, one that appeared to be leading in the right direction, that I met

Harakka. Or should I say, she met me (is that another song lyric?). I was lying in what I took to be a very deep cavern with shiny strobe lights of various colours, which was a bit odd because only moments before I had been in the sitting room of my acquaintance Aoife as we downed the chemical in question. I had begun to formulate the words in my head to consider this conundrum when a bird landed beside me and looked sideways at me, (which I have since learned is the way birds have to look with their eyes so far apart on opposite sides of their heads). It was a bit surprising, what with the bird flu and all—kids today, most of them have never even seen a real bird and barely recall what they looked like, apart from corporate logos and such. I didn't know what kind of bird it was. Although it was kind of big, it didn't look threatening like the eagle on the back of a Sacagawea. She was black and white and almost shiny in the darkness of the cave.

It was strange enough to see a bird like that, and in a cave of all things. But it was even stranger when the bird spoke to me and said, "So is this what you'd like? I only ask because you don't seem particularly ready for death."

"Death?" I finally said, each phoneme calling forth great effort.

"You don't even know where you are, do you?"

Great, I get a sarcastic bird in a cave. "I'm in a cave. No, wait, I'm at Aoife's."

"Yes and no." That's an answer Harakka gives a lot. 'Tell me, do you desire to start a new path?"

I wasn't entirely sure what she meant by that, but I could begin to feel the individual parts of my body drifting in a way that was somewhat disturbing, but also kind of anesthetizing. I wouldn't say it was pleasant, (in fact, it was kind of terrifying), but I was beginning to lose the ability to be upset by it. I at least had enough brain cells to think that perhaps that was not a good thing. Fear has its uses. Anger may be an energy, but fear is a motor. It was time to put the pedal to the metal and cruise out of the cave. "Yes," was the best I could do, but it was good enough.

"When you get out of the hospital, go to the library. You have a lot to learn."

"Hospital?" My brain was moving too slowly to grasp what the words meant, but suddenly there was a fluttering of wings and I awoke to the disconcerting sensation of Aoife pounding on my chest and muttering, "not in my house, not in my house," over and over and over. Within minutes the medics arrived and confirmed that I was alive and that Aoife had broken two of my ribs. They kept me overnight for observation but kicked me out in the morning. Somehow the staff wasn't really interested in assessing the finer points of the health of chem recs. I stumbled home alone and in so doing, passed by the library.

Now it's a common misconception that there are no more libraries. It's not true—despite the wide access of the 'net, there are still people paid to find information that other idiots can't locate. Not that idiots are the only ones who need their specialized skills—information doubles every five minutes, as rumour has it, so finding your way through such dense circuitry requires considerable skill. It's one thing to look up tonight's vid offerings, but quite another to know how fast the Wags are eating us, how many were killed or captured in the war today, or even how many different mutations of cockroaches now fill our walls and ceilings.

Our local lib had been in the same place since I was about ten, although it seemed to have shrunk considerably, which was not simply my imagination. Sold off for more profitable endeavours—the remaining librarians perched behind the small counter with ever-present headsets, poised to find information come what may. I felt a bit odd strolling up to the counter to face all those eager eyes, but I swallowed and croaked out my question, holding my bandaged ribs for safety. "Where do I find out about birds in visions?"

Until the words were out of my mouth, I hadn't really known what I was going to ask. Somehow the right words spilled out, perhaps planted there subliminally by my new pal. In any case, the librarians quickly turned to the task and figured out the appropriate keywords for the searching. They found me a number of promising leads which they conveniently sent to my addy. It was all kind of weird and at first, I really didn't know what I was doing. It was a good thing I was already an experienced reader or I would have given up. This vision stuff was a whole other kind of mind-altering. There were techniques with breath and concentration and such that were really difficult for my slack brain functions in the beginning. Then I found this historical audio file of Siberian drums and that did the trick—it helped me find my way back to that cave. I was inordinately proud of myself. Until, of course, Harakka said, "Why do you want to be in this cave?"

"Can we go somewhere else?" I had worked for months to get back to that cave, so it had never occurred to me that there might be other places. All I knew was that I had to get back to that bird. Which might seem strange at first—we tend to think of birds in the abstract, on money or in pictures or vids. A real live bird—one that talked, no less—not only was this a novelty, but clearly it knew a lot of things that I didn't. So I was more than willing to go where it led.

I had no idea what I was in for. We walked out of the cave and as soon as I stopped blinking in the light, I fell to my knees. "What is this?"

Harakka hopped up on a big rock in the cave's mouth. "This is your world. Well, this is what your world used to be, say, oh, maybe a few hundred years ago."

I know how stupid I must have looked, but I just stared and gaped. There was just no way to process what I saw. It was like a switch went off in my head and from somewhere in its depths, a snatch of poetry from childhood welled up to my lips: *verde que te quiero verde.* Everywhere I looked it was green. Not just green, every colour of green—who knew there were different greens?—it was more than any paint chip demo, more than any fabric swatch guide. Dark green, light green, medium green, yellowish green, bluish green, leaves of green, grass of green. It made me want to just take up mouthfuls and chew. That was weird. It must have been the shock. This was our world? What the hell happened? And it didn't end with the green: there were birds everywhere, birds of different colours and sizes and shapes and they were all singing and cawing and croaking and flapping. It was a cacophony the like of which I had never heard, but unlike city street sounds, it wasn't entirely unpleasant. But it took a long time to get off my knees, close my mouth and step out onto the soft greenery and walk around.

That was the beginning of my visits. Eventually I saw animals too, and more kinds of landscapes than I knew had ever existed, but no people. "There are some here," Harakka told me when I finally thought to ask, "Some like you, but they tend to shy away from people." I had to admit I wasn't eager to see people in this wonderland. I was greedy to keep it all to myself. I suppose that's why I never told even Simon about it. I got so adept at shifting my consciousness that I no longer needed the drums and the incense and the darkened room, but I could go at will with a little concentration. The dangerous thing was that I was apt to fall into travelling while I was bored at meetings, so I had to become more vigilant over time. I could do it anywhere; however, it is safer to do it at home in my darkened room because I hate to leave my body slumped over on the seat of a bus. People are liable to poke you unnecessarily and take liberties.

That day I needed to get some quick advice on how to deal with Simon and his memory and what I should tell him when he came home. In minutes I was popping out of the cave and rubbing my eyes in the sunlight. It looked like just after dawn this visit—time worked differently in this world. I could never anticipate just when it would be but every time I was knocked speechless by the beauty of it. This time I let myself revel in the exquisite sight of the morning dew in the clear sunlight—sunlight! unfiltered by smog—for about thirty seconds then looked for Harakka. Sometimes I had to wait for a while for her to show, which normally was fine by me, but I couldn't wait now. "Harakka, Harakka!" I have to say I felt pretty stupid yelling for a bird.

It seemed far too long before she appeared, but it was probably only a couple of minutes. She landed about ten feet away and walked up to me with that strangely jaunty stride she had, wobbling a little from side to side, one eye crooked up toward me, the white on her wings and belly bright in the early light, the black tail and wing tips shining almost green. "Welcome, traveller. What do you seek?"

This was a standard response to seeing me. I tried not to think that she greeted everybody that way, that I was somehow special, (is that not the *cri de coeur* of every living being?), but I didn't even have time for self-pity that day. "Harakka, what am I going to do about Simon. He's awake! He'll be coming home. He's going to have questions!"

Harakka hopped up closer as I sank down onto the grass, idly picking a few leaves as I gave into fear and despair. She snapped her beak a few times, then told me, "The truth would be simplest."

Oh, sure. "If the truth were that easy, the land might still look like this in my world."

Harakka hopped over and made a grab for the eyelet in my shoe with her quick beak. "I didn't say it was the easiest thing to do—I said it was the simplest."

"So I should just say, sorry Simon, I put you in a coma, kiss kiss, all is better?"

Harakka cocked her other eye up at me. "Do you think that would work?"

"No!"

"Well, then, what will?"

I sighed violently. "How should I know! Aren't you supposed to be my wise spirit guide?"

Harakka stretched her wings out and swivelled her head to dig under her shoulder (is it shoulder on a bird?) with her beak. "News to me," she finally deigned to say. "I'm just a magpie."

"Argh!" I threw myself back on the ground dramatically, trying to punctuate my despair with an appropriate gesture, but only succeeding in knocking the wind out of myself. This was not helping at all. I closed my eyes, not just for melodramatic effect but because the unfiltered sun was quite bright here.

Harakka hopped up on my rib cage. It was weird to feel those little birdy feet on me. They dug into my skin just a little too much. "Would you rather he remembered? Would you rather he found out from someone else?"

"I'd rather he never knew."

"You can't count on that." She picked at my shirt playfully, trying to get me back up, but I was going to enjoy my sulk as fully as possible. If only I could have cookies and milk. I was old enough to remember real chocolate and I had a real taste for it suddenly. I suppose it's not unusual to drift off like that, off onto unconnected tangents, especially here, but I wasn't going to be allowed to get away with it today. "Hey, wake up! I have important things to tell you."

"How can you," I reasoned, eyes still stubbornly shut, "if you're not my wise spirit guide?"

"Oh, all right. I'm your wise spirit guide. Now listen to me—something's coming, you need to be ready for it."

Did I mention that Harakka had warned me about the Wags, but I was too stupid to realise what she was saying? 'From above it will come, with fire,' I think she said. I thought it was all about me, the warnings of disruption, of severe and irrevocable change. It sounded like a weather report, I guess. I didn't really put together all the clues until it was too late. But that's the nature of this kind of communication I guess: Too many filters. Including my brain, I suppose, but that's not really my fault. I blame genetics, environmental concerns and, perhaps, poor nutrition. "What's coming? Why do I need to be concerned? It's not like I could have done anything about the

Wags, you know." Who feels guilty? Not me.

Harakka pulled at my shirt again. It was beginning to get annoying. "Listen, you have to be ready because they'll be coming after people like you."

"People like me? People with witty repartee and killer dress sense and a fabulous collection of books?" It was amazing how the warmth of the sun drained all sense of ambition and worry from my brain, as if the rays were leeching anxiety from my skin itself. I could lay here forever. You know, that wasn't a half bad idea. If I stayed here I could avoid all those other problems. Good plan—why hadn't I thought of it before. I could feel a smile reach my lips and stretch out lazily.

"Ouch! Damn it!" Harakka had pinched my nipple with her shiny black beak. "What the hell was that for?"

"You can't stay here. You don't belong. You have things to do in your own existence."

"Oh yeah, the thing with the thing." I rubbed my offended breast while sitting up at last. "What do you mean, people like me?"

"People who can change consciousness at will. You'll be the most susceptible. You must be on your guard." She shook herself, fluffing her feathers out briefly, then just as quickly smoothing them down. "It's not just for yourself. A lot of beings are depending on you."

"Depending on me?" I laughed. "They're making a big mistake, then."

"Well, that's abundantly clear," Harakka said without rancour but also without much pity. "But there is little to be done. There are so few with the skills anymore to fight back."

"Fight? Oh no, not me. I just need to know what to do about Simon. I'm not fighting. Look," I added, holding up my right arm, "weak as a blade of grass. Useless."

"You're left handed."

"The left is no better."

Harakka gave me one of those looks, swivelling from right eye to left and back again. "You need to be careful. What's coming is bad."

"Worse than the Wags?" That was hard to believe.

"You have no idea," she said in a strikingly cold voice. "But you will. And too soon."

"What about Simon?"

"I already told you: Tell him the truth. Now go."

And just like that I was falling back into myself with a rather jarring crush of consciousness. It felt like a hammer to the head—well, what I assume a hammer to the head would feel like; I had not yet at that point experienced the real sensation. The result was that it took some time before I got up, staggered around and finally put a kettle on to have some tea. Thank the gods that there is still a tea trade across the world. Coffee died out with the fungus and bugs, but there was still tea. I don't know what I would do without the elixir of the morning—although I have to admit, afternoon tea is a reason to go on living. The citrus tang of a good Earl Grey can be better than a good shot of whiskey. Did I mention it's my only vice these days? I needed it today. Simon was coming home.

He was still weak as a kitten when he walked through the door he hadn't seen in ten years. An appropriate enough metaphor, I suppose, given the circumstances. After I helped him onto the sofa, he just sat there breathing a bit too hard for having walked up only one flight.

"You want some tea?" Thrust into the unaccustomed role of hostess or caregiver, I was floundering, woefully unprepared.

Simon grimaced and flopped a lock of his straw-coloured hair out of his eyes. His hair used to be so carefully cut, every four weeks whether it needed it or not. It never did. "You know I can't stand tea. Don't you have any soda?"

My turn to grimace. "Sorry, Simon. It's been a while since I needed any."

He looked around the room as if it were all new, even though he'd really only been away a couple of weeks by his reckoning. I think the enormity of the gap was beginning to sink in. He sighed. "All right, tea it is—but none of that herbal cack. I want something with caffeine at least."

I dashed off to our little galley and threw on the kettle. Food, food—why hadn't I thought of food? Well, I could run around the corner to the market. "You're not hungry at present are you?" I asked as I spooned out the tea, muttering under my breath, "Say no."

"No."

Sigh of relief. "Is there anything else I can get you? Do you want the vid screen on?"

"God no. Let's give it a rest. That's one thing I haven't missed at all."

I had to grin at that. Who could never go out at night without checking the latest fashions on line? Who had three different Milan shoe stores bookmarked? Who never started a day without checking the latest celebrity walks of shame? I smiled at my reflection in the cupboard. It was good to have my best friend back.

However, when I brought the tea tray into the front room, (why is it called a front room when it's in a flat in the middle of a big building?), Simon's next words made me almost wish him back in the coma. "Where's Mr. Tolliver?"

I put the tray down on the coffee table, (why is it a coffee table if we only ever use it for tea and sometimes an impromptu bar, back in the day?), and cleared my throat a few times as if I were going to say something. What I was going to say, though, I didn't know.

"Ten years," Simon said quietly. "He's dead, isn't he?"

What a great friend, softening the blow for me. I'm such a yutz. "Well, yes, you're right, your cat's dead." Why did I have to tell him? I sat down beside him on the sofa and angled an arm around him. "I don't know that it will help any to know, but all cats are dead. And dogs—birds, etc. Well, you knew about the birds already, right? That was before." It was a new marker of time: pre-coma, post-coma. "It's kind of like that one movie. Do you remember that one movie...?"

"Yes, of course. Which movie?" Simon asked trying to pretend he wasn't wiping away a tear.

"That 'Planet of the Monkeys' one. You know the one. There's the misunderstood monkey king, Caesar?"

"Sounds vaguely familiar."

"You know, monkeys became the new pets because a virus wiped out all the cats and dogs? It was sort of like that. Except no monkeys. The virus got them, too."

"Jesus wept!" Simon shook his head. "Was it some kind of mutation of the bird flu? Are all the animals dead? That is just too weird."

"You're telling me. We were knee deep in carcasses for a while. Sorry," I added hastily seeing him wince. "They disposed of most of them quickly—there was some fear of it transferring to humans. Certainly the vid heads were going nutty on the topic."

"I didn't think the bird flu could jump to humans." Simon rubbed his eyes more with fatigue than anything else, I think, while I poured out some tea.

"We didn't think it could jump to other animals. But then, we only have *their* word to go on. The powers that be—"

"They be awful strange," Simon finished. Just like the old days. But it didn't feel like the old days anymore. It felt really late—and it was only mid-morning. "I think I need a wobbly," he said at last.

Fortunately, despite my recent abstemiousness, I did still keep a drop around. It was only fair—I had probably drunk up all of Simon's booze a week after he was in the coma. It was a bad week. But I did eventually replace some of it, just about in time to give it up. There was a bottle of very dusty brandy in the back of the cupboard, so I wiped it off and after considering for a minute, brought it and two glasses with me. I poured out a measure for each of us.

"Here's to you, back again."

"And to Mr. Tolliver." With a strange solemnity, we drank the brandy which burned in my throat like a cosy fire.

"I did save his ashes," I said at last after the silence finally began to feel awkward.

"Thanks."

I never did know what to do with them, so there they were in a little white box in a little green bag at the back of the closet next to some dusty board games, waiting for Simon to wake up and come home.

"So what happened, Ro? How did I develop a coma?" As if it were an ability to play the piano, or a good fastball; it was actually kind of sudden. Not like that at all.

"Oh, for god's sake, let us sit on the ground and tell sad stories of the deaths of kings," I said, trying to buy time.

"What?

Just then the vid alarm went off. I thanked every spiritual leader in the cosmos for that, even though normally I would just ignore it. "We better see what that is," I said nervously reaching for the remote. *Videus interruptus* trumps again. But I better start thinking about how I was going to break my own news.

The screen faded in from rest mode with a blinking red border. Must be important.

"Wow, they've ramped up the visual rhetoric," Simon said with a touch of admiration. "Good font." Did I mention his being a graphic designer? It was obvious. Mere days out of a coma and he was admiring fonts. And people think I'm odd.

It took a minute or two to untangle the sense of the running text, side bars and overlapping video feeds, but it seemed like there was something new with the Wags. I looked over at my friend uneasily. "Um, I think you're going to see one of them in a minute."

"One of what? Oh." He leaned forward a tad too eagerly. I don't think it's a good idea to sit too close. I know they probably can't see through the vid but who wants to take chances. We didn't think interplanetary travel on their level was possible either, but more fool us.

There was one now, in all its purple glory. I heard Simon's involuntary gasp. I could explain them and describe them, but there was no substitute for seeing them. This one was waving his arms—can I call them arms accurately? But what can I say, appendages?—and talking, I guess, to the camera. I would guess that the camera operator was using the best telephoto lens possible, keeping as far out of reach of that hungry tummy as possible. The one big eye stared unblinkingly at the lens. Once there had been a president or vice president or something like that who had unblinking eyes. After the Wags arrived, someone actually suggested that he had been an advance agent, some kind of clone of human and Wag, but I don't think anyone took it seriously. Probably.

The Wag apparently wanted to convey something important, but what came out of its face, (well, it didn't really have a mouth—how could it talk? Psychic powers?), kind of sounded like "Whompbompalulaahwompbampboop." Somehow, I didn't really believe that they had crossed the galaxies to partake in a little karaoke. Well, crossed galaxies is a speculation, too. We don't really know how far the Wags have come, or how they came or when they might leave, although everybody hopes they will soon. We know they're not from next door. Beyond that, who knows? Our best scientists have been on it since they got here, but they've come up with little more than guesses—those who didn't become lunches. Mostly what they say is there's a whole galaxy of we-don't-know-what, which is humbling, I suppose, when it's not terrifying.

"Is it always like this?" Simon asked with a mouthful of revulsion coating his words.

"Um, well, no," I said, trying to be accurate. "They don't really tend to say much at all. Just gesture and eat. Or gesture to eat. This seems like something new."

That's our culture all over: Everything is seen, but nothing is understood. We're under constant surveillance in our streets and our jobs, but it's all a thin veneer of sight and sound, no comprehension. We don't understand the people next door let alone these creatures from another world or another dimension. There're a thousand and one theories about what the Wags are, but not one has managed to take hold. The most omnipresent fact of our lives and we don't even begin to understand it. I have heard there are those who have begun to worship them as gods, offering up sacrifices and composing verses in their honour. I suppose it's no stranger than most religions, but I guess I find it hard to believe something that only consumes can be a god.

Get this—they don't even seem to excrete. Now putting aside for the moment questions of power, deity and possible vulnerabilities, that's just wrong. When I say wrong, I mean that it doesn't fit any model of being alive. There are efficient bio-systems, but I don't think there's a one that doesn't have some waste to emit. In some ways, that's the scariest thing of all to me. Maybe I'm just ignorant about the nature of things. Maybe they discreetly used some kind of intergalactic toilet in their ships. But in five years not even a stop at a chemical station? It's not natural, as my Auntie Betty would say.

"I think he looks worried," Simon said at last, jarring me out of my rambling thoughts. We both leaned in closer to the screen. The big ugly creature wiggled its appendages and bore into the camera with its unblinking eye.

"I don't know, there's not much that they have to worry about." It was hard to admit it, but there wasn't much you could tell about these creatures at all. That damned eye—it was spooky.

Simon sipped the last of his brandy and set the glass down. "Well, if they're worried about something, don't you think we should be, too?"

Damn.

He was right. It made me wish that I was another girl on another planet. Hopefully one with oxygen and a friendly climate. "Uh, well, uh..." and then I remembered what Harakka had said, about something coming worse than the Wags. Frankly I didn't think there was space in my brain to think of something worse than the Wags. I was beginning to reconsider this whole tee-totalling trend. Perhaps it was time to begin ingesting serious mind wipes.

Then again, what was all that drivel from the early years of the war? The enemy of my enemy is my friend? Couldn't it work that way here? I suggested as much to Simon, but he wasn't feeling confident. In fact, he was starting to look like death warmed over. "Maybe you should be resting," I suggested, trying to get him toward his room and away from the screen. It was barely noon, but hey, he was recovering from a coma.

"Wait," he said, delaying bedtime like a naughty child, "I think they're going to say something." 'They' being the authoritative talking heads of the vid yack news who would no doubt tell us the latest absolute rubbish about what nobody knows anyway about what the Wags will do next—or not.

"Who's that?" Simon said pointing to the yacker overlaid on the upper left hand corner of the screen.

"Oh that's Razi—she's the hottest thing in the 24/7 feed right now." She was certainly a gorgeous woman with her green eyes and carefully tumbled waves of black hair.

"What's *angra mainyu*?" Simon was reading her words off the bottom of the screen rather than looking at her face. Old habits die hard.

"It's one of the Middle Eastern names for the Wags. Everybody's got their own. I think the British started the use of 'Wags' here. BBC reporters were less shell-shocked than our own that day, or at least they seemed to be. The Swedes call them '*sviskonar*' and the South Americans call them '*bexigas*.' Everybody's got a nickname for them, whatever stuck on the first day." Yes, I went through a phase of looking up all the names used for the Wags. Knowledge is power, or so I believed then. I finally gave up when I realised that none of the names were their own and that was the knowledge we really needed.

"Stepping up the pace? That doesn't sound good."

Indeed—first would be the pace of feedings, which meant

inevitably the pace of call ups for the war. I thanked my lucky stars for my government pass, once again—but what about Simon?

Let's think about that tomorrow.

"You should really be getting to bed. You need to rest." It was easier to persuade him then, because he was beginning to nod, although whether it was the brandy, fatigue or shell-shock, it was hard to tell. But Simon allowed me to steer him toward the bedroom where he kicked off his shoes and lay on the bed. I dropped his bag beside the bed. There wasn't much in it, but in case he needed anything it would be there.

"It's going to be hard to sleep without Mr. Tolliver curled up by my feet," Simon said before gently beginning to snore. I pulled down the window shade. I don't think the afternoon haze would disturb him, but it seemed like the right thing to do.

I wandered back out to the front room, wondering whether to make an effort to wash the glasses or simply veg in front of the vid, when there came a sharp rap at the door. I am largely untroubled by visitors on the whole. In the ten years I have been without my roommate, the buzzer may have gone off maybe a dozen times, so you'd forgive me for being a bit surprised—particularly when it was not the buzzer but that peremptory knock. It was probably nothing—some of the new Wag evangelists who wormed their way into the building and were going door to door. But for some reason, to use an anachronism, my spider-sense was tingling. I briefly considered ignoring the summons, but then I felt a bit silly and walked over to the door.

They might have been evangelists. The plain charcoal suits fit, but the dour expressions did not match the usual stereotype of shiny born-agains. They also did not seem to have the garish brochures and Chick tracts of the newly-converted.

"We're looking for Simon Magus," the lead clone said.

I smiled. "I don't know anyone by that name," I said, which was not strictly true, but it was not Simon's real name. It was his business name, but hey, did I have to admit to knowing it?

"He is also known as Simon Marcus," offered the third one.

"You do know that he's been in a coma for ten years," I said with all the sadness and hurt outrage I could muster.

They were beginning to lose the patience, especially the lead clone. "We also know that he has recovered consciousness this week. Do let us in. We need to see him." There was a smile without any warmth in it.

"He's sleeping."

"Wake him up, then."

"He's not well."

"We have to see him."

We stared at one another for a moment or two, then I sighed and opened the door a bit wider. "All right, it'll be a minute. Do sit down." I knew the sofa wouldn't be big enough for all three, but I wasn't about to stir myself on their behalf. Clearly gov, so it looked like the inevitable was here. They continued to stand and I walked around them to Simon's room.

Kneeling down next to the bed, I laid a hand on his shoulder. It seemed such a shame to wake him. He had barely had time to get to REM level, although his eyes were darting back and forth under their lids like he was speed-reading. "Simon," I said softly, trying to shake him awake gently. "Simon, I'm sorry but—"

Suddenly he was up, shouting in my face, "They're coming!"

"Ow, Simon. No, they're already here. Gov clones, they want to talk to you. I think it's probably—"

"No, not them." He looked up at me, but his focus still seemed to be on his dreams. "They're coming and we have to be ready."

"You're dreaming, Simon. Sorry."

"No, Ro, this is real. We have to be ready."

"Who, Simon? Who's coming?'

He shook his head. "I can't remember. It's gone. She was telling me, but I couldn't quite hear what she was saying."

"Who was saying, Simon?" I was beginning to have a bad feeling about this dreaming stuff.

"She had a funny name," Simon said, rubbing his head and sinking back down on the bed. "I think it was Japanese."

"Japanese?"

"Haruka? Haraka? I'm not sure."

"Huh," I laughed unconvincingly, knowing I was going to turn around and see the clones in the doorway. "Dreams, huh?"

"Simon Marcus," said the lead clone in a perfectly even gov tone, "You are hereby invited to join the esteemed ranks of the National Army Ground Reserve Service. Report to duty 15 July at 0800 hours to the Northeastern Recruitment Centre. You will be issued proper kit and trained in accordance with the finest military techniques with the best in twenty-first century technology."

"So you can round up people to feed to the Wags or get fed to them yourself," I muttered, still kneeling beside the bed. The clones ignored me and the leader thrust the paper into Simon's hand while he was still blinking in surprise. "Get out!"

The leader gave me a smug smile, then they turned around and headed out. I heard the door click behind them.

"Simon, I'm sorry. I shouldn't have let them in."

"Ro, you know they would have got me one way or another." He looked at the form. Good old paper. Induction notices are about the only thing outside the archives that still gets printed on good old paper. What a waste. "July 15. That gives us plenty of time."

"Time for what?"

"We have to take Mr. Tolliver to his final resting place. You know what that means?"

"Huh?" News to me.

Simon smiled. "Road trip!"

43

3

"Simon, we don't have a vehicle of any kind," I began reasonably, but it was too late. I could see it in his eyes. This wasn't really about Mr. Tolliver. Don't get me wrong, I loved him. I cried like a two-year-old when he died. Well, there's another circumlocution: he was put to sleep. He actually lasted quite a while longer than expected. As all the other pets were dropping like so many ball bearings, tough old Mr. Tolliver hung in there. He actually died of the maladies of old age—heart murmur, thyroid problems and such. He finally got so weak that he couldn't get up to feed himself or relieve himself and I knew he was miserable. I delayed it as long as possible, because he was beginning to feel like my last friend.

I finally had to admit it was no good and went back to the vet one more time. He was surprisingly kind. Consider: he was phenomenally busy with hysterical people whose pets were keeling over minute by minute and seriously threatening his whole career—after all, no pets means no vets. In the midst of this maelstrom, he was kind. Sometimes there is no better word to describe what a living being can best achieve. I have been kind too seldom.

As Mr. Tolliver lay there on the cold metal table, warmed only by his favourite towel (favourite since Tuesday when he lay down upon it and decided no longer to move), the vet said "Well, there are a few things we can try. They are very expensive."

"That doesn't matter," I said, trying not to dab at my eye like a movie heroine. "I have plenty of credits."

"They also won't do very much to make him more comfortable. He is very old and his heart cannot hold out much longer."

"So you think I should—should...?"

"It's your decision. I can't make it for you."

And in the end I said yes, even though it wasn't my decision to make. But Mr. Tolliver wouldn't have lasted until the time Simon woke up. If it hadn't been his heart, it would have been the pet flu. I stood there beside the examination table with his head resting on my hand as the vet gave him the shot, left a box of tissues within reach and then slipped out the door. He purred as I talked to him, making him vague promises of a kitty heaven even I didn't believe existed, and then finally he was silent and I closed his little eyes and he wasn't there anymore. I wrapped the corner of the towel around his still form, as if he might catch a chill, and made myself walk to the door. I turned back before I closed the door behind me and my eye jumped to his little pink pads and then I couldn't see any more. I stumbled out into the late afternoon haze and walked all the way home, bawling.

And then I got very, very drunk, completely drenched up to my eyeballs.

It felt as if the end was coming, what with Simon in the *krankhaus* and Mr. Tolliver no longer mewing in my ear. Little did I know. It was only a few days later that I met Harakka and everything began to change again. For the better? Well, who can say? I had to go back to the vet a week later and they handed me little green bag with a little white box inside it and Mr. Tolliver's name on it. When I got it out of the closet to hand to Simon, I felt like there was something I should say, some final words of comfort I ought to produce, but nothing came to me.

"It's not much, is it?" he said finally after looking down into the bag for a minute or two.

"No, but they give you a card." I reached in to pull it out.

"It's addressed to you."

"They didn't know." More awkward silence. "So, where will his final resting place be?

"Mount Auburn," Simon said, setting down the bag with a sigh.

"You're putting him on a mountain?"

Simon shook his head. "It's a cemetery. In Boston. A lot of my family have been buried there over the years. Good old Brahmins."

"What, you don't mean that swanky one we went to years ago?" I still remembered it though—back in the day when things were still green. It had fancy headstones that were more like sculptures, even a little lake. We even saw a kid playing a wooden flute that day—we danced a little to the music because it felt like it was that kind of tune. "You're joking, right?"

"No." Behind that single syllable was the look of determination I saw only occasionally on Simon's face, but knew well. There would be no gainsaying. We were going to make that road trip.

"We still don't have a vehicle. Not even a bike. A lot has happened in those ten years, pal. Hardly anybody has their own transport. No one can afford it."

"What about Maggie? You're telling me Maggie doesn't have some kind of vehicle?"

Damn. I was hoping to avoid this. "Well…"

"What?"

"Uh…"

"Oh, Jesus wept! You didn't sleep with her, too?"

Have I mentioned my inability to maintain a romantic relationship? Terminal inability, I should say. One thing that's kept my relationship with Simon safely intact is his utter lack of interest in me. Even completely drenched, he's never been the least bit inclined to experiment. I don't think he's ever slept with a woman. Just zero interest. It's not that I'm such a goat, I just can't maintain the interest. It's not that I don't enjoy them. Perhaps I do a bit too much. The greeting card industry should invent a line of cards for it: "I am no longer interested in your body, but I don't mind chatting once in a while." Think of the convenience. It's not such a stretch—they did come up with a whole line of "sorry the Wags ate your wife/husband/son/ daughter/friend" cards. There are even cards for those left behind when the army claims a loved one, "Wishing you strength and courage while your beloved is off fighting for freedom/democracy/truth/honour/food." Let the card say it. Is it my fault if I don't get all googly-eyed and want to share my innermost secrets with others? We're at war, as the vids tell us every hour on the hour. Shouldn't short term comfort romances be the order of the day? Here today, gone tomorrow. Admittedly, I have known Maggie for much of my life, although most of it slightly, so I'm not sure that would qualify, but the spirit of the thing is there.

Simon looked at me and sighed noisily. "Well, that's just wonderful. But unless you can think of someone else with a vehicle, you're going to have to make it up to her. We need a vehicle."

"Why do you assume it was me who made it a mess?"

Another glare.

"Well, all right, but I don't think she's going to change her mind about things."

"What did you do to her?"

What did I do? I don't know. What do I ever do? I approach a new lover the way I approach a new meal: to see what tastes good, to see what I like, and to leave behind what I don't like. Even if you use the same recipe, the meal isn't quite the same ever—the ingredients have changed, being less ripe or more so, or more tart or less sweet or some other combination of flavours. You know the sort of thing you might like to try again (green curry) and the thing you'd just as soon leave behind (anything with lima beans). "I didn't do anything to her. It just didn't work out."

Simon put his fists on his hips in what seemed a tolerably feminine gesture. "So, she's not going to be peeved to hear from you, or refuse to lend us a vehicle because of you?"

"Well, who can say? Life is unpredictable." Where was that brandy? Jesus, out of the hospital a single day and he has me retreating to bad habits.

"You could have been nicer, I'm sure."

"What good is a body perfect in outer ways, if inwardly it is impaired by lack of love?" I read that in some old book of Indian wisdom when I was looking for more information on these mystical sorts of happenings. Oddly enough it was one of the few things that stuck to the sides of my unpredictable accumulator brain.

"Jesus, Mary and Joseph," Simon said. "I'll call." He walked over to the vid and switched screens. It was just another story about the Wags latest peculiarities, so undoubtedly it was of no importance. I made sure to slip out of view. A little brandy wasn't going to hurt, right?

After Simon fiddled with the keys for a minute or two I finally remembered to shout, "add 01!" and he got through right away. Sheesh, sit by the phone much? Although to be fair, Maggie did run a business from her home, so I suppose it was conscientiousness and not desperation.

"Oh my god, Simon!" She smiled broadly and I remembered why it all happened anyway. She had the kind of grin that lit a face like a halogen. "You're—you're awake!" I could tell she had been going to say alive, but awake was a good catch. "Oh my god!"

"I just got out of the hospital today," Simon said, matching her grin with a smile of genuine warmth. Good old Simon, he could always seem so sweet—mostly because he was. "How have you been?"

"How have you been, stranger?! Oh my god," she said for the third time which I couldn't help noticing, uncharitable as that observation was. I'm just that kind of person, but the aesthetics of repetition are a tough line to toe. "I can't believe you're back!"

Simon smiled wider. It seemed hardly possible, but there were always a couple of teeth held in reserve for a slightly bigger smile. It was a secret I must learn. "I'm still a little shaky, but I'm getting back on my feet. I can hardly believe it myself."

"Can we do dinner? I don't have much, but we can have a little wine, we can share a little nosh, it will be just like old times."

"Oh, I wish I could, Maggie," Simon said with what seemed liked genuine regret. "This is just awful of me, but there's something I have to do."

"Oh." Was it my imagination, or was there a hint of frostiness in her reply. Perhaps I was just reading into it—and her inevitable realisation that I was in the room. "What's up, Simon?"

"It's Mr. Tolliver. You probably already know..." He trailed off as if it were too horrible to mention. Well, it was too horrible. What was wrong with me?

"Oh, yes, Simon, I am so sorry! I wasn't there, but I know how terrible it was for the poor little guy."

One, two, three: "Oh, is Ro there, too?"

I wish I could convey all the emotions that inquiry contained. There was the arctic cold, of course, but there was also a disgust of someone who had gone out for an hour and returned to find their best wardrobe full of cockroaches, along with the contempt of a high-roller in a Gucci soy-suit for a change-begging insectivore in the streets. I was that most contemptible of creatures, after all: the lover who had ceased to be a lover.

"Yes, she's here. In fact, we were just talking about you."

"She can rot in hell for all I care," Maggie stated flatly.

Simon regrouped subtly. "I understand there has been some...history between you two." An awkward way to put it, but no less than the truth. "I really need your help, though, Maggie. Can you put aside your disgust to help a friend?" He didn't need to add, that it was a friend who had been in a coma for ten years, but it was there in those big brown eyes.

I peeked around the corner at the screen. She was thinking. A sigh—and then, "I suppose. For you, Simon." Her words were almost pathetic in their belligerence. "What can I do?"

"We need a vehicle of some kind for a short trip. Can you help us out?"

"For both of you?" The coldness lasted just a moment. "I guess you don't know how much transport has changed in…the last few years." She had the good grace to swallow those words. Never good to remind the coma patient that he's been away awhile.

"I noticed I didn't get a ride home from the hospital."

"Well, electric has become the wave of the future today. With the war and all, no oil; with the crap economy, nobody much can afford a car at all. The roads are so bad nothing but trams get down them anyway."

"Even the highways?" Simon looked over at me. He really was determined to get to Boston. I was beginning to suspect that it wasn't all about Mr. Tolliver.

Maggie exhaled thoughtfully. "Well, haven't been on them much. I've heard that there are a lot of disruptions here and there, and not always a charging station when you need it. I could check the 'net. There are a few traveller groups that would know. Where you headed?"

"Why don't we come over and talk about it?"

That more than anything made me really wonder what Simon was up to. Normally he was as voluble as a drunken salesman. He was hiding something, but what could a man in a coma for ten years be hiding?

Maggie's thoughts, however, were heading in another direction. "We?" she repeated with all the warmth of an arctic ice floe. "You're both coming?"

Simon's voice got very soft and velvety. "I know she's messed things up—as usual, but I'm asking you, for me, to put aside your hurt and anger. I really need your help, Maggie— your expertise."

Add the cow eyes and who could resist, (as if anyone knew these days what cow eyes looked like anyway)? Maggie certainly couldn't resist. She muttered something half-hearted, shrugged and said, "Okay. See you in half an hour."

Simon flipped back to the news feed, where they were showing some maps charting Wag movements in the last few days. Damned if the crazy buggers weren't hot-rodding around the country. Just when we thought we had them figured out, they're up and running again. Crazy aliens anyway. Probably just bored, looking for new flavours. Don't we all?

"Well?" I asked, as if I hadn't heard and seen exactly what Simon had.

"Well, let's get ready." He rubbed his hands together like some kind of cartoon character ready to put a cunning plan into action.

"You look sneakier than a cartoon weasel getting ready to sneak up on someone and weasel him. What are you up to, Simon?"

He gave me that innocent look, the patented Simon Magus "who, li'l ol' me?" look. "We're going to Boston to lay Mr. Tolliver to rest. There's nothing so odd about that."

I tried to give him a searching look, as people always seem to do in novels of the early twentieth-century, but my search did not turn up any survivors. "How much are we packing? Lunch? Overnight? I need to know."

"A change of clothes, or two, I'm sure will be sufficient," Simon answered carelessly. "You never know, we might find some interesting things to do. Bring some money in case we see something we want to buy."

I knew that was a quote from one of his favourite films, so I didn't bother to correct his anachronism. With a sigh, I went to my room and started jamming a few odds and ends into my rucksack. Whatever was up, he wasn't ready to tell me. I was hemming and hawing over whether to throw in a real book, when I heard Simon pause at the door.

"Is my passport still in the safety deposit box?"

"Yes," I said without looking up. Should I take a gothic or something philosophical?

Simon got down on the floor and reached under the bed. Within seconds he was coughing. He dragged the old shoebox out along with a lot of dust. "You might consider cleaning away some of the dust bunnies," he said between choking breaths.

"Those are dust elephants," I told him, deciding on the Radcliffe and shoving it down into the bottom of the bag. "Outside my jurisdiction. What do you need your passport for, anyway?"

"I need some kind of identification. My driver's license expired eight years ago." Simon flipped open the passport. "Hello, handsome."

I smiled over at him. "You have a standard issue ID. It's on the refrigerator. I didn't think to bring it to the hospital. It has the picture from your old license. Nobody has licenses anymore."

He shrugged. "Well, I like this picture better. Yours up to date, too?"

I nodded. "Haven't used it in three years."

"Where'd you go?"

"Iceland."

"Ah."

He didn't ask me to explain. I wasn't sure I wanted to do so anyway. "Anyway, I have an ID, I don't need the passport."

"I just wanted to see the old you." Simon had my passport open to the picture. "My, how times have changed."

I didn't really want to see that picture from thirteen years ago. Who was that crazy-eyed woman with the wild hair anyway? "Put it away, please."

Simon smiled, but he closed the passport. "Anything else useful in here?"

I shrugged. Things that had once seemed so important just vanished into detritus. "Put it back in the vault, if you can choke down the dust." He poked through the box, then closed the lid and shoved it back under the bed.

"Ready?"

I looked at him. No way was he done packing before me. Simon couldn't leave for work without packing and unpacking his bag about three times, forgetting something essential and changing his mind about what he was wearing. "You're packed? You. Packed. Where is the real Simon and what have you done with him?"

"I've turned over a new leaf. Nothing like a coma to change your priorities."

Maybe he meant it. Despite the pale weakness that seemed to permeate his skin, there was a resoluteness that didn't really fit the old Simon. "All right, let's face the music."

"As long as there will be dancing," Simon said, laughing and gathering up his natty leather case that made my rucksack look like a lost hobo bindle.

It was only about a fifteen minute walk to Maggie's little house. Unlike everyone else I knew, she actually had a free standing house with a garage of all things. It seemed like luxury, except for the fact that it was always getting broken into by various desperate types, who inevitably went away disappointed because there was nothing of interest to anyone but another gearhead. Well, they often didn't just go away, but smashed up as much as they could because they were disappointed. I could never tell if it really made Maggie angry or not. It was inconvenient, sure, but it also meant one more thing for her to puzzle her way through fixing, and that always made her as happy as the proverbial clam, which always made me wonder: were clams really ever known for their happiness? I know they were eaten by people, which wouldn't seem to inspire all that much gaiety. Did they write little happy clam songs or paint pictures of smiling crustaceans? Were pearls perfect little shiny bits of happiness hardened to a high gloss? I should look it up sometime. But clam-like or not, Maggie was certainly cheerful whenever she had something with a motor to take apart, to put back together and to rev its engine with a satisfied smile of accomplishment. Like all the other artists we know (Simon included) she made things. Me, on the other hand, I have only ever been a consumer of things, but I suppose someone has to be there to ooh and ahh to make the crafting all worthwhile.

Let's not say I never made anything. I made Maggie hate me.

We walked along the streets toward Maggie's gingerbread house, occasionally stopping to gape at something that had changed in the ten coma years. Mostly things looked a bit more dilapidated. There were few people about, even less than usual—probably all watching the latest news on the Wags. When we were kids, people still sat out on their porches and stoops, talking to neighbours and passing the time. It was easier to breathe then. I regretted not picking up masks, but we could always pop into Stewart's and buy a disposable. As we passed one of the blasted tree trunks on the corner of the park, I suddenly remembered what Simon had said upon waking. "Simon, who were you talking about? In your dream, you know?"

He had been walking along the curb as if it were a kind of balance beam. "What?"

"When I woke you up, when the gov clones were there? You were telling me something, something that seemed important."

Simon stopped and stared off into the distance. "Dream?" he finally said.

"You said, you said, that someone was coming. That we had to be ready. There was a girl, maybe Japanese…"

He rubbed his forehead with his hand. "It sounds sort of familiar, I think. I don't know."

"You said her name. It started with an H, I think. Har-something?"

"Haruko?" He said it uncertainly. "It think I remember, she had black hair with white streaks, like whatshername in the X-Men comics."

"What did she say?" I tried to keep the creeping hysteria out of my voice but it was just too weird.

Simon shrugged. "I don't remember. It was a dream, Ro. It was only a dream."

"Yeah, you're right." I was going to have to see Harakka soon. This was too strange. It had to be related. It was too bizarre to be a coincidence—and I didn't much believe in coincidences anymore. Was he picking up on my thoughts? Or was he having similar experiences?

I was still preoccupied when we got to Maggie's house, so I didn't hear her yell to us from the garage. Simon had to pluck my sleeve and drag me from my forward trajectory toward the front door. I should have guessed that was where she would be.

While her house is miniscule, the garage is pretty good-sized. That was of course the draw for Maggie in the first place. She was never too concerned about her living quarters, but she needed the garage and driveway and space for her tools. Just then, she was carefully returning the tools in her hand to their place on the bench, rubbing her hands briskly on a towel, then running to hug Simon.

"I can't believe it's you!" Her eyes were closed as she and Simon wrapped their arms around each other. I found my eyes wandering off in another direction, knowing that a different reception was ready for me.

"It's so good to see you," Simon said enthusiastically when Maggie finally let him go. "It feels like it's only been a few days."

Maggie reached up to touch his cheek. "I can't imagine how that feels. So much has changed..." Why did she choose that moment to throw me a frosty glance? "It's all so different. The Wags, the war—"

"Well, the war had been going before," Simon said, slipping his arm around Maggie as we walked toward the house. "But I hear it's changed."

Maggie snorted. "It used to be all about freedom and courage, like we ever believed that. Now it's all about feeding the Wags. 'We must feed or be fed.' Not quite what we thought would be the rallying cry of a generation."

"You didn't used to be so cynical," Simon said as we sat

around the tiny kitchenette. I always liked the retro-floral Formica tabletop. It was amazing how girly a grease-monkey could be. Once you left the garage, everything was frilly and floral.

"A lot of things have changed," Maggie said, making sure to look right at me then. Bad luck, because I happened to be looking at her just then, too. I flushed and my embarrassment started to change to anger. After all, it took at least two to tango. It wasn't all my fault. Well, okay, it was mostly my fault. But I wasn't going to be anyone's martyr. Suffering was not my mission in life. I crossed my arms and stopped cringing.

"All right, you two. We're going to have to clear the air a bit, I can see." Simon looked more than a tad exasperated. "I don't want to know any of the details. Believe me, I so do not want to know the details. But you're both my friends, so we have to get through this."

Neither of us said anything. A few minutes ago, I might have been willing to bend my head to the cheap and chippy chopper on the big black block, but not now. Maggie looked just as resolute. Simon looked back and forth between our stubborn faces and then finally drew a deep breath. I thought it was going to be a prelude to further pleading.

Instead he opened his mouth and shouted, "You maggot-sucking, thorn-fisting, ungrateful shrews! I've been in a coma for ten years and you can't be pleasant to one another for half an hour. I don't care if she screwed you," he said pointing at Maggie, "And I don't care why," he said turning on me. "Just shut the hell up and be nice."

Simon sat down, exhausted. Maggie and I rolled our eyes away from each other and then back. Well, crap. "Sorry Maggie, I know I was thoughtless and callous and a jerk."

"You were." Her hands gripped the side of the table tightly. "I hate you. But I will be nice." She smiled the most insincere smile I have ever seen, baring her teeth at me aggressively as any jungle cat. Then she smiled for real at Simon. "My word, I think that coma might have had some unexpected side effects!"

He laughed and put his hand over one of hers. "I know. I think I have a lot to...find out. Things are going to be strange for a while." He smiled over at me. "We all have some weird shit to sort out." Simon didn't know the half of it. Wait until I told him about my visits to the mystical past with some kind of talking bird. But that could wait. "Maggie," he continued, pressing her hand, "We need to borrow some kind of transport. I don't mean to just barge in here and demand things, but it's important."

Maggie smiled. "Don't worry, it's not going to seem rude. A ten year backlog of things to do, I know." She looked ready to cry. "Simon, I've missed you so much."

Simon smiled in return. "Thank you, sweetheart."

"I have a small car," Maggie said, getting up to grab a pitcher of cold water and some glasses. "It doesn't hold a long charge, but it's fairly reliable. I got it about a week ago, was going to work on it some, but I haven't had time. Still working on the Indian." She grinned.

"Still?" Simon laughed. "It will never be done, will it? You'll be working on that when you're ninety."

Maggie pretended to look hurt as she handed him a glass. "Parts are nigh on impossible to come by. I have to save up and bid. Sometimes I win, sometimes I don't. I just got a transmission end cover this week and I've been cleaning it ever since. One piece at a time." We all laughed at that. "So, where're you headed?"

"Boston. We have to take Mr. Tolliver to his final resting place."

"Oh, I am so sorry, Simon. He was a great cat." She patted his shoulder, comfort for a pet years dead. Could things get much weirder? Oh yeah, even then I had no doubt they could. "This is too strange. I just got a message from a friend asking if I would be heading out that way anytime soon." She went to the fridge and grabbed a piece of paper held up b a magnet. "This might be convenient for me, too."

Oh, great—what a comfortable ride that was going to be.

"You wouldn't mind stopping by my friend's place first. It's in the Berkshires. We could overnight there and charge the car."

"All right, sounds good to me." Simon looked over at me and I shrugged.

"It's nice of you to want to do this for Mr. Tolliver."

"He deserves a fitting place. We're going to take him to Mt. Auburn Cemetery and scatter his ashes."

"Do they allow that?"

"Who cares?" Simon said with some pugnaciousness. "He's my cat, I can do what I like. There's a little place I know that will be perfect."

"It's not going to be like you remember," I cautioned. Leave it to me to be the killjoy. "No more green, no more pretty lake, probably not even any trees. Stumps maybe."

"I know, I know." Simon waved away my words of warning. "But this is important to do now."

"He got a call up notice," I told Maggie.

"Those bastards!" It was great to see her anger thrown at someone else for a change. "You're barely out of the hospital. What were they thinking? I can't believe it."

"Hence the urgency," Simon smiled again, but there was a little strain in it. "Can we go in the morning?"

"Yeah, yeah. I'll make a couple of calls, leave a couple of messages. I'll call my friend—she'll be pleasantly surprised. It's so strange—but, well, it was meant to be, eh? What time you want to leave?"

"Eight?"

I smothered my groan.

"Okay, no problem."

Sure, for her—she was up with the sun. Simon got up and hugged her again and we made our way toward the door. I tried to smile ingratiatingly, but she only muttered, "Don't push it." I was tolerated, but not forgiven. It would have to do for now.

"Simon," I asked as we strolled back under the darkening skies, "why is this so important to you? I know you loved Mr. Tolliver, but why Boston?"

Simon kind of laughed. "I dunno, it's hard to explain. Just trust me, it's important."

I let it go. It was enough that he was out of the coma and we had him back, if only for a short while. They could take him into the services, but I had a feeling they wouldn't be able to keep him. Look at him! He's weak as a puppy—or a kitten, whichever would be weaker. They would have to let him go. It was the only possible answer. I didn't dare say it to Simon, but I was confident in my heart that it would happen.

Simon went to bed as soon as we got back. It had been quite a day. Within hours of being sprung from the hospital where he lay for ten long years, he had been served with induction papers, found his pet to be years dead, and had begun to see how off-kilter the world had become during his slumber. In the morning we'd be off to the east in a borrowed car. Good thing I didn't have to be back to work until Monday. It was going to be some kind of weekend.

As soon as I was sure Simon was deeply asleep, I lay down on the floor in my room to fall back into the world of the past. I found my body a little reluctant to relax at first—probably due to, oh, I don't know, stress, alcohol and more stress. Facing down ex-lovers was never a favourite task of mine. Simon's return, welcome as it was, also was going to prove an adjustment. Ten years of privacy was now going to fade back into a roommate situation. It was going to be different. At some point, he was going to ask again about how he went into that coma and I wasn't going to be able to dodge him forever, especially with Maggie along. But I wasn't going to think about that then. Well, I was going to try not to think about it. That's the thing with meditation—the more you try to empty your mind, the more you discover just how full it is.

At last I felt the room slip away and I found myself crouching in the obsidian temple somewhere in my brain whose door opened to the green world of the birds and bees and funny creatures that once existed. I went to the eastern wall of the temple and threw open the door. For a disturbing moment, a cold wind blew into my face as if to discourage me from entering. I blinked and it was as if dark storm clouds parted, and suddenly the bright day was back. I had been in showers before in this land, but never had they seemed to be anything other than invigorating and life-giving. This was different. I couldn't tell you how, but I could feel it.

Harakka was waiting for me. Unusual, but not unprecedented. However, it made me feel a further jittery unease. I couldn't help wondering if I had got there a few minutes before I would have caught her tapping a little birdy claw impatiently.

"You're here," she said needlessly. "When do you begin your journey?"

This is the sort of remark that never ceased to annoy me. "It feels like you're eavesdropping on my life, sometimes," I said with only a modicum of irritation showing. I think.

"We have a bond." She made a movement that seemed an awful lot like a shrug. Who knew birds could shrug? "I am trying to help you. There is a—"

"Danger coming, I know, I know. Worse than the Wags. But can't you tell me more? That alone is not much help. I'm kind of dim that way. I can't imagine much worse than flying purple cannibals."

"Technically, cannibals are those who eat their own kind."

Great: a pedantic bird. "Point taken. But what's worse? If they eat the Wags, I'd think that was a good thing. At least until they get hungry again."

"You cannot comprehend the breadth of the cosmos, the layers of time that exist. I'm sorry, but your mind is not sufficiently expanded to grasp the enormity of what lies beyond your universe."

"I'm not sure it's even up to that," I said, sitting down on a nearby rock. This was giving me a headache. "When I think about the infinite expanses of space I get all woozy. I don't think it's possible to contemplate the idea of eternity."

Harakka looked up at me in that quizzical way that birds do so well. I was beginning to wonder if the eradication of birds wasn't done out of annoyance. They look at you with those beady eyes from the sides of their head and those quick movements back and forth, regarding you with those shiny black orbs. It's kind of spooky when you think about it. This wasn't even a real bird, just a memory of one or something. What was Harakka anyway?

"Are you a real bird, or a memory of a bird, or a dead bird, or what?" I finally asked. Not that it mattered, but it was a way to put off the inevitable lecture.

"A little from column A, a little from column B," Harakka said at last. Shecky Birdstein, I presume. "I am a spirit guide. I come out of your memories, the world's memories, the past, the future, the alternate present. Think of it as a great mythic well of possibility."

"I think I read a book like that once," I said, trying to cast my mind back to a book read years before, something about a dream sea where people swam only on deeply resonant occasions. The name escaped me, but the idea remained vivid. Great, here was another secret show that lay behind the conscious mind, some secret that I could not understand or even begin to comprehend. "But are you real?"

Harakka sighed. I had asked this question a hundred times and got the same answer in a variety of guises. I knew them all by now, but I still asked. "I am real. I'm not physical. I am true, but I am not visible in the mundane world. I am what I am, but I am not what you think. I will do what I can, as must you. Why do you always question? Why do you never accept?"

"I think that's what we call human nature," I said, as I had said on other occasions. It was our impasse. Nothing much was going to change in that direction any time soon. "We're heading off east tomorrow. But it's not a great spiritual quest. We're just going to bury Mr. Tolliver. Well, no—not bury.

Scatter, I guess."

I wish it were easier to see if a bird were smiling. Her words certainly seemed to have a bit of smile behind them. "If you don't think the burial of a friend is a spiritual journey, you haven't been paying attention."

"Oh, all right, all right. But I doubt it's going to do much about this threat you see coming. We're just going to go to Boston and come back."

"No other stops?"

"Well, Maggie wants to stop at some friend of hers, but I doubt that will mean much of anything. Some old pal. She's probably going to pick up an exhaust manifold."

"What's that?" Harakka asked, cocking her head again.

"I have no idea."

When I returned to my room, I felt a vague sense of disappointment. Was I waiting for something to happen? Or was I afraid that Harakka wasn't preparing me for worse disasters? What was I doing anyway? Wasn't part of this my job?

Well, I'll worry about that tomorrow, Miss Scarlet.

4

"So where's your friend live?" Simon asked as we took off down the dim city streets. The car was tiny, little more than a bubble around us, but there were few others on the road and we enjoyed the feel of zipping past the long queues at the tram stops in the little yellow bug, as I had already begun to call it. I was in the back seat as usual, because I hated sitting up front. As soon as we were on the main roads I would slip my book out and do some reading, but while we were in the city I didn't mind having a look around.

You never really get to know the city in which you live. You're always on your way somewhere, somewhere specific— to work, to a friend's, to a restaurant—so there's never time to just wander. Back in the day, I guess people used to do that all the time. When you could breathe the air for more than half an hour at a time, and when there were parks with green lawns and trees with leaves, (I'm old enough to remember), maybe it was different. But I'd lived here for years and in the area for most of my life and still I didn't recognise half the buildings we passed. The red gothic spires of the capitol, the old tower, and the big silly ovoid—they were all touchstones I seldom saw any more and nearly forgot were so near by. As we drove on the bridge across the wide grey gulch, I looked back through the rear window and felt a momentary stab of irrational loss, as if I might never see those sights again.

I had lost track of Maggie's answer to Simon's question, until I heard her say something about the Berkshires. "Are they mountains? Do they qualify as mountains?" I interrupted. Trust me to make things more difficult.

Maggie just glared at me over her shoulder and continued

what she was saying. "I have to see my friend there. They have a kind of, I dunno. Collective, I guess you might call it. I said I'd do a little maintenance work for them. Probably take a couple of hours, but they'll put us up for the night and we can charge the car. They have a lot of space apparently."

Collective—the very word struck dread into my heart: A bunch of back-to-nature types, living in a dream, hoping for the grass to grow, not bathing, singing folk songs. I shivered. The horror, the horror. I squirmed around in my seat. There wasn't enough room and I was feeling cramped with my knees pressed up against the back of Simon's seat. It was almost as bad as being shackled, except that there was even less room to move. I decided to swing my legs around on the seat to see whether that was a bit more comfortable. Part of the seat was taken up with a box of tools and tubes and wires that Maggie had thrown in at the last minute, part of the maintenance work she said. If it needed fixing, she would be the one to do it. Unless it was people.

The road was pitted with holes and cracks so we had to go kind of slow. There were a few other vehicles out on the road, mostly scary-looking truck things with oversize wheels and darkened glass. They might be privateers, I supposed. That must be some life, I couldn't help thinking, free and easy, running from the bronze and the feds, but not chained to a desk. I tried to fill the idea with a smack of romance, but all I could think of was the constant need for energy off the grid. It was like getting illegals when you were a teen, asking around, "You got any? Know anyone who's got any?" Rolling around in unsavoury parts of town, eyes peeled for trouble and never knowing how much you were willing to dare. When you get older you can pay other people to do the hard work and just sit at home, or even settle for the legals, which are cheaper and easier, if not a whole lot effective. Then again, there's always alcohol. Centuries, no, millennia, and it's still the best mind-altering drug around. Tastes good, too, and unlike ayahuasca and peyote, doesn't make you vomit. Well, that's as long as you don't over-indulge. I'd never do that, you know.

Not more than once or twice—or a few thousand times. But not more than that.

So far.

"Are we there yet?" I felt obliged to ask. Maggie ignored me and Simon turned around to stick his tongue out at me. "Will this little thing make it up the Berkshire hills?"

Maggie failed to rise to my bait. Pity. She was behaving herself—why couldn't I? I supposed it was just the idea of being trapped in this small container for not just hours but days on end. It was hard to believe that people used to make a habit of this. I am stuck all day with my co-workers, but I barely have to speak to them. I had a bad feeling Simon was expecting me to make amends to Maggie over the next few days.

Prospects: unlikely.

I leaned my head back and stared out at the grey skies. What a bleak old world this has become. The sad thing is that I'm still old enough to recall the tail end of family car trips. Not that we made many; oil was already getting expensive and the electrics hadn't taken off. There was still drinkable water flowing in some of the rivers. We'd got to my aunt's who lived outside Worcester with her duck pond and cats. The cats weren't in the duck pond, you know. They were inside. Nowadays you have to explain the idea of a duck pond. And ducks. Hers went swiftly. And the cats? I looked down at the little green bag that held Mr. Tolliver. He was getting a more personal send-off than my aunt's menagerie did. Her crazy next door neighbour who thought the end times were coming set his house on fire, which spread to hers and to several of the surrounding houses. They poked through the debris to find my aunt but not what was left of her cats. I heard a bulldozer just knocked down what was left and they buried cats and house together. Could be worse, I suppose. Not sure how, really. I suppose if they had not rifled through the ashes to find Aunt Dana that would be worse. For her family anyway—I doubt she'd have minded being recycled with her pets.

Car trips were an excuse to fight with my sisters. Hence the need to flex my annoying capabilities. But it was no fun to fight against the two marshmallows up front. You needed a good sparrer, like my oldest sister. She'd rise to almost any bait back then, including ones she had invented. We could often keep my mother busy for the whole of the journey, issuing ultimatums and slaps until we arrived at the doorstep of some relative or site of natural beauty. Even then they were looking seedy, but we didn't really know that. I suppose if I had ever paid attention in my classes I might have retained more of a memory of the great land this once was, but honestly, until I met Harakka I hadn't a clue.

Now, here we were speeding toward a sad little enclave of people desperately trying to bring back that lost cause. In all the visits I made, Harakka never suggested that it might be possible to restore this land to what it was. She did make an off-hand remark once that I guess I ought to have picked up on sooner than this.

I had mentioned the sorry state of the once green hills of this land and wondered at the fact that even with a much smaller population we weren't making much of comeback plant-wise. All she said was "Not enough died."

"Enough what?" I asked, puzzled, thinking she meant not enough plants had died which seemed a conundrum. But I was looking for conundrums about then, they seemed to be the order of the day.

"Not enough people," she corrected me.

"How many would that be?"

She laughed. Picture that, will you: you may not have seen a bird talk, but try to imagine one laughing. It's a peculiar sight. Her answer, though, surely did not make me laugh.

"All of them."

It put a chill on conversation for a moment, I can tell you, but I didn't really think about it then. At least not to the point where I might get the full gist of the implications. If we wanted to bring the land back to health, we would all have to vacate the premises. Grim thought, and one I was still not too willing to grapple with for any length of time.

Much easier to crack jokes about Maggie's friends.

As the auto laboured up the inclines at the Berkshires' base, my musing thoughts turned to what drew them there. "So what kind of people would choose to live in such a remote spot?"

Simon gave me a warning look. "Why don't you shut up and enjoy the quiet?"

"People who have a purpose in life," Maggie cut in. "It would take too long to explain that concept to you, but many people have a point beyond sucking up valuable air and water."

Now, I was happy. "I take it you mean I am a worthless use of such resources?"

"Will you two not do this?" Simon said. "Is it too late to play the coma card? Do you think I missed the sound of bickering for ten years?"

"I'm not bickering, I'm just curious about where we're going. Will they all be wearing Birkenstocks?" Those were shoes worn in the last century to mark one's status as a caring individual with regard to the natural world. I think they were made from puffins, a renewable source of energy back then. I was trying to be as reasonable as possible.

Maggie, too, was maintaining a veneer of reason. "I believe they all go barefoot, probably naked, too." She threw a quick glance my way. "But don't get excited—I think they practice celibacy as well."

"A real struggle I'm sure." It was my sincere belief that people practiced celibacy because they had little choice. Like myself of late, which I can't begin to explain. Nothing deliberate, you know, just a kind of accident. If I cast my mind back, it had indeed been months, but it only struck me just then. I felt a sudden surge of panic. Was I becoming unattractive? No, wait, there was that guy down on the third floor who flirted with me and always asked me out for coffee and whatnot. I had assumed I would get around to him sooner or later, but that was three months ago.

Not that he'd lost interest, I should add as a salve to my vanity. When did I? Well, not interest, just practice. Well, we were going to fix that, I promised myself. Nothing like a collective of celibate folks to pose a good challenge. "Are they just women?" I was kind of in a man mood that day.

"All the genders are represented," Maggie said with a little bit of a laugh in her voice. It made me a tad suspicious. What did she know that I didn't? Or was she aiming that toward Simon. Shit—he'd had ten years of celibacy thrust upon him. Beware the next man in his path. He could well explode with ten years of celibacy to release.

"I'm not singing 'Kumbayah' with anyone."

"Duly noted."

Simon was still giving me a stern look, but I was bored. "Are we there yet?"

You can imagine how it went on. There were no explosions, not so much for lack of trying as for the cramped confines and the lack any real malice. On my part anyway—I couldn't speak for Maggie, but she seemed to have taken Simon's exhortations to heart. I was too sleepy and bored to work up much of a head of steam. By the time we were winding around the remnants of small tourist towns, I was almost beginning to get excited about arriving.

At least it would be a change.

We had weaved through yet another ghost town and were passing by what might have been a lake at one time, when the car began to slow. "Mothersuckingrabbitfelcher," Maggie muttered under her breath.

"Are we going to have to walk?" I added helpfully.

"No, we're going to have to push!"

Well, crap. "C'mon, little auto. You can do it." I tried to gesture imploringly to the car, but it was continuing to slow and it finally just puttered to a stop. For a moment, there was nothing but silence, which was odd. Things were quiet back in town, but silent—this was silent. When Simon and I finally unfolded ourselves from our seats and stepped outside, the silence seemed to thunder in my ears. I could tell immediately that this was part of the fire-scorch side of the hills. They had burned for weeks back then. What was left behind still wasn't pretty. There were no people, there were no buildings, there weren't even any other cars. It was spooky.

I looked around for something other than the blasted tree stumps and brown dirt. Nothing. I rolled up my sleeves and joined Simon at the back of the car. "You feel up to this?" I asked, looking over at his pale arms and face. He shrugged. We would do what we could.

With Maggie steering and shouting encouragement, we bent our backs to it and shoved. Even though there was a slight incline, once we got the auto rolling it wasn't too bad. Getting it started proved to be the worst part—at least until it came to stopping it once the momentum was going.

"Stop, stop here!" Maggie yelled. I let go and straightened up, but Simon stumbled a little, so I grabbed his arm. The auto quickly came to a halt in front of a large wooden gate with some kind of Sanskrit symbol on it. Well, I had read enough in my seeking to be pretty certain that it was Sanskrit, though I hadn't the slightest notion what it might say. Must be hippie haven.

Simon was breathing a mite heavy beside me, but Maggie was jumping out of her seat to run up to the com spot on the doors. There was a vid trained on the entrance from up above. It was looking like some rather humourless security for a bunch of back-to-blasted-nature folks. The wall was easily ten or twelve feet high, I guessed. The weird thing was, it looked like real wood. Maybe it was old.

Maggie spoke her name into the com and there was a crackle of greeting. After a minute we heard the whine of machinery and the gate began to roll to the right. As it jittered open, two people stepped into the gap. They were similarly dressed in loose-fitting clothes that looked both comfortable and breathable. Natural fabrics! Wow, it had been a while. I still had my wool scarf from high school wrapped around the lamp by my bed, but it had to be the last organic fibre I had felt in some time. But there was no fooling the eye when it came to drape. A man and a woman, both young and thin—all right, let's say it, ungodly healthy looking—stood in the middle of the drive to greet Maggie.

"You are Aleria's friend," the woman said to Maggie, gravely taking her hand in her clasped hands. "We've been expecting you." She looked up at me and Simon, chests still heaving from the exertion. "You've brought friends." It wasn't exactly disapproval in her voice, so much as it was leeriness. It seemed like she was afraid we might infiltrate their nirvana.

Fat chance.

"Can we lend you a hand?" the young man asked us. Maggie jumped back in the auto to turn the wheel in the right direction. The two hippies joined us behind the bumper and we put the vehicle back in motion, running it through the gates and into the compound. I was somewhat distressed to see that it was all uphill from there by the look of it. We paused to let the door roll shut behind us and then everybody prepared to get the auto moving once again.

"Do we really need to roll it all the way up the hill?" I asked. "Hear me out—aren't we just going to have to roll it back down again?"

"I'm going to have to work on it," Maggie said with more than a tad of irritation in her voice. "Do you propose I work on it down here by the gates, or up where there's some light?"

I was going to say there was plenty of light down here, but I wisely shut my mouth and turned back to task. But before we got it rolling again, I stopped. "Wait!"

"What now?" Simon said irritably.

"Look—all around. It's green!"

Indeed it was. Inside the walls there was a distinct greenish hue to the ground, not the patchy brown that could be found elsewhere. It wasn't like the lush verdant colour of

Harakka's world, but it was a damn sight healthier than anything I had seen since childhood. I bent down to poke at the grass on the side of the driveway and sure enough, it was real grass. I couldn't resist pulling out a blade and lifting it to my nostrils. Green, real, green—just like I smelled when I visited Harakka.

I looked up at the two hippies. "You guys have a little goldmine here."

That drew frowns—I am the genius of the spoken word, did I mention that? "This is sacred land," the woman said with a touch of frostiness. "It is not a cash crop."

"I didn't mean it that way—"

"Ro, let it go. Push." Simon was right. Plenty of time to admire the scenery later. I put my shoulder back to the auto and slowly we pushed it up the hill. It hadn't looked all that steep, but it was a mother of a hill. By the time we reached the top, we were all dripping, even the cool customers who had met us at the gate. At least Maggie was content with the lower parking lot and didn't demand that we trundle it all the way to the front door of the headquarters.

And what a place—it was the strangest thing. It had a kind of industrial look to it, as if it had been a hospital or a school for disappointing children. It was set back in the hill and no doubt from the top floors gave what had once been an impressive view of the Berkshires and the valleys between them, on a clear day anyway. The walls stretched around a good bit of the local real estate, disappearing into a grove of burnt stumps and blasted trunks on either side. Who knew how far the land went.

The woman who ran from the big double doors was undoubtedly Aleria, this dear friend of Maggie's. I tried not to think about the fact that she had let us push the auto all the way up here without helping. She was dressed similarly to her two friends, but in a light blue colour while their clothes were more natural tones. She hopped down the steps light as a feather and graceful as a dancer.

Who's jealous?

That's envy actually. It's not that I was jealous of the evident bond between her and Maggie. I had my own fish to fry. I would, however, have liked to look like her, to be delicate and dainty instead of the clod-footed beast that I am, crashing into breakables and always saying the wrong thing. I suppose it might be possible to be physically graceful as this Aleria certainly seemed to be and still be a social degenerate. Need I add that her voice was musical and her hair shiny and bouncy? No, that would be overkill. She greeted us as if we were all long-lost friends and welcomed us into the centre. "This is Garbhavihar. You are safe, you are welcome."

Well, we'd see about that. In the meantime, we had to carry all the stuff from the seats and the trunk up the steps to the entrance, where suddenly there was a crowd of people all murmuring in soft tones. Where were they when the auto needed pushing? We were divested of our burdens and taken to rooms. The accommodations were Spartan but scrupulously clean. The young man who showed me to my room, shyly gestured down the hall to the communal bathroom where he said I could take a shower if I wanted.

A shower?!

Maybe it was a euphemism for the moist rubdown, I thought quickly. At my shocked look, he smiled. "We have our own spring. We filter and reuse the water, but we do have our own well." Guess that's why there was a hint of green hereabouts. He handed me a towel and slipped away down the hall.

"What's your name?" I called after him. Hey, you never know.

"Wyn." With that he padded down the hall and I went to explore the wonders of a real water shower. I found Simon there before me, looking somewhat askance at the visible tubes and machinery of the shower. "My person told me that I should lather up before I let the water run," he said, gesturing to the industrial size container of body wash. We shucked off our clothes, lathered up and ducked into our separate compartments. I gave the dial a spin and gasped as the water hit me. It wasn't that it was too cold or too hot—apparently they regulated the temperature with solar heating, we found out later—it was the novelty of water pouring over my body, a feeling I had not had for so many years. I just stood there, revelling in the feeling until I heard Simon bark with pleasure, too, and then raise his voice in song. The tune was an oldie but a goodie, but even as I joined him singing, I could only think that much as it was enjoyable to have love reign o'er me, I was rather pleased at the moment that it was water raining down on me. No wonder people were dying of dehydration—as much as you might drink, there's no substitute for being sloshed on the outside.

I didn't even dry my hair off, instead enjoying the streaming water trickling down my back as I wrapped myself in the borrowed robe. It was a little threadbare, but I couldn't have cared less. The bodily sensation gave me such a charge that I wanted to laugh out loud. I could see Simon shared my exhilaration, both of us grinning into the mirrors lining the bathroom. As we stepped out the door into the hallway, we were both jabbering excitedly and nearly ran over Maggie, who was coming to have her own shower. I was grinning like an idiot and it said something that she did not scowl at me but shared the mood enough to grin in return.

"Come on in, the water's great!" Simon said with a whoop, stepping out of her way with exaggerated gallantry.

"They're serving dinner in the cafeteria, second floor. You may actually enjoy the food," she added as the door closed behind her. We went to our rooms, threw on our clothes and went back up the stairs, smelling the food all the way. Another woman greeted us at the door. When I say greeted, what I mean is she smiled and pointed to the sign on the door. It said "Please maintain silence during meals." Simon and I exchanged a glance, but he shrugged and stepped in to join the buffet line. The plates were bright orange, yellow and blue, which seemed quite cheery for the rather institutional room. It was cavernous for the amount of people that were currently eating there, spread out in groups of half a dozen or less, here and there at the long wooden tables.

The smell of the buffet, however, quickly took centre stage. There was a variety, for sure, but the smell—there was something I couldn't put my finger on until I saw the greens. When had I last seen greens?

I looked up at Simon and he was grinning from ear to ear. He hadn't even had ten years of endless soy with the occasional ear of corn or oaty bread, but God knows what they fed him in the hospital. Soy gelatin, no doubt. But it wasn't the same as being conscious and eating endless permutations of soy, disguised and diluted, flavoured and spiced but still the same beany flavour and the same hormonal effects. I'm sure there was soy here, but there was also real rice, real fresh vegetables, real leafy greens. I cast a quick glance around the room. Maybe these weren't hippies but privateers. If so, the hippie get-up was a good camouflage.

In the mean time, I heaped my plate high and looked with relish at the meal. At the end of the buffet were big pitchers of water, presumably from their well. I filled a tall glass, then waited for Simon who was still agonizing over choices. We didn't quite know where we ought to sit, but Aleria waved us over to her table where a small group sat. We pulled up chairs, overcoming just barely the habit of making small talk. Aleria smiled at our plates full of food. Clearly they were used to more modest portions, but who knew when we would have another meal like this.

Unless, of course, Maggie couldn't fix the car. I was beginning to have some ambivalence about that fact. It might not be so bad to hang out with the hippies, although I would have to go back to work Monday and we still needed to get to Boston. Well, you know, I had a backlog of vacation days. Look at you, I thought to myself, willingly thinking about spending more time with these strange folks just because they had fresh vegetables and running water.

That was no small thing, though, to be fair. While I had thought of the silent meal as a hardship, I ignored everyone at the table while I chewed each bite, treasuring the flavours that spilled across my palate, the crunch of each vegetable and the texture of every grain of rice. Flavour was such a novelty. Twenty years ago there had been a lot of hand-wringing about obesity. Funny how all that changed after the Blight. All the lawsuits against The-Corporation-Who-Must-Not-Be-Named did nothing to change the fact that nothing much edible was growing anymore, other than the supersoy that was muscling aside every plant in its path. How quickly things could change.

Aleria, who had gotten up from the table with a smile I assumed to mean farewell, returned and handed something to both Simon and me. I had to stare at it moment to realise it was an apple. Aleria was grinning as Maggie came up with her tray of food and joined the staring. I held the red and green orb in my hand and ran my fingers over its smooth surface. I remembered some words from a poem about daring to eat a peach—was that before or after the poet imagined being pinned like a bug to a wall—and something about believing that that mermaids were crooning in his ear, or that he wished they would. Mermaids might well have been singing in my ears when I bit into the tart sweetness of the apple and felt its juicy ripeness spring into every pore of my mouth. It seemed, anyway, as if a chorus of some kind were sighing in my ear.

Simon broke the mood, leaning over and whispering in my ear, "Do you need to be alone with that fruit?" I grinned back at him and bit deeper again. I didn't care. The juice ran down my throat, the slight acidity tickling my tongue. To think people used to eat things like this every day. Curse them all to the blackest perdition for poisoning this world and its greenery. I could understand Harakka's disdain for our world so much better now. What I couldn't understand was why she let me see the beauty of hers—who could trust us?—and why she would bother to help such a worthless species.

Aleria was still smiling as she watched us all revel in the

food. Exchanging a glance with her other friends she said, "Since we're the last ones here and I won't disturb anyone, I have to tell you: If you like that meal, just wait, because you ain't seen nothing yet."

"What do you mean?" Simon said, laughing just a little in the sudden echo of the empty hall. "There's more?"

She grinned unselfconsciously and looked eminently pleased with herself. "We have such sights to show you!"

I had the vaguest memory of that phrase being a tagline to some film, so it distracted me for a moment from the conversation as I tried to remember it. The sensation of the voices ringing in my ears seemed to continue, too, as if that tintinnabulation were real and not just imagined. I shook my head a little and tried to pop my ears. Maybe it was the effect of all this fresh food—surely it must be a shock to the system.

"Are you all right?" Simon finally asked me as I sat there waggling my lower jaw.

"Yeah, it's just there's a kind of ringing in my ears."

"Maybe it's the elevation."

I gave him a look. "We're not that high up. This isn't Peru."

"Well, maybe it will go away soon."

When Maggie had finished her meal and devoured her apple, we took our trays to the kitchen area and dropped each item into its properly labelled receptacle. It was a model of efficiency and scrupulously clean. Everything here conspired to make me feel lumpy, dirty and useless. Aleria led us back down the hallway and paused before a large set of double doors. I could hear a murmur of speech within as if the rest of the folks had gathered after their meal to do all the talking they had saved up. Who knew—maybe they kept silent the rest of the day, too.

Aleria looked at us as if she were about to tell us we had won the golden tickets. "This is our temple," she said, laying a hand on the door as gently as if it were a frail and beloved elder.

Temple! Oh, I didn't like the sound of that. Fill us up on rich food and then, wham! Ask us for money—or lifelong dedication. I wasn't going to join her temple, no Kool-Aid for me, thank you very much. Now is it the symptom of a cynical world that I would have these thoughts, unkind and uncharitable as they might be, or the sign of a somewhat less than gullible inhabitant of this continent in this century who is not too stupid to learn from the mistakes of others? The Purges were fresh enough in my mind so as to not make me too inclined to forget. Indeed, the weeping and wailing and loud vid haranguing day and night in the wake of the Wags' arrival will no doubt keep its vividness until my final days.

The opportunity to observe a seismic shift's fissure through society is rare. I doubt all such alterations need be accompanied with so much yowling, weeping and gnashing of teeth. The Wags, however, were. It wasn't so much the Wags themselves, as the pointlessness of them. There was a cleft between those who accepted what their eyes, (well, by way of a multitude of screens), told them and those who refused to acknowledge that input. They tended to be the oldest of the population, who had the luxury of simply ignoring that with which they did not wish to occupy themselves. Then there was the crevice between those who saw the arrival as something interesting—if dangerous—and those who found it horrifying.

Oddly enough, either group was as likely to contain people of what we call a religious persuasion. There were people who could wave the strange incursion away with a few words from the Bhagavad Gita or the Mahayana Sutras. Then there were the people who used the Wags as an excuse to go bat-shit crazy. We not just talking wild-eyed gibbering in the street manic preaching. No, this was the grab a submachine gun and do Saint Warren's Roland proud kind of crazy, not just dying but taking a small village worth of people with them. Most often it was family, so there was no one to bear the tears, but sometimes it was strangers and we all felt the fears. I think the biggest was a guy in Durham, North Carolina who took out most of the people in a Marriott Hotel. They said it was the Wag-fever, but I heard another version where it was the bad service he got. I guess we'll never know.

The worst by far, though, was the Purges. When the heads of religions go crazy, they take a mighty big crowd down the drain with them. With the 'net word can fly so fast; instantaneous crazy across the globe. I forget which one it was that started it all—one of those megachurch jokers, Reverend somebody or other and his massive congregation of people who like saying they been to church more so than they like to have any involvement in the process. Face it, we have become a nation of passive receptors. Most people did nothing more at the arrival of the Wags than gape at the vid screen and drool.

I suppose it would have been better if more had done so. Reverend Moody—that was the name, and a fitting one it was—apparently brooded over the Wags arrival and decided that he had been taken for a ride by his good lord. All that bible-learning had been nothing but a smokescreen and promises of the sweet hereafter a pipedream of the most insidious kind. And if there's one thing I learned from reading that Irishman's play, it's that a dead pipe dream makes a lethal weapon. While a lot of people were soaking in a happy and drunken denial, (hands up, everyone I know), the Reverend and his network of until-recently-believers were putting the word out—fire sale, everything's got to go. They tried to say it wasn't anger, but when you're counting on the Big Daddy in the sky and he lets you down, wrath follows fast upon the heels of despair and it's usually wearing its heavy boots.

The Reverend thought he would save all the followers from the same infuriated outrage that he was suffering by relieving them of the pain of continuing to exist in a world plagued by Wags but Jesus-free. Crazy as his logic seemed, there were many who shared it. Thousands, in fact hundreds of thousands wound up dead. Worse yet, historic buildings of great beauty and majesty were levelled into rubble. It was the Buddhas of Bamyan all over again, but this time the destruction wasn't ignored by the rest of the world. Our fearless armed forces—at least the ones that weren't watching the Wags—were called upon to put a stop to the Purges, but the momentum had grown so fast and so wildly, it took a good bit to calm things down once more. The Reverend Moody had already shuffled off his mortal coil by way of a little cocktail of morphine and cyanide, but they dug him up like Cromwell and paraded his head around Las Vegas like some kind of spectacle, which I suppose it was. By then the backlash against the Purges was so strong and the vitriol running so high that the counter-Purge (if you will) threatened to draw as much blood in return.

Part of what made that movement run out of steam was the lack of substantial bodies. People who didn't lose anyone in their immediate circle were disinclined to get too passionate about killing those whose killing upset them in the first time. Some were just lazy, but I like to think most of them were sickened by the idiocy of the Purges. Around the world funeral pyres raged and bodies piled high. The smoke filled the skies but it was a healthier kind of pollution than the usual, so the gloomy grey firmament just settled like mourning clothes upon us.

The weird thing was the people who still insisted upon burials. Simon's family was among them. Yes, there were even a few of those Boston Brahmins who gave in to the madness of the Purges. I guess it was the old "banned in Boston" spirit. His maiden aunt on his mother's side was even on the news spool, which took some doing in the midst of the Purges. I guess maybe it was the contrast between this priggish Boston blueblood and her vitriolic violence against the church that let her down. Simon always said that she had had a highly developed sense of propriety, which always seemed to mean she had a stick up her butt about a foot wide, but he insisted it was a matter of aesthetics.

So it was all the more surprising that she could bring herself to blow up that beautiful old building. Well, beautiful in a prim kind of Bostonian way, I guess—not really my kind of thing. I much prefer the gothic when you get right down to it. There was far too much Puritanism in the old church for my liking, but I could still feel the horror of its destruction just as painfully. When I saw the footage of its starchy white steeple charred and blackened, it felt like a punch in the gut. While the destruction of centuries old cathedrals in Europe made me weep for hours on end, the destruction of this little church I had seen with my own eyes struck me like the death of a friend. Not a close friend, maybe, but a near one who had heretofore seemed bubbly if dull and miles away from death, but suddenly was hit by a tour bus or crushed by an elevator. It was senseless, stupid and familiar.

I saw Simon's aunt spitting and snarling at the vid eyes, a kind of madness in her glittering eyes and it was the single most frightening sight I have ever seen. The Wags were scary, but there was a different kind of unreality to seeing someone I had known and filed away in the drawer of my brain for starchy old women, who clearly had to be moved to the ravening lunatic bin. The little church where she had served on any number of genteel ladies' guilds, (or so I always imagined), had been pockmarked and blasted by her own hands, even though she had bragged of its place in American history. "Two if by land, one if by sea," she had told us with a sniff that made clear our unworthiness of such titans. Paul Revere had been a bell ringer there for a time (a likely story). Yet she had turned on that little brick building as upon a mad dog, filling with the explosive wrath that detonated from her heart. I saw her dangling from the arms of the big bronze, shouting her truth to the skies and filling me with one thought:

Where on earth did she get the bombs?

Here was a woman who would not whisper the words "toilet paper" aloud, who could not bring herself to regard her little terrier without a sweater hiding his nether regions. How does a woman like that get explosives, put them in place, ignore the neat rows of hymnals lined up and commit the oldest church in her beloved city to rubble—or half rubble? She didn't turn out to be too good at placing bombs. Practice, practice, practice, I guess.

Simon didn't even know about that yet. It hadn't really come up and well, there had been other things to talk about. For once, I was glad his family had disowned him all those years ago—left me with a lot less to have to explain. Maybe when we got to Mount Auburn, I could tell him about his aunt and we could visit her, too.

So, no—I wasn't too thrilled when Aleria said this was their temple and invited us to come in and join the rest of her folk. I steeled myself and looked over at Simon, who was doing his best to look polite and guarded as we stepped out of the way of the opening doors. So I saw his reaction before I looked inside.

"Jesus, Mary and Joseph!" It was a whisper of pure surprise.

I turned to look for myself. "Shiva H. Vishnu!"

The room was full of trees.

5

It was not just trees, although trees were the most remarkable sight in that room. There were all kinds of plants, so many in fact that I had no idea of the names of most of them—they didn't even look familiar. But many did: purple loosestrife, chicory, Queen Anne's lace, witchweed—they were all things once considered weeds, to be routed out with all alacrity and grim imprecations. That's what made them valuable here: their strength, their persistence. I didn't even know all the trees' names either, but I marvelled at the sight of them reaching up toward the high ceiling of the hall. The smell permeated my senses.

"Oh, my America, my new-found land," I said, lacking any words of my own. That was the flea poet, although I couldn't think of his name at that moment. I would have to look it up when the trip was done. Simon, too, gawked at the greenery and Maggie bent down to touch a knot of crab grass with her fingertips, as if it might break.

Aleria grinned at us. "Not what you had in mind, was it?" We shook our heads. "I couldn't resist a little bit of dramatic effect. It's such a wonderful sight, I can't imagine someone who could take it all in without feeling joy."

"But how...?" Simon gestured toward the trees.

Aleria laughed. "A lot of hard work and a lot of incredible luck. The previous tenants of this place took good care of the land. They were careful stewards and worked hard to keep it GMO-free. Nothing could save everything, but as you can tell, the hardier plants were able to survive.

"With a little help," said the thin African-American woman whose name escaped me. "Aleria and the others who were first to recover this spot from ruin learned all they could about indoor farming and preserving the habitat."

"How long ago was that?" I was beginning to think Aleria was a bit older than I had thought.

"Before the war started," Aleria answered, confirming my suspicions. Good god, she must be my age. Damn her for looking half that. "During the first years of the Green Evolution. The last tenants had been decimated by the draft and the economic downturn. A small group of us bought the place with the promise that we would do what we could to preserve it."

"You've done a great job at that," Maggie said, her admiration evident as she stared up at the trees. "I can't believe all you've done here."

Aleria led us through the little forest where people were busy tending the plants, looking for yellowed or brown leaves and shoring up wiggly trunks. "We had a good start with the previous tenants. They had protected the lands while they could and when they could no longer shield the grounds sufficiently, we were able to step in and take over. Some of the fires got up here—the orchard up behind us on the hill got hit rather badly—but for the most part the location helped guard us from further encroachment by the Blight or by meddling observers."

In the back, the wall of the building had simply been knocked down and the trees continued out into what must have been another parking lot. There was a clear ceiling overhead, but it didn't seem to be enough to hide these wonders from prying eyes. "What about snoops? Don't you get them flying over? They're going to see the tree tops, surely?"

Aleria looked up. "It looks like a clear roof from here, but it's actually filled with solar-heating cells that mask the visibility. The light gets through but on photos they tend to show up as solid. We've had no sign of trouble in all the years we've been here." To my surprise, she leaned over to knock on one of the tree trunks. "For luck," she winked.

She led us through the trees, pointing out this kind or that, explaining which ones had been easy to maintain and which proved more problematic. We all cooed over a wee peach tree that had barely got beyond the twig stage, as if it were somebody's precocious offspring, touching the tender nap of the single miniature fruit as if it were solid gold. It was certainly as good as or better than a Fort Knox brick at this point, they being more common than real peaches for some time now. There had always been rumours of private gardens, whistled about on the web or talked up on the vids, but somehow crazy millionaires far away in Switzerland seemed more probable than a bunch of hippie types practically next door.

"Can you believe this?" I asked Simon as we gaped at a little weeping willow next to a little pond they had made from an offshoot of the spring.

"I expect to see little animated bluebirds flying in to light on my finger." Simon poked a toe into the pond and grinned at me. "Could you imagine we'd be seeing something like this when we set out this morning?"

"I'm beginning to hope that it will take Maggie a while to fix the auto."

Just then a sort of gong sounded and people started putting away their tools and other paraphernalia, then gathered around Aleria in the most open section of forest temple. "Quittin' time," I muttered to Simon, who snorted with suppressed laughter. There were smiles and a lot of chatter so it did kind of seem like socialising time. Voices had been subdued while they toiled, but now laughter tinkled through the boughs.

"Shall we join them?" Simon looked over at me, raising his eyebrows.

"I suppose so. You know, you have a dopey grin on your face."

"So do you."

We followed one of the winding paths back to the centre.

Maggie was there in hushed conversation with Aleria, looking serious. Probably getting details on the needed maintenance work, no doubt. Or so I thought until she looked up at our arrival and immediately shifted her eyes away. Call me a tad suspicious and paranoid, but I read something into that motion—something not charitable. I glanced at Simon to see if he shared my misgivings, but he was staring vacantly up at the ceiling where an adventurous vine of some kind was struggling against gravity toward the roof, soft green tentacles clutching at any kind of purchase on the stuccoed walls. I set my mental phasers to stun and stretched my awareness out around me like a hurricane fence.

It was almost a relief to hear Aleria say as we walked up, "I have to admit, we had a bit of an ulterior motive in bringing you here."

Simon looked at me and I gave him a guarded look back. I could see his deflector shields go up, too.

"You know that unusual things have been going on of late," she continued looking from me to Simon.

Unusual, eh? You mean like aliens taking over the world? Hot-rodding around the planet and, just lately, getting all agitated and jumpy themselves? That kind of weird was what I suppose she meant, but I just kept my mouth shut for once. She didn't know weird. Try a talking bird in a world that no longer exists but somehow I can find my way there to jabber on about this and that.

"You have had an unusual experience." But she was talking to Simon now. Oh yeah, coma—true enough, that was a tad uncommon. "What you may not know, is that people all over the world who had been in comas for years are all waking up now."

Simon looked at me, and I looked at him. Who'd 'a thunk it, Aleister Plunkett? So it wasn't my witty repartee. "Why?" Simon was the obvious one to ask, but I got there first.

"We're not sure," Aleria smiled what was probably meant to be a reassuring smile, but I was past being placated now. Too odd, too odd by half. "But we have a ceremony that may help us to discover the special link that has been forged."

"Link?" Simon now, sounding like he was far from reassured, too. "Forged by whom? With whom? Why?"

"That's what we're not sure of yet." Aleria put out a hand to encourage Simon's trust. I could tell by the narrowing of his gaze that it was not having the desired effect. "But it is a world-wide phenomenon. People who have been inexplicably in comas for years are all waking now. It must be for a purpose. Have you not seen the news vids?"

He shrugged. Somehow in the busy whirl of events he had been less than glued to the screen. Something about regaining muscular control and the ability to walk, I guess. Besides, Simon had always been too easily bored by the endless parade of splashy images. Always the artist—images were to be selected, not lumped together like porridge.

Aleria and her people were looking excited now. I could see Maggie trying to slip into the background. The rat! "It's the most amazing thing. Those who have awakened have had an incredible gift bestowed upon them"

"Ten lost years—must be quite a spangly gift," Simon said so quiet you could hardly hear the fury rumbling beneath his words. Unless you knew how he could blow up when he lost his temper, and I knew. I had a feeling everything was going to go pear-shaped very soon.

Give the gal credit, Aleria seemed to realise that she was getting onto shifting sands with the object of her intentions. She drew back a little to try another tack across the icy surface of my friend. "It cannot seem like much of a gift to you, I know. Your loss can never be sufficiently repaid." She should patent the soothing tone of her voice, she'd make a mint. Fine china could balance on those dulcet tones. The most delicate Georgian eggshell porcelain could slip between its waves and safely resist any impact up to a thousand pounds, (was that wording from some long forgotten advertisement?). "But you have an opportunity to help us all, to give us insight at a time of great need."

Simon shot me a quick glance. I shrugged. He looked back at Aleria. "What do I have to do?"

"You're not going to slice him open to read his entrails are you?" I had read about that in some book on ancient Roman traditions. Apparently it was considered a very trustworthy method of divination.

Aleria had the good grace to laugh. "Nothing like that. It's more of a ceremony, in fact. We drum to put you into a trance-like state and then with guidance of elders, you will make a visit to the spirit realms."

"Oh, you mean journeying," I said with surprise.

Aleria looked surprised too, but not as much as Maggie and Simon. They gaped. That's not a word I get to use much: gape. They gaped quite demonstratively. Aleria said, "I wasn't aware you had some training in esoteric techniques."

"I have many skills," I said trying not to look too smug or annoyed. Simon was staring at me with patent disbelief. I wondered where to begin telling him how much things had changed in ten years.

Maggie snorted. "We're not talking drugs here, Ro. This is serious stuff."

"Maggie, you don't know dick about what I've been doing for the last few years."

"Girls," Simon said in a placating sort of tone, while stretching out the word to ridiculousness. "Let's not make this personal. What were you saying about this business, Aleria? It's new to me."

Aleria looked a bit concerned, brows knitted as her eyes darted between me and Maggie. I knew I shouldn't be getting my hackles up, but Maggie was really giving a bag of moonshine about me. It had been quite some time since that I had given up dipping rather deeply. Just because she had been nursing a bit of spleen about me, because things hadn't worked out between us, didn't mean she had to darken my name with the others—those who didn't know me as a perennial toss-pot of ambition-free carnage and full-time dissolution.

It wasn't like that anymore. I wasn't like that anymore. And I resented Maggie still casting me in that role. "It's an ancient technique," I said, "by which people walk between the layers of consciousness—if you hold to that belief system—or between the temporal worlds, if you hold to that one. All I know is that I have learned a lot about the past and some tantalising facts about the future by doing just that." No need to mention that I had initially come to that path by means of an accidental overdose—things were different now and I deserved to have that recognised.

Aleria nodded in response to the questioning looks of Maggie and Simon. I smiled with triumph of a sort as she continued. I have to take my conquests as they come. "All we're going to do is some drumming, first to get everyone to dance and work out the excess energy, then we'll switch to a kind of repetitive beat that will help you to move into a trance. Then we'll just see what happens. If all goes well, you'll have a transcendent experience that you can share with us to offer some insight about the new phenomena that are occurring at present."

I had to laugh. It wasn't mean; it wasn't a "superior" laugh as they say. But the thought of someone without any journeying experience just moving into a trance state without any training or help or preparation was patently ridiculous. Not to mention having a transcendent experience that you could just share with a big crowd of people in a totally articulate manner.

Ha, as they say.

Simon looked a tad dubious as well. "I don't mean to throw a rub in the way, but are you fucking crazy?"

I love the way that man can turn a phrase. How I have missed him these ten long years. You don't know what it was like, having that dry humour and scathing insight to rely upon for so long and then being robbed of it for so long. I might have been sucked under, but for Harakka. I remember once Harakka asking me about Simon when I had mentioned him for the umpteenth time, "What is the bond between you?"

How to explain? It wasn't sex, it wasn't family, it wasn't even mutual dependence of the sort where sad folk rely on each other to keep themselves from looking like the losers they are. He was a swell of the first stare, rolling in lard, and I was a funny-looking spaz with no money, no friends and far too much trouble trailing in my wake. As kids, it might have been just coincidence, but we stayed friends from something more than mere habit. He was always clear-sighted. I usually imagined him as a William Blake for the modern age with a singular vision of prescient clarity. His art was surreal, singular and compelling. Unlike Blake, though, he was surprisingly successful. As little as people understood his images, they recognised the power of them and paid well for his work. I can't say for certain what on earth I offered to him, other than the fact that I recognised his artistry. Anyway, that's what I told Harakka.

Don't make the mistake that it was ego on Simon's part. He was—and is—a handsome guy who needed nothing to make people fall into his bed and to woo him from the sidelines. But I always knew what his work was worth, even if I had nothing of myself to offer. I'm no artist, never have been, likely never will be. But I know incredible creations when I see them, and maybe that is some kind of art in itself.

Stretching the idea, sure—but if art falls in a forest and there's no one to hear it, is it art?

Aleria was clearly taken aback by Simon's discouraging comment. To her credit, she took it well, not exactly disguising her surprise so much as mastering it, considering it and then responding to it with a thoughtful remark. "It is a daunting task. What we're asking is not easy. But we are desperate and we need your help. Both of you. Perhaps the two of you should go discuss it privately. We will not force you to do anything that you do not feel comfortable performing, but we are very eager to encourage you to consider helping us in this way."

Maggie looked with astonishment from Aleria to me and to my rather small credit, I did not crow my success but only maintained a serious air and waited to hear Simon's decision. 'If you don't mind," he finally said, "We would like to talk this over."

Aleria nodded. She pointed toward the back of the room, such as it was, overgrown with trees and flowing out into the wild. "There is a door at the back that leads to what used to be the orchard. You can talk there without any observation, away from all this. We will wait as long as you need, days if you like. If in the end, you say no, we will accept it." She chuckled in a delightfully sexy way, which I'm afraid she knew was rather delightfully sexy, and said, "We may not be very pleased, but we will accept it."

Simon reached out to take her hand. "Thank you. I think we'll go now." He took my hand and off we went through the trees. Through the trees! What an exciting phrase to hear, a phrase not heard since childhood, but one that evoked such magic that I felt once more we were running away from home, as we did about once a week as children—to start a new life, to create a new world, to pretend we were without roots and families and boring lives of normalcy. But now we were heading into the unknown, a ten year gap sitting uneasily between us—or so I saw it suddenly as the memories flooded back. Perhaps I was just worrying too much, but I was really a different person and not just because most of the cells of my body had been replaced in that time.

We pushed through the double glass door and stepped out onto the tarmac. It retained the heat of the day and hastened our steps across it. Up the hill, where brown grass lay disconsolate as if robbed of all ambition, we struggled trying to find that place distant enough to show some sign of privacy so we could talk like we used to do. I have to admit, I wasn't entirely trusting the kindly folk of Garbhavihar. Electrosnoops were invading every other aspect of our lives, why not here? Every word I wrote, every phrase I uttered was recorded, scanned and picked over for sedition, contrition and subversion. I was not so confident that we might escape it even out there.

Yet the blackened trees of the orchard seemed far less likely a spot for snooping, I had to admit. The gnarled limbs and blasted trunks were far too sad to encourage light-hearted espionage. We finally paused in a nook of blackened branches where once, no doubt, apples had fallen to the ground in happy harvests. I perched upon a blasted bough, charcoal coating my pants, but I did not care. They weren't mine, after all. They were nice and comfy though, like all the clothes here. "What do you think, Simon?" It might have been ten years since anyone asked him, but I was more than willing to ask him.

"What do I know? What's all this journeying business?"

Unlike everybody else, he was willing to give me the benefit of the doubt. Simon knew that I was a fuck-up—big time—but when I said I knew something, I knew something. I bit my lip for a minute or two while I organised some thoughts and honestly attempted to explain it, tried to give an idea of what it felt like to be a walker between the worlds, to step out of time and into the rift, to trespass on spiritual time. I'm not sure that Simon had much of a context for the information I was offering. It probably all sounded like Greek to him—or worse, like insane ramblings. But to his credit, he listened and then he asked a few questions.

"So—how long have you been doing this?"

"Well, Harakka came to me about seven years ago. Admittedly, at first it was by mistake, but I soon figured out how to do it on purpose. I was a mess, Simon, but I have gotten better. It's taken a while to find this path, but I'm making my way down it."

"Is it dangerous?"

Good question. "I haven't found it to be so, but there are all kinds of stories in the histories about people who bring things back that they ought not to have done, or who get trapped in another place and never fully return to their bodies.

It's like they're crazy or," I paused nervously, "or like in a coma."

"Ain't that a kick in the head?" Simon thrust his hands into his pockets and kicked at a small limb lying in front of him. "But what's it feel like? I mean, is it just kind of using your imagination?"

"Well, yeah—and no. It's the same thing. Sort of—it's like tapping into the deepest part of your mind. Some people see it as no more than that, although that's pretty profound when you think about it—memories in your cells, from your ancestors, from the rest of the human race."

"And others?"

I kicked my heels against the tree. "That it's all real, and that our physical reality is only one of many realities, that even if it's 'all in your head' it changes what happens in this world."

"You believe that." It wasn't a question.

I nodded. "Crazy as it sounds to say it out loud, I know it's real. I don't pretend to understand how it works or if it's a real place or just in my head, but it's real, all right."

"So do you think I ought to delve into this too?"

"Well, I think it was Emerson who said one should beware of all enterprises that require new clothes. Or maybe it was his buddy, the other guy with three names."

We looked at our new clothes, freshly acquired after the wild sensation of the showers. "I suppose they're not actually required clothes, are they?"

I shrugged. My fingers worked their way into a hollow that bit into one thick arm of the tree. The tips touched something curious and round. Pulling it out I saw it was an image of a woman with two thick braids, surrounded by triskelions and some kind of curling birds. There was something about her that filled me with a sense of well-being, as much for the kindly person who left it behind as for the woman—or goddess, I corrected myself once I had given it a bit of a think—who seemed to radiate a serene sort of confidence. I slipped the metal disk into my pocket. I don't know why I didn't tell Simon. He was looking back down the hill toward the forest.

"That's quite some science project they have going on down there," he finally said. He looked over his shoulder at me. "I don't know about you, but I have to admit, I'm impressed."

I hopped off the tree to come stand beside him. "That they could do it at all, let alone hide it so well all this time. I heard one of them say it had been here ten years."

"Trees grow that fast? I guess I never really thought about it."

"We were always surrounded by such old trees. That's one of my cues for journeying. The old maple tree at the end of the field—there was that knotty lump of root that something had dug a burrow into. I jump down that hole and I'm...I'm in another place."

"Tarnation." Simon smiled down at the strange building and at the utter absurdity of finding himself here of all places after ten years in a coma. "If I go, you're going with me."

It was only fair.

We walked back down the slope, stopping only to wipe the soot from my forehead that had somehow gotten there. "Honestly, Ro. You're worse than a child," Simon scolded me as we stepped back into the forest.

"C'mon Hansel, let's follow the breadcrumbs back."

Oddly enough, every head turned when we squeaked the doors open. Every head but Maggie's that is. She had steadfastly refused to crane her neck in curiosity, but everyone else was too excited to pretend not to be interested. I could feel the force of their held breaths like a soap bubble. When Simon said, "I'll do it," there was a nearly audible pop.

Aleria's face burst into a supernova grin and she clapped her hands together with delight. "I thought we'd have to try harder to convince you," she said thrusting her PDA before us, its screen filled with headlines about people all over the world waking up from comas, relating strange visions they had after awaking, visions which were of course discounted by those in the medical profession as mere side-effects of the extended twilight times. Simon scrolled through the headlines skimming for facts.

"Have you had any unusual experiences?" Aleria asked him while he continued to scan.

Simon shrugged. "There was that sort of...waking dream." He looked up and smiled. "Same day I got called up. At the moment I got called up, in fact." His eyes clouded for a moment. "Something about someone coming, with some sense of alarm. Some Japanese girl talking to me."

"It might not be a Japanese girl," I said with some hesitancy. Did I want to get into this? Or try to explain Harakka? Maybe I should just let him discover things for himself. After all, different travellers had different experiences of the other realms. It could be that Simon would have his own world in which to travel—even if we started in the same place. Now that the two of them were staring at me, I would have to decide.

"You have had a similar...contact?" Aleria groped to find the suitable term. "You have also met this woman?"

"Well, no." I looked back and forth between Simon and Aleria. Simon's brows were furrowed now, whether it was irritation or concentration was hard to say. "It's just that when he was waking up, the name he said—well, I'm not sure. It sounded kind of like someone—that is, a person, well, not exactly a person." The weight of all those gazes was beginning to buckle my self-confidence. I could feel the colour rising in my cheeks.

"Harakka," Simon said, nodding his head. Aleria stared intently, which made me squirm.

"It's, um, hard to talk about this to other people. I never have." Sometimes the truth is the simplest thing. As soon as I had that thought, it echoed in my brain. Where had I heard that very phrase? For some reason, it increased my sense of discomfort. I could feel sweat forming on my brow. This room was too hot. It must be all the trees and plants, insulating the place and trapping all the moisture—humidity, that was a killer. I remembered, I couldn't stand humidity. It saps your strength and kills brain cells. I had to get out of here, had to get some fresh air. "I got to go," I mumbled and moved toward the hallway.

Out the doors, into the white-painted walls of the corridor, I began to feel my heart slow. Not for long though; Simon came out a minute later, looking at me with concern. "Ro, you all right?"

"Just had to—had to get out." I closed my eyes and leaned against the cool plaster. The shiny paint kept me from sticking to the surface even though I could feel sweat seeping through the fibres.

"You're getting soot all over the walls, Ro," Simon said without his usual biting wit. It made me jump nonetheless and I quickly turned to try to rub the sootiness off. I succeeded in making it worse, smearing charcoal blots against the pristine paint. "Maybe we can get some towels or something," Simon said as he watched me furiously spreading the muck.

I finally stopped and closed my eyes again, but I was unable to turn and face him. "I have something to tell you," I started but was startled to hear my voice crack.

"What is it, Ro?" Why did he have to be so kind, so understanding, so caring? It only made it harder. I would tell him and he would be gone and I would lose the only person I had in this world. But it had been pounding in the back of my head like a bad hangover since he had woken up. I managed to put it away from my waking thoughts since then, but it rapped at the doors of consciousness, demanding entry, demanding release and if I didn't let it out soon, it was going to turn to a wild screaming shriek that would drown out all other thoughts. I had really thought there was more time left, that I could let it lie for a bit longer until by some unaccountable miracle, I would know the right way to say it and I would not have to lose my friend. Maybe it was the thought of journeying by his side into another realm, maybe it was his absolute faith in me, but I couldn't hold out any longer against the truth beating like a tell-tale heart against my forehead, ready to burst.

"It was my fault."

"What?"

"It—the coma, it was my fault."

"What!" The puzzled look on his face seemed to inflate to amazement, but not yet to anger, but that would come soon, I knew.

"My fault," I repeated, jamming like a DJ's scratch. "That last night...when we were...you know..."

Simon shook his head. "No, I don't know, I can't remember anything about that night. I tried. It's all a blur."

I swallowed. It was show time. I thought of Harakka's encouraging voice, but it didn't sound that way in my head now, just scratchy and harsh, like her pointy beak and her spiky little toes. "I—"

The door opened yet again and out came Aleria and Maggie. Christ on a crutch, wag me to the colon—just what I needed. Aleria halted at once, picking up on the discomfort of the scene—either that or she was noticing the big smudges on the wall. Doubtless those would need explaining, too, but one disaster at a time. Maggie was looking ready for a barney, and I was regretting suddenly becoming the gabster at such an incredibly inauspicious time. But Simon was looking at me with a very painfully sober expression and I felt the situation had become rather inextricable.

"That night, the night you, you—that night, it was my fault." I swallowed, but it didn't seem to clear the lump in my throat that was threatening to choke me and cut off the words. "We had been out late, drinking and whatnot, we came back and were drinking some more."

"Nothing so odd about that," Simon said, his voice even.

"I know." I pointedly looked away from Maggie but I could feel anger rising from her direction and it was filling the hallway. "But I was kidding you about trying that new drug, you remember the one? Lusios. It was supposed to, to give you a trip like no other. Take you on an ecstatic jolt that shamed X and left glint in the dirt. I picked up a couple of hits that night and I was bugging you that we had to try it together. You don't remember, do you? You don't remember telling me no, telling me that it was a crap idea, something no one knew, only stories, something that was nigh on lethal in its potential. I was so keen to try it, but not alone."

Simon was silent and the corridor seemed to have shrunk in size but grown in pressure and it was making my head feel like it was a balloon attached to my neck. "We were drinking cognac, I remember it now, remember? Cognac and it seemed like nothing, like a little thing, such a tiny thing..."

I did not dare look up and meet Simon's eyes. How could you even respond to the knowledge that some so-called friend had poisoned you and then robbed you of ten long years? A decade, decaying, he was lost in a fog, unmoving, asleep, wasting away, losing years, losing friends while I sat there in my muddled guilt waiting for things to get better, hoping for him to wake up and be all right again so I could lift that burden from my conscience. The only thing worse than putting your friend in a coma is forgetting over time how bad it is that you have done so, beginning to let the guilt fall away as the years roll by, allowing yourself to settle that guilt like an unpleasant but manageable ache in your gall bladder, that seizes up on the occasion of a too rich meal, but mostly fails to trouble you, because you changed your eating habits so long ago you hardly feel it anymore. I let my betrayal slip away.

Now it was coming back like a suddenly matured late bloomer on the first day of senior year, twice the size it had been when the summer started, looking rough and swinging a lead pipe. I had to look up, but Simon was looking down—not looking, eyes shut, face sorrowful and lined, lined with those ten dead years, ten years of novel reading and waiting, then not waiting, goofing on the other veg in the ward, coming out of duty, out of fear—admit it! Fear that he would wake up battled with fear that he would not, and as the years went by, forgetting that fear and living with what was, as if it had always been that way. Tears rolled down Simon's cheeks and I sank to the floor, hugging his knees, but he did not move. I could feel a couple of drops hit my hair. I had made such a cake of myself! But I didn't know how to tell him, I couldn't just announce it—what a thing to hit him with when he was still weak and wiggly on his pins. He had to have some strength. It wasn't just my sad little fear.

Maggie apparently didn't think so, because she strode across the tile expanse and seized me by the hair, shouting, "You maggot-headed, selfish, stupid, dangerous blowhead! You might have killed him. You coward, not to tell him before now!" She threw me to the floor and it was a point of my abjectness that I did not fight back, but curled into a ball waiting for the inevitable blows that would be my lot.

Aleria broke the jagged noise with her soothing voice. "Maggie," she said, her voice muffled, "Maggie, please." I peeked out over my clasped arms to see her wrap her arms around Maggie's shaking frame. "It wasn't the drugs. It wasn't her fault." I am a very bad person to have felt a spark of hope at that remark. As if it would make me any less culpable—I was still at fault, I had to admit that. I didn't dare look at Simon beyond his knees, as he seemed not to have moved at all.

But he must have, for he said, "What do you mean, Aleria?"

"Just that. The stories are the same all over the world, those people who are waking up now. They all went into comas within a few days of each other, the same time you did. Look here." She must have handed him her PDA again to scroll through the links and read the headlines. "All over the world, the same times, then and now. It is not random, it is not an accident—it is an attempt to communicate." I did look then. Her eyes were shining, full of a kind of inner light. In the midst of my self-pitying, self-immolating shame, I had a bad feeling about that shining light in her eyes. I never liked to see the spark of fanaticism—I saw it in the eyes of the people who started the war fourteen years ago, of those who embraced the Wags in a newly-founded religion, and of those who murdered their families and anyone else in the vicinity when they decided the Wags had the end times in their picnic baskets.

"Who's trying to communicate?" I asked, my voice still rough from my own struggles to communicate. I had a bad feeling that the problems of we little people weren't going to amount to a hill of beans in this brave new world. It reminded me of the words of Huxley, something about we being the ones to pull the strings of the gods we created, but I seemed to recall there was something, too, about our letting those strings pull us in turn—and that's where things always went all pear-shaped.

"We don't know," Aleria continued, pulling a still-fuming Maggie to her feet. "But we have been getting closer. We're simply not trained at the level of someone like you." She turned to Simon's slumped figure and continued, "Or you. Something extraordinary has happened to you that will give you unexpected advantages. We have tried learning the ropes, studying the techniques, but our success so far has been limited."

"Normally the skill is taught, passed on from teacher to initiate. There's been a bit of a disruption in traditions the last hundred years or so," I said. "I have actually been working on my skills for over seven years. I'm still struggling in the dark most of the time, and I have the advantage of someone being there on the other side. I don't know how Simon feels about being thrust into the ether without any experience or a guide. It's a dangerous thing."

"We will all be close at hand," Aleria said, but she seemed to falter a little, her smile drooping ever so slightly. "We will be protecting you while you journey, watching you from here and keeping our minds in concert with yours."

"From here," I said beginning to finally sit up. "We will not be here. We will be in another...consciousness, land, call it what you will. Your thinking happy thoughts won't keep us buoyant. If there's something out there trying to contact you, why assume it's your pal? The Wags haven't been our pals. Or had you forgotten that?"

I think she was unaccustomed to people speaking to her with anything but flowery accolades and gushing joy, but Aleria quickly rose to the challenge in a kindly yet firm manner. "We are well aware of that, in fact that is part of the reason for doing this. The entities that are trying to reach us have told us that they may be able to help us with the Wags. And that they are already making inroads into their consciousness, too."

I thought on that for a minute, recalling the news stories about the Wags going apeshit and screaming around the globe like children caught scrumping apples. If these new things were going to help—but then I remembered Harakka's warning, too. Something was coming—what if it was these creatures?

"If it will get rid of these hideous Wags, I'm all for it," Simon said quietly, but with a resolution that made his voice sound a lot stronger than its timbre. "Let's do it."

I looked up and his eyes still reflected a world of pain, but his chin was jutting out in a way I knew so well. I sighed, but said, to no one in particular, "Once more unto the breach, dear friends, once more; or close up the wall with our English dead." We were going to set our teeth and stretch our nostrils wide and jump into another world. Let us swear we are worth our breeding, I thought, though my eye lacked a noble lustre and I was not straining in the slip.

But what could I do? The game was indeed afoot.

6

As we re-entered the temple, all faces turned toward us with eager eyes. It was more than a tad disturbing. Nobody kept them anymore, but we still had the term: fishbowl. Even a fake one was a waste of water. But that must be what it felt like staring out through the distorted glass at a whole lot of eyes looking back at you—and you have nowhere to go.

Aleria put a chummy arm around my shoulder and another around Simon's. "They have agreed!" she said to her friends and they all cheered. How bad could it be, I was beginning to argue to myself. We get in, get out and probably nobody gets hurt, because we're all in this together, right? Somehow the words had an unpleasant ring to them, like it was a line from a play I couldn't quite remember—something South American, or at least that was the detail that rose up to the back of my mind. The maggots have done their work, as we say: brain like Swiss cheese, which I can only assume meant it had holes in it. Why would the Swiss put holes in their cheese? Normally I would ask Simon a question like that, not that he would necessarily know the answer, but that he would have a lot of fun coming up with a somewhat plausible response. However, I was leery of making the first awkward step toward a hoped-for rapprochement and more than a tad worried that my attempts would be rebuffed. Aleria's news did not get me off the hook. I knew that. So I couldn't quite bring myself to search for his gaze and see whether I might meet it.

For the moment, anyway, there was little I could do, caught as we were in the arms of Hurricane Aleria. "Let's get the drums and all the rhythm instruments! Michael, will you get some folks to help you with the fruit water? Liesel, bring a couple of the yoga mats for our travellers. Yes, everyone, let's get things organised under the linden tree."

Everywhere smiling people rushed to arrange the impromptu party, which was looking a little more planned than the scurrying conveyed. All the preparations were fairly near to hand. They may not have been counting on it, but they certainly had hope in our response.

The forest was alive with laughter and light and, within minutes, singing and a steady drum beat. "We have to get warmed up," Aleria explained, jumping into a ring of hands and swirling off. The shadows between the trees even seemed to dance but I was left with an after-image of some blackly fuliginous riddling hex lying in wait for our foolish daring. I sneaked a glance at Simon. He was looking solemn. I guess he wasn't getting into the spirit of things yet, either. Generally, given a bit of music and a rowdy crowd, we would both be diving in without a thought. Back in the day before the water problems went wild, we once danced in the fountain at the Plaza Hotel like Zelda and Scott, before running wetly into Central Park, laughing and whooping all the way to Strawberry Fields, where we collapsed singing songs of our parents' day.

I wanted to talk to Simon, to say how sorry I was, to say how much I had missed him, to say how I had suffered endless day upon day as I watched his still form wither and shrink, my heart jangling so loud I could only pretend to read my book, holding back the tears in my eyes through sheer force of will and violent self-loathing. Worse, I wanted to tell him how ten years wore away like an old stone stair, chafed away inexorably but imperceptibly by thousands of feet. I would tell him how my self-flagellation wore away the same way, never forgotten, but dulling through repetition, through familiarity, the soft bruise of my soul hardening to a scab, to a scar. My conscience was never clear, but it grew around my horror, enveloping it in new skin, new leaves, hiding it in shadow as the steps of each day accumulated.

Only my dreams never forgot.

Part of the greater dissolution that followed in those first years was an echo of those dreams. In sleep I had been denied rest, so vainly I had sought to borrow in chemicals some surcease of sorrow, but found it nevermore, or only fleetingly. To be beyond the fringes of consciousness, if regrettable, was at least an absence from the dull ache of that blow on the bruise of my memory, my regret, my grief—and my loneliness. We have greeting cards and platitudes for every kind of loss but this: the friend. For ten long years, it was as if Simon were dead and no one understood. "Were you lovers?" they asked. Those who knew better, condoled me, but denied me the place that should be accorded a friend. My loss, they seemed to reason, could not be so much, not so much as an intimate partner. But it was so much more.

"This is folk music. I'm not dancing to folk music," Simon said suddenly, in a voice just audible beneath the seductive baladii rhythm now looping between the trees. I flushed, I could feel it, then I feared being obvious, I wanted to play it cool.

Naturally I tripped over a tree root just then, landing hands down in the soft earth that covered this once-indoor room, choking back my breath with the sudden surprise and barking it back out in a laugh that was three parts ruefulness and two parts hope. His hand at my elbow, just politeness, I was certain, but I couldn't stop the filament of wishing that ventured forth to test his flesh for answer. I did not make the stupid mistake of looking up, at least not at first. And when I had, he was already looking with curiosity at the whirling dancers who wove their way between the trees. But that little vine from my heart, it thought there was a welcoming spark, just enough of the force that through the green fuse drives the flower, which might be enough to patch the scar between us two.

"Look, there's Maggie." I pointed off to the left where our friend danced somewhat self-consciously behind the always graceful Aleria. The line of frisking nature lovers were laughing so hard they could hardly keep from bending over with the effort, while their faces shone with fine layer of sweat and happiness. It was kind of revolting. Or perhaps I was feeling a tad envious. There's always that weird moment for joining in with something and if you let it pass, it's just too late.

Or not: "Come on," Simon said and like that, we were running through the trees and laughing like ten year olds, stumbling and looking like spaztastics, but we were dancing after a fashion and things were good. It carried on like this for some time, with strings of folks weaving in and out of the little trees. I could easily imagine the tree spirits rolling their eyes at such insanity, but it was a party, it was a celebration and it was friends and food and green, green trees and plants everywhere. It seemed careless to tread them underfoot, but the caretakers seemed unconcerned, so I could only shrug and assume it was all right.

When we finally collapsed near the bevy of bevvies, I figured out that Aleria must have planned all this just so we could feel united and chummy. It worked. Everyone was chatting happily, their voices burbling to the treetops as they guzzled the juice water that was clearly the celebratory beverage of choice. That included Maggie, who was the picture of reckless enjoyment as she sat cross-legged on a rug. Looking sweaty, blissful and satisfied, all of Aleria's people leaned back against the trunks of their friendly forest as if they hadn't a care in the world—which I suppose they didn't as long as the snoops didn't spot their riches from the sky. What're the odds, I thought.

Aleria was moving among the folks like a politician on the campaign trail, clasping hands, sharing jokes and making sure everyone was having a good time. Everywhere she went, people seemed to cheer. But I could feel myself tensing up as she got nearer. It might start that way, but it wasn't going to be a simple glad-hand for us. We had work to do tonight. I couldn't decide if I was more nervous for Simon or proud that he would see I could do something worthwhile. Of course, there was that little niggling bit of doubt, too, that refused to be quieted completely. What if things went haywire? What if this was a big mistake? What if there really was something less than friendly out there? What if the sky began to fall? Ha, ha—what if aliens from another planet or time zone or reality decided to pay us a visit? Oh, that's right, they already did.

All too soon, Aleria was before us and smiled back and forth from my face to Simon's. "What do you think?" She couldn't hide how much this mattered to her, to her people, to her trees even, I suppose, and I couldn't help dropping my gaze for fear that I would screw up as usual, given enough rope, as they say.

"Whenever you're ready, I guess," Simon said. His voice betrayed no anxiety, but I peeked a look at him and I could see the strain in the corners of his eyes, a fatigue that had everything to do with ten long years and a whole lot of unwelcome surprises since. Yesterday seemed like a year ago already.

"What about you?" Aleria looked at me with such kindness. She couldn't know what an unmitigated cock-up I generally made of things. Well, she might have a bit of a picture after our Broadway production in the hallway. Befogged at the best of times, I suppose, I can really be quite shockingly loose in the haft. What difference did it make now? We were all in this together, as they say down in Brazil.

"All right," I said with a diffident shrug, hoping against hope that I didn't turn into some kind of bonnacon and begin spewing my inner works at random. Or even something less embarrassing—let's aim for not at all mortifying in any way and just try to be happy with whatever emerges.

We went to the centre, more or less, of the room, and the flickering candle lights made it feel as if we had somehow stepped back into a previous era—either that or the power had been knocked out again by overloaded summer air-conditioning use or wandering Wags with a propensity for target shooting of tower-like objects. It really had been a pain the first couple of years, when they decided that our clearly primitive power systems were fun to machine gun with their laser pointer thingees and watch the sparks fly. They are rather easily amused for superior beings. In this case, Aleria's people seemed simply to like the warm of the natural light and probably the economical and reasonably green factor. Are candles greener, I suddenly wondered, or am I only assuming? Why do candles burn? They are made of wax, but what is wax anyway? Doesn't it come from bees? And wouldn't they hate to kill bees? Don't they need bees, what with all these plants here? Perhaps they were secretly the enemies of bees and couldn't wait to boil them into wax. They look like a bunch of bee-killing wax-hoarders, I decided.

Was there something in my drink? Had I foolishly sucked down some illicit bee poison? I could feel sweat oozing from my pores and tried to peek through my eyelashes at Aleria and at Simon. He seemed fine. Maybe I was just being paranoid. Wonder if it had something to do with trotting too hard to be all right, or perhaps with displaying my oh-so-mystical powers in front of the masses and my maybe-still best friend? Get a grip, Ro. Worst that could happen would be you would die and then you wouldn't have to worry about it no more.

"We tried to make this area as comfortable as possible," said one of Aleria's folks, a young Asian girl with a strong Revere accent, which made me blink with surprise. The "are-ah" looked fine. A few soft rag rugs criss-crossed together to make plenty of space for the two of us to lie down, side by side.

Simon looked at me and smiled weakly. "You're the expert. What do we do?"

I tried to unclench my jaws, but they cracked and gave me away. "We lie down, they start the drums, and you just concentrate on the beat. It will probably relax you and you'll get into a more productive state. If you want the scientific name, that's Alpha, that's where the brain slows down when you're creating something cool, drawing or messing around with that unfortunately named picture manipulation program."

Simon smiled, a real smile this time. "You mean the Gimp?"

"Yeah, that's the one. Then we're going to try to go slower yet—that's Theta. It's like meditation. We'll be travelling then. Here's where I always start: you remember the gigantic maple tree on Comm Ave right near your building? Too big for three kids to reach around? Good; picture it as clearly as you can, focus on the little hole on the low side where we always figured a badger or something must have lived."

"It was probably only a squirrel," Simon said, settling down on the rugs, wiggling his ass a little to make the spot comfortable. "There haven't been badgers in Massachusetts for a hundred years, I bet."

"Yeah, I know, but picture that opening and when you can see it really clearly, dive into it. It'll be like going headlong into a black hole at first, but look for me. I'll take you to Harakka and she'll help us out. Okay?"

Simon nodded and lay down. I got down on the rug and crab walked over so I was hip to hip with Simon but facing the opposite direction. He craned his head up with a puzzled look, so I said, "This is traditional for people travelling together." I looked up at Aleria. "If we show any signs of distress, bring us back. You know how to bring us back with the drum?"

She nodded eagerly. "Three quick beats, a pause, repeat, repeat, and then faster and faster until you wake up. We have Tina and Jesse ready to monitor you, too." Aleria gestured to two painfully young-looking people with a black bag between them. Oh brother, let's play doctor, kids.

There was no point in delaying further. I lay down and closed my eyes. Let the gods watch over us and be kind, I thought as they began to beat the drums. "I'm counting on you to be my Ninshubur," I muttered toward the group of drummers. They might not have heard me, but I felt better for having expressed it.

Journeying was such an automatic process for me by now that I felt a bit unnerved when I couldn't fall into the proper state at once. C'mon, c'mon, I scolded with a mental shake: forget all these people, forget all the pressure, forget Simon and all that pain, forget everything. I blocked out everything but the steady beat of the drum, pound-pound-pounding like a heart. I took three deep breaths and let each one out slower than the one before. I brought the image of the old maple tree—many years dead and gone by now—sharply to mind, moving like the fleshless spirit I had become, across the greenery that no longer grew, toward the looming presence of the stark branches and around to the west side of the tree. There it was: the mini cave I had entered a thousand or more times, more vivid in my mind than it was in my memory, and in a trice I was landing in the onyx-walled temple where my journeys inevitably began.

I thought I would have to wait quite a while for Simon to arrive, but it was only a short time later that he fell suddenly to the floor from the darkness of the ceiling, as if out of nothing. He landed with an audible thump and it shook him a bit to suddenly be staring at the muffling black walls.

"Hullo," I said, grabbing his arm to try to help him hoist back astern.

"Jesus, Mary and Joseph!" Simon shook his head and I could almost see the whirling stars circle around his noggin. "You do this a lot?"

"I usually land on my feet, makes it a little easier."

"Even the first time?" He rubbed the back of his head where contact had been made.

I frowned. I didn't like thinking about that first time, but it only seemed fair to say, "I was a bit panicky the first time, so I'm not too sure. I suspect I wasn't filled with cat-like grace. But you get used to it fairly quickly. Did you have trouble finding this?" As if it were a house on a poorly-labelled street, or an apartment in a giant complex. Look for the blue trim! We've got a ficus benjamina outside the door—plastic, don't you know—you can't miss it. As if travelling in the astral planes were as simple as motoring through the physical world—or should I say worlds at this point?

"I don't know," Simon was still answering my initial question while he fastidiously brushed his clothes off and I wandered in the labyrinth of my own revolving thoughts. "I was beginning to think nothing was going to happen and then it was sort of, oh—what was that movie? 'My god, it's full of stars!'"

I grinned. "I love you, man."

Simon sobered for a moment. "You really thought you put me in that coma, didn't you."

I hung my head. Apologies weren't enough. Why couldn't I let it lie? Why keep rubbing salt into a wound? Why risk the one thing I still had in this world, (or should I say, the other one), with such cavalier words? I suppose deep down I had a breaking point. If we could not repair our friendship, it would be more painful to carry on in awkward distance than to sever the bond completely. I had to know.

"I think it was your William who said that it was easier to forgive an enemy than a friend."

I looked up at his face and saw fatigue and worry. "So are we enemies? Because I want forgiveness more than anything I can think of."

"We're not enemies," Simon said, giving a weak smile. "I just might need to hold it over your head now and then that you put me into a coma, just to keep you in line."

"Hey, it wasn't me, probably, you know. Like Aleria said—there are things out there, doing stuff to us. It was them. Probably." I wasn't quite ready to smile myself. "And Huckleberry Twain said that forgiveness is the scent roses give to the heel that crushes them."

Simon laughed. "What's that supposed to mean."

"I'm sorry."

"I know, Ro. I know."

"Can I get a hug?"

"I suppose."

There in that black temple, whose walls had welcomed me countless times, I felt a little piece of my heart return and lock into place like a lost puzzle piece as we wrapped our arms around each other. "I'm sorry," I whispered again, though whether it was for my ears or his I couldn't be sure.

"So, how do we get where we're going?" Simon asked when we finally broke our embrace.

"There's a door here, when you need it." I pointed to the place in the wall as I surreptitiously wiped away a little leakage from my eye. "I can't wait for you to meet Harakka! You'll be so amazed, she's so smart and funny, well, sometimes. She can be really mean, but mostly when you don't listen to her, as of course, I sometimes am too stupid to do. Here, see? It opens and look!"

I didn't even have to say more. Who could look at that green world and not become breathless? The most urban philistine lover of steel and glass would have to be agog just from the sheer novelty of so much green. Forget the institutional green that seemingly every place of work was awash with, mostly for reasons of calm and tranquillity—how many studies had shown that it was the best colour for soothing the angst of the trapped worker. Not that anyone proved no worker had kept from chewing off her shackle solely because of the green walls of the faceless corporation, but it was a firmly-held belief. In the higher echelons of my own rubble-router, the walls actually had a distinctive leaf motif, (upper echelon folks being like ravens and writing desks, I suppose, their fewer numbers allowing for more expensive decorations).

But none of that could prepare Simon for the shock of a landscape greener than our brightest lamb-white days of sky-blue trades and heedless ways. We had had a rare privilege of some of the last green trees still living in our memories before the blight, before the droughts, before the dithering politicians and postulating evangelists and endless, endless war. And still it wasn't enough. I, who had seen this verdant vista open before me times without clear number, even I could not face the sight without a sob of loss and a sigh of joy.

Simon stared, his eyes burning with tears unshed, his mouth a little 'o' of surprise. "Is it real?" He reached his hand over to grab mine. "Is it? Is it real?" He looked at me, awaiting confirmation.

"Touch it," I said, my voice grown husky as I squatted down to run my fingers through the twining green. "Smell it."

Simon threw himself down on the ground and buried his nose in the grass. He laughed and lifted up his head, plucking a blade to thrust between his lips, chewing it with satisfaction. "I don't believe it," he said at last. "It's real, it's all real. How can it be real?"

I shrugged. "It's real, but it's not our reality. We can move back and forth between them but they're not the same thing. I used to think this was just the past of our world, but it's not that exactly. It's hard to explain."

"If we can come here," Simon continued, marvelling at a leaf dropped on the ground before him, "Can they come to our world?"

I nodded. "Apparently there are ways back and forth, but it's easier where there are linkages. There is something like an infinite possible worlds out there."

Simon laughed. "*Something like* an infinite possible worlds?"

I could feel myself redden, but I tried to keep my thoughts organised. "Harakka explained it. There are any number of worlds, which is what makes this a bit risky. I don't think Aleria grasps that part of it. Coming here is fairly safe because I build my own sort of bridge here."

"How's that?"

"The temple. That's mine," I could hear myself sounding a bit proud about that, but it's true; it was mine and I was quite proud, damn it. "Of course it helped to have Harakka. Back in the day, people never went alone without being trained and apprenticed and all. You had to know the methods for walking between the worlds."

"But you just figured it out?" Simon was curious now.

"Well, sort of by accident the first time. Then I did a lot of research to find out more about it and then, of course, I had Harakka, too. I got lucky there." I was beginning to finally grasp just how lucky I had been. Odd, but explaining a process to someone else really helps you to understand it better, even if you've done it a hundred times. I wondered if that was how teachers felt. "We should find her now."

"What? She doesn't just come when you call?"

Oh boy, did he have a lot to learn. "She's got her own life, things to do. She doesn't just stand around waiting for me to come. Besides, time doesn't work the same way in this world as in ours. I've asked her. Things unfold at different rates."

I started to walk through the low brush toward the sound of the babbling river. Things were never quite the same from one visit to the next, as if this world kept turning, too. Seasons passed, weather changed; but the landmarks mostly stayed the same. At least I felt as if I knew my way around here. Sure, I was showing off a little: Simon was straggling behind a little, gaping at everything we passed—goggling at a velvety sumac fruit, marvelling at the intricate veins on a leaf, starting at the chatter of a rather obnoxious squirrel.

I could hardly wait for him to meet my friend, my guide, that dumb bird. Harakka, although very strict with me and a rather stern task-master at times, had been my saviour in a way. Everything might have ended quite badly—I could be a blip on the horizon, forgotten by the only person who bothered remembering me when I was heading toward my worst. I really needed to remember to ask her about Simon and the coma and all this weirdness. I would have thought she'd have mentioned it if she knew, although I suppose if it were one of these seemingly endless mystical things I have to find out for myself—which seems to constitute a very large portion of unpleasant things that come my way—she would just leave me to get on with it. Sometimes, when things were apparently painfully obvious to anyone but me—which admittedly, took in most of the rest of the unpleasantness—it would not likely occur to her to say anything at all.

I was just turning around to tell Simon not to lag too far behind when I felt something pinch my shoulder. Perhaps 'pinch' isn't really the right word. It was more like giant talons sinking into the soft parts of my skin about the shoulder area with great force and considerable pain and probably not a little blood.

Which is exactly what it was, after all.

Two sets of them, actually, and they were dug in with a firmness not unlike a harried mother might use with a particularly obdurate child. It was not a feeling I would have enjoyed in the best of humours, and certainly having said pain arrive swiftly, vehemently and unexpectedly only added to the aggravation. That the talons were attached to the legs of two enormous barn owls did not help in the least. Even under normal circumstances, I would have been reluctant to be in such close proximity to these predators because first of all, their cry is a rather screeching unpleasantness particularly when uttered in one's ear, and second of all, their ghostly faces caused me an especial dread ever since I had seen an Italian film with a serial killer who wore a large barn owl's head — seriously creepy. I made the mistake of watching it on my lonesome one weekend and — unable to stop — kept on to the bitter end, chewing my nails to the quick with the tension, watching him pick off the theatre folk one by one.

Now the two natty lads who had me by the shoulders probably weren't serial killers, but they were far too large to be any kind of normal barn owl. Stranger yet, they were each flapping only one wing as they carried me away. With eerily perfect precision, they flapped their single wings in unison and flew swiftly but evenly through the air. I was lifted above the tree level in no time and seemed to be heading for the mountains.

I did yell, by the way. At first it was a kind of yelp of surprise, but then as I saw panic on Simon's face below me, I began to yaffle in earnest, shouting the usual things I suppose

113

one does when being shanghaied in this way. But clearly it was having no effect and, as the dull pain sank into my flesh along with the talons, I rather uselessly recalled a similar phenomenon from nineteenth century novels—or was it even eighteenth century? Men grabbed for naval service—pressing, it was called, or I suppose being pressed. Pressgangs, they were the ones who did it. I had my own personal two-owl pressgang. I did wonder why, but as there was very little to do about it at that point, I let my mind go slack into idle musings; its natural habitat, I suppose. I did talk to them. True, I only asked them one question—who are you?—but I only got a scratchy shriek in response, which might have been a name, but not one I could have accurately pronounced. Hello indescribably screeching call, how's the wife and kids? We were too far above the ground for me to want to struggle much. So I just tried to enjoy the ride despite the intense shooting pains.

This was a good time to consider that not long before I would have been somewhat less relaxed at such a predicament—not that it wasn't unsettling, of course, and I did appreciate that fact in the sense that I knew it, not that I enjoyed it—primarily because I was terrified of heights, and flying in particular. Harakka had cured me. She'd had me flying beside her on one visit, me in bird form by her side, and I'd kept gasping and gurgling with fear. "Why are you afraid?" she'd asked me without turning her head away from the wind. I'd only thought my answer, but of course she could hear my thoughts when I'd said that I was afraid of falling. She'd laughed, in fact, as she often did when I spoke my little thoughts. "Birds can't fall."

Now I am not a bird—so far as I know, being rather large and generally flightless—but somehow that ended my fear at once. I never again dreaded getting on a plane. Of course the irony as we all know is that was about the same time that most commercial flights were grounded because of the Wags. Safety first, but I had really wanted to enjoy my new fearlessness.

Who knew I'd get a chance to try it out courtesy of a couple of ghost-faced thrillers.

The land below me was wrenching in its beauty. Rivers led to lakes and ponds. I could see waterfalls at the foot of the hills toward which we seemed to be heading. I saw an even greater profusion of trees than I had ever previously, my wanderings with Harakka never having given me a good picture of the breadth of this world. They must have all had names, like these persistent owls, families and genus (genii?). Funny how I could recognise animals long departed from our sphere, but name only a handful of trees and plants. People once chose to be vegetarians; my youngest sister was virulently so. "I won't eat anything with a face!" she'd declared at dinner one day, under the spell of some new friend or vid program, little knowing we'd all be vegetarians soon. But even then I had failed to understand the lack of empathy for plants. If they'd had faces, would people have been kinder to them? If the cries of tomatoes had been audible, would we have held them close and stroked their firm flesh? I suppose it's just as well soy doesn't smile—we'd have nothing left to eat. Everything that isn't soy is becoming so year by year. Super.

My attempts to keep from thinking about the pain in my shoulders were beginning to lose power. "Are we landing soon?" I asked my kidnappers, expecting no answer and receiving the same. I decided a more direct attack would be useful.

I took a deep breath and screamed as loud as I could.

I was lucky they didn't drop me. Their grip loosened for a second and I felt adrenaline surge through my veins as I imagined plummeting to the pines below, impaling myself on a medium-sized point. I felt reasonably certain that dying in this world would lead to dying in other worlds, which was something I was keen to avoid these days. Fortunately, they tightened their grip again and increased their pace, flapping with large muffled fwuhps that struck my arms with their tips on each down stroke. They must have a destination in mind at least. That was reassuring. Before long I could see what it was: a cave in the side of the small mountain that loomed before us. It was triangular and black. If Simon were here, I know he would make a rude remark about its shape, but I couldn't quite motivate myself to be funny. My only thought was holding on until the pain in my shoulders might stop. I was surprised to find the cave looming immensely huge as we approached it; it had looked so tiny at first. Life is different from the owl perspective.

We flew into the cave and they released me a foot or so above the floor, but I crumpled happily to the ground and began at once rubbing my shoulders, trying to see whether there were indeed tracks of blood from the talons. The two moon-faced owls fluttered to the back of the cave and landed without a sound. Almost at once their shapes distorted, shrinking while the shadows they cast against the wall grew larger and took on a new shape. I would say they were human, but the proportions weren't quite right, as if drawn by children. Returned to something resembling their original size, the two owls stretched their wings, then huddled together and promptly fell asleep. I knew the feeling. If I got back from this, I was going to sleep a good long while.

I knew what was coming next, but that didn't make me any happier about it. "Greetings," a too cheerful voice said. It seemed to emanate from the shadows on the cave wall, which was peculiar enough, but they didn't quite sound like they ought to have—how should the voice of a shadow sound? I don't know, but it didn't seem right.

"Ow, why'd you have to do that?" I said irritably, ignoring their attempt to be cheery. "I am in a great deal of pain here."

"Pain?" A slightly different voice this time. Was it the other shadow?

"Yeah, your owls' talons dug deeply into my tender skin leaving lasting marks and a great deal of pain behind, for which I am not terribly grateful, nor am I pleased to see you."

"Pain in the area you are rubbing with your appendage?"

116

the first voice again.

"We will address," continued the other voice.

All at once I felt a kind of golden light suffuse my shoulders and even the fingers of the hand that was chafing at the tender spots. Just as suddenly as it came, it departed and with it the pain. I pulled at my shirt to look at my left shoulder. There were a couple of faint red marks, but the pain was pretty much gone.

"Well," I said. "Thanks. I think." Yes, they healed the agony, but they had also caused it in the first place. "Who are you and what do you want with me?"

"We're here to help."

"We want to help you."

This double voice thing was getting to be a bit disconcerting. It was beginning to give me a headache, and while I was certain they might be able to cure my headache, too, I wasn't too sure I wanted to have them messing with my head in that way. "Why do you want to help me? What did I ever do to you?"

"We do not understand your query."

"We are puzzled by the nature of your questions, which do not seem to be mutually reliant."

"Reliant?" This was only getting worse. "What do you mean?"

"Perhaps we use the wrong term?"

"We are doing our best to understand and communicate."

"Maybe you could do less of the Morecambe and Wise bit," I said with a bit of a grumpy unkindness, deliberately making a reference that few people were likely to know these days, let alone folks from some other reality. This actually succeeded in puzzling them into silence. For a moment, anyway. The shadows wavered on the wall and seemed to mutate into more amorphous shapes.

"You dislike the two voices intertwining?"

"You might say that." I'll give them this—they seemed to be fairly sharp out of the box. "It's a bit disconcerting to talk to both of you at once."

"We see." And with that, the two shadows became one.

If I thought the two voice interrogation was a bit off-putting, the two-become-one was even stranger. I stared at them for a moment wondering what in the name of Asphodel had brought me here.

"Is this better?" the now single voice asked, eager to please, I suppose.

"Sure." Did it really make a difference? It was all so weird.

"We want to help," it began, but I cut it off.

"So you're plural even when you're one?"

There was a slight hesitation. Were they translating my words somehow? "Yes, that is correct. I speak on behalf of all."

"All what?"

"Our...people."

Uh huh. "Where are your people?"

Was that a kind of chuckle? "We are in a differently reality from this. We have managed to come to this place with some effort, but we cannot reach your reality so far."

And I thought my head hurt before. "This reality? How do you get to this reality?"

"The same way you do, via the forking paths."

I was completely nonplussed now. "Forking paths? Sounds like a curse to me."

"No, it is in fact quite beneficial and we find it stimulating."

"That was what we call a joke in my reality, which isn't this one by the way." That punctured my thick skull. "I get it now, forked path—we call it journeying." Listen to me, now I was speaking for my entire reality. "But I thought my reality, or my planet's reality or people's or whatever... I thought that created this particular reality." It's a sad thing when you lose the thread of your own conversation.

"Many have a hand in this place. It is as real as any other path."

"I suppose."

"You create this reality."

"So do you, though."

"All right; co-create reality."

"Well, I certainly don't think I had anything to do with piercing my own skin with owl talons."

"Are you certain?"

Well, they had me there. "Why not just come into the other world in which I sometimes reside? If you want to help us so badly?"

"So far we cannot, although we know much of it—and the terrible struggle your people undergo at present."

"You mean our droughts and poisoned genes?"

"No, the foreign invaders you call the Wags."

"You can help us with the Wags? We could sure use the help." Maybe this was going to be a good thing after all. "So who are you—all of you?"

There was that chuckle again. "Call us the Wits."

Christ on a crutch: aliens with a dry sense of humour.

7

"So," I said at last when the silence began to turn awkward, "You think you can help us?"

The shadow (or shadows?) on the cave wall seemed to smile. How does a shadow smile? I would say very carefully while waving an imaginary cigar and raising dark eyebrows, but it was in fact a rather careless sort of move, free and light-hearted. It felt like a smile, that's all I can say. I suppose I ought not to call them the shadows anymore but the name they had given me, the Wits. Translation is a funny thing.

"Yes, we can help. But you will have to come to our world to receive the training. Would you like to do that?"

Hmm, would I like to abandon all I know, head for parts unknown and trust strange beings I had only just met? Perhaps if they had some candy, I would take that, too. Well, maybe I would do. But I didn't need to tell them that yet. "I'm not too sure about that. Can you tell me more?"

It was just about that time that I felt a strong pull in my solar plexus. I had always thought that term sounded like a belt around a planet rather than the belt around a human body, but there you are. I didn't name it, after all. I did, however, know well what that pull meant.

It was time to go back.

Just when things were getting good. "I have to go now. Can I come and see you again? I think I would like to hear more about your world and your...er...life."

The shadows seemed to be splintering. "You are leaving now?" The words seemed to echo with reverberations that filled the empty space of the cave. "We have not completed our interlocution."

"Well, sorry but I have to go. Now can you embiggen those owls again and fly me back tout suite?" What were the odds they'd know French anyway? Surely they would assume it was correctly said in my own language, like my cousin's habit of saying "horsey durvies." Mares eat oats and does eat oats, but little lambs eat ivy.

"We believe you can go on your own. Remember, you create—or co-create," they said in a slightly different voice, "your own reality. That is the first lesson!" Another mildly humorous and disturbingly inhuman chuckle followed, and I decided I might as well test that theory as the pull in my belly was growing stronger.

I went to the edge of the cave and looked out across the pine forest below. There were tall green tips everywhere I looked, swaying in the mountain breeze. My temple was a long way off. I closed my eyes and breathed in the chilly air. How could nothing smell so good? All right, air's not nothing, but it feels like nothing, unless you suddenly run out of it.

I looked back over my shoulder at the interior of the cave. I couldn't see the shadows, but I was pretty sure they were still lurking inside. "Where are you from, anyway?"

It didn't seem as if they were going to answer, but then the two voices joined into giddy duet to repeat, "Second star on the right, straight until morning."

Wits, yeah. "All right, don't tell me." I let my gaze drift off to the south where the pull seemed strongest. The feeling was very nearly tangible and I narrowed my eyes as if that could somehow make it more visible, like a safety rope of some etheric silk. Would it be strong enough?

"We are from another consciousness. It is not on your maps. You have only dreamed of our world, you have not located it." Their voices drifted away like mist, but I knew they were still there, waiting for my reply.

Fair enough. "I'll be back." *Sure, I say that now,* I thought, *but what if the fall kills me?* Yet I was somehow certain that it wouldn't. Somehow I trusted that non-existent thread, I trusted

Harakka's teaching, I even trusted—may all the gods help me—my own stupid self. I walked to the edge of that cliff, lifted my chin, raised my arms and pushed off as if I were on the edge of a swimming pool and about to belly flop. I was distracted for a moment by that distant childhood memory. I couldn't have been much more than four the last time I dove into a pool. Some friend of the family owned one, some summer day with kids running and screaming, eating hot dogs made of real meat, (well, some kinds of meat), and adults sipping beer and exchanging languorous glances of barely disguised lust. The perfect picture—was it even real? Was it a dream or a story I had read—hung in the air before me, behind my eyes? The sudden adrenaline rush of knowing I was plummeting through air was just enough to make me concentrate instead on the task at hand and to soar once more above the pointy pines, pulled by the string tied to my navel by nothing more than the force of my will.

It was no surprise to find myself a raven, black wings thrusting back and forth in easy rhythm. Occasionally I paused to feel the wind glide across my feathers and ruffle them familiarly, before beginning the instinctive motion again to wheel to the right or the left as the pull of the cord demanded. I had flown on several occasions with Harakka but somehow this was different. Flying under my own power seemed like so much more of an accomplishment and filled me with inexpressible joy. I could imagine the very first human consciousness looking up at a soaring bird and thinking, "That's the life, all right." Do ravens gloat? Do they cackle with laughter at the sad plodding critters below them? Do they preen with pride in their ebony feathers and the precise wedge of their tails?

I did. And I marvelled at the curl of the feathers at the end of my wings, the smooth caress of the wind along my pinions, and the joy of floating on the zephyrs, those intangible pathways of the sky. I swooped far more than was necessary, weaving my way between trees and hills. It was almost a disappointment to find myself approaching the nook where my temple lay, but the tug on my belly was becoming insistent and I picked up speed as I approached the narrow opening and landed with a few ticking steps on the midnight stone floor. My horny feet and claws became once again my feet, feathers retracted into skin and my vision returned to my usual short-sighted squint. Could I change even that? I wondered, straightening with a few vertebral cracks. At that moment, anything seemed possible.

In a moment I leapt up to find myself once more on the floor of the strange forest room. I blinked several times and was rather taken aback to see several pairs of eyes repeating the motion in what felt like a vacuum.

"She's back!" All at once a sigh seemed to fill the air and I could hear knees crack as people got up.

"Are you all right?" That was Simon now, peering closely at my face as I nodded energetically. For once, I was not immediately spewing pithy remarks. My thoughts were still captivated by the exquisite bliss of flight, but I nodded vigorously to show I was fine. "Are you sure? No broken bones? No mental damage of any kind?"

"No, I'm fine. In fact, you won't believe this, but—"

"I don't care! What the hell were you thinking?" I had always read stories where people's eyes blazed, but I don't think I had ever seen it happen until I beheld Simon's glittering orbs just then. "You dragged me to another world and then you ditched me. There were dangerous animals there, there were boulders, there were...diseases!" He was too angry for articulation. I was too disconcerted by my sudden return to immediately respond. I felt logy and more than a bit off-kilter, no match for the continuing barrage of accusations that spewed forth until Aleria stepped in.

"Let us check her pulse and vitals, Simon. We have to make sure she's come through all right." She put her hands on Simon's shoulders to stop him from shaking mine. I could see halos around the lights that flickered between the trees. The fire in Simon's face made me want to shrink away. While I was relieved to see Simon's anger eclipsed by the vaguely troubled faces of Aleria's people, their murmuring anxiety clouded my fevered thoughts. It was all too much for me to take—and the thought turned into song in my head.

I think it was fatigue. Every sound echoed in my head like a bell that wouldn't stop ringing. Images and sound skittered across my brain pan, beetles insubstantial but itchy and persistent. Everything around me—the people, the trees, the lights—seemed less real than in the world I had just left. I thought somehow that was a rather dangerous thing to be happening.

"Ro, are you there? Ro, come back to us."

I wasn't gone. What were they thinking?

"Ro." It was Simon now, calmer, focused. "Get your ass back here."

I opened my eyes. "What? I'm here." The faces looking down at me had little haloes around them. I blinked several times. "I'm fine," I said, suddenly flashing through the memory of countless drunken nights, stumbling, lost, ecstatic or embroiled in a life or death struggle with a lamp. The recollection made me laugh.

"Here, drink this." Aleria now, one hand behind my head, the other bringing a smooth glass to my lips, pouring ambrosia over my lips. I could taste the apples in the juice, see the trees from which they had fallen, smell the seeds from which they grew and hear the winds that caressed their buds. The sugar in the nectar seeped into my pores, into my arteries and veins, racing to fill my brain with the thrill of life itself.

"Apples," I said and I could feel the grin across my face. "Up now, I need to get up." With a few helping hands, I was on my feet again, staggering about like a wino on South Pearl. At last the room stopped pulsating and I stopped grinning and things went more or less back to normal. By then I had drunk two glasses of apple juice and my stomach felt pleasantly full. "I'm sorry, Simon," I said sitting once more, legs crossed beneath me and still clutching the empty glass, my sticky fingers imprinting on the smooth transparent surface. "I didn't mean to leave you. Was it awful?"

Simon shrugged, arms folded across his chest. "It was terrifying! I knew I was in the suds when I saw those two big things whip you off like helicopters."

I saw Aleria's puzzled look. "They were owls. Larger than normal, but owls all the same. They were the harbingers."

"Harbingers!" Simon continued. "I'd rather have seen harbingers. There was this enormous black cat. I thought it was sure to eat me, so I jumped up in a tree and watched it drink water out of a brook for ages. I figured you were going to kick up a lark and leave me stranded there forever."

"I wouldn't do that."

"Oh, wouldn't you? What about Belgium?"

"Belgium doesn't count." Nonetheless I could feel the flush rising up my cheeks. "What happened next?"

He uncrossed his hands—he was going to need them to gesture, which I took as a good sign. "The cat was this big, no lie. It finally drank enough water to fill a bathtub I think, which made me really thirsty, too. When it seemed like it was really gone, I climbed down and drank from the stream, too. Do you know what water tastes like? Real water? Oh, I guess you all do, but damn, it's still a big surprise to me. I had it running down my chin like a four year old, but then I heard that voice. It wasn't a Japanese girl."

"I know," I said with a smile.

"It was that bird. That funny black and white bird that hops. Harakka. You told me her name but I didn't remember it until now. She's real."

"Yup."

"I saw her, that made it real, right? Can we have the same dream? It's not a dream."

"It's not a dream. It may not be the same real as here, but it's real." I could feel the crowd around us drawing closer and closer as they hung on Simon's every word.

"She came to me and she even knew my name. She asked where you were and I told her you had fucked off without a word."

"I'm sure I remember saying 'Argh' or something like that."

"Whatever. I asked her if she knew where you went, yeah, I know she had already asked me, but I asked her anyway." His glare dared me to criticize. "I asked her how to get the hell out of there. And then we sat and talked for a long time. Or what seemed like a long time."

"What about?" Aleria was trying to hide the eagerness in her voice but the rest of her body betrayed her. I could almost hear the ca-ching in her voice, but it wasn't so much the real gingerbread she was looking for, but a kind of spiritual capital. She wanted to quaff the cup of life with eager haste, as the man said, but I wasn't too keen on spilling over the brim.

"You ought to know that much of the journey is private," I answered as Simon stopped to think. I knew well that it was probably getting a bit hazy in the details for him already. It's important to write them down as soon as possible, like a dream. While many details will stay with you all your life, a lot of them will slip away like summer snakes. "He'll tell you what he can."

"It wasn't much," Simon said, sounding puzzled and somewhat uncertain. "I was asking about the land. I forgot what we had gone there to do. Really." He looked up at Aleria and the others standing around. "Harakka told me about the land. It's amazing! You have to see it," he said trailing off a little lamely at the end.

"I did see the ones you hoped to meet," I said finally, feeling my way through the words as if through a darkened labyrinth. How much did I want to tell? How much should I tell? How much would they want me to tell? Probably everything which made me a little suspicious. Probably my unevolved lizard brain, but something made me cut corners as I told them a bit about the Wits. Most of the crew looked gloriously happy, shiny with sweat still from the dancing—had it gone on while the drummers played for us? There was a look of giddy happiness that made me glad I had not told everything. The look on Aleria's face seemed somewhat more clouded. It wasn't quite what she expected.

"I have to sleep now," I finally said, getting up from the ground while my knees cracked, then swaying a little, light-headed still. Aleria immediately stepped to my side, taking solicitous hold of my elbow to make sure that I was safely stable. I looked over at Simon, who was also staggering to a standing position. "Are you coming?" I had hoped he would—we had a lot to talk about without the glare of the public radiating upon us. Like the man said—or was it a woman?—there are certain kinds of limelight that do not flatter a gal's brow. I was feeling myself to be in the firing line of just such a pallid light. It would be a far, far better thing to repair to some privacy and discuss this at greater length between just ourselves.

If I had any hopes of Simon reading my mind at that point they evaporated in the next moment, when a familiar young man put the same sort of solicitous grip on Simon's appendage. I had forgotten his name, but I recognised the shy young man who had brought us our towels earlier. A quick glance shuttled between the two of them, accompanied by the flash of a smile on each face, and I knew I wouldn't be seeing Simon that night.

I sighed, but allowed Aleria to herd me down the corridor while Simon and his paramour shuffled along behind us. While I could feel no exhilaration of lust in my nether regions, I could understand Simon's zing of thrill at the discovery of this new-found land, even if I walked in white like an evil sprite. It was not my colour.

Aleria moved to detain me further at the door to my room, even as Simon and his pal slipped swiftly behind their door, no doubt to thrash noisily upon the floor, casting their linen hence without penance or innocence. It made me feel distinctly wistful. But I had no interest in such grappling then, and there was little about Aleria at that moment to interest me. Don't get me wrong—that was one beautiful armful. But she was far too hungry for information. I could see it in the shiny glint in the corner of her eye. It was entirely possible that Aleria would not be averse to any amorous moves I might make if they might result in spilling of knowledge.

That's irony by the way: the libertine unresponsive and the ascetic precipitously inclined.

I made small noises and gestures—so tired—and she regretfully relinquished my arm, though clearly burning with curiosity. She had patience, I'll give her that. Undoubtedly Aleria assumed she would be able to winnow the details out of me gradually as the days unwound. Little did she know we would be on the road again tomorrow. I was going to make sure of it.

My head had barely struck the pillow when I fell into a nigh insensate sleep, despite the desperate groans coming from the next room. I must have dreamed, but the details were lost to me by the next morning when I awoke at dawn. I was so disoriented by the light and the smells that I couldn't figure out where I was for some few elongated and blinking seconds of breathless terror. Where am I? A question I had once asked with regularity and little curiosity, now it leaped forth like a well-paid bodyguard ready to assess the dangers and muscle away any intruders. The sense of panic subsided quickly with a glance taking in the Spartan efficiency of the room. I sat up and swung my feet to the floor, gathering my thoughts for a moment before downing the glass of water I had made sure to put nearby. Habit: a glass of water, a step through my tai chi routine, a short meditation of thankfulness, and I was ready for the day. The thin futon was more comfortable than I imagined it would be and my stretched muscles seemed eager to find what the day would bring. I hadn't forgotten about the night that had passed, though.

Listening at the door was not part of my usual morning routine, but it seemed prudent. I didn't seem to hear anything or anyone outside my door until a sudden series of knocks set me back on my heels so fast I nearly fell over. "Yes," I said cupping my surprised ear protectively, "who is it?"

"Me." Simon shoved his way into the room and closed the door behind him. He looked considerably in sorts (is that the opposite of out of sorts?), grinning broadly. "Morning!"

"No need to be quite so cheery. In the words of the immortal saint, 'only dull people are brilliant at breakfast.'" I sat back down on my futon and Simon plopped down on the single chair. He looked a lot better than he had since waking up. Ah, the restorative powers of a good night's shagging. "What was his name again?"

Simon grinned. "What do you care?"

"You don't remember, do you," I sneered. "Slut!"

"Bimbo." It was a perfunctory insult, he didn't really care all that much. "You're just envious." He picked up a book of Zen poems and idled through its pages.

"Not true. I could have had Aleria last night if I didn't mind her probing my mind as much as my body."

Simon looked up then, tossing aside the book. "You don't trust them?"

"No."

He shrugged. "Well, they were a bit keen. What do you suppose we ought to do?"

"Leave. We were going to anyway."

"I suppose—do you think we can?"

"What, they're going to stop us?" Admittedly the idea was a bit intimidating. Even vegetarian yoga twisters could be powerful in a crowd. I had sudden visions of the lot of them stalking toward us as we cowered against a wall, all of them moaning in vaguely zombified fashion and trying to get hold of us with dead fingers. Didn't take much to turn just about any situation into a horror film. When did George Romero take up residence in my subconscious? Oh, that's right—about the age of fifteen.

Simon got up and smacked the top of my head playfully.

"No, dummy. Car trouble. I don't think they'll try to keep us here, but they will try to get us to come back. I don't think they're evil, you know."

"They're good/bad, but they're not evil," I agreed. "Are you getting breakfast?"

"Yeah," he grinned. "I'm hungry."

I rolled my eyes with what I hoped was a sage world-weariness but probably just looked like my usual self. "Enjoy. I'm going to go find Maggie and see what the skinny is on the car."

I found her about fifteen minutes later, pointed to the parking lot by a smiling and cheerful resident at whom I tried not to scowl. Maggie was already at work on the little yellow bug, pulling out a spaghetti of wires from the engine and soldering here and there with a little gun. She did not look up when I arrived even though my cast shadow fell across her shoulders. "How's it look?" I finally asked.

I was beginning to think she wasn't going to answer me when she finally lowered the little gun, (which made me oddly nervous), and rocked back on her heels to regard her handiwork. "Should be all right now," she said, still eyeballing the profusion of wires as if she might have missed a rogue here or there.

So Maggie wasn't ignoring me, just caught up in her work. I think a train could run next to her workbench and she'd pay it no mind if she were in the middle of some project, even if it blew three long whistles as they used to do back when they still ran all the time. I couldn't believe we were still waiting on the electrics in most regions. Criminy! They could make kid's trains run on electric—why not adult ones? I looked at Maggie's back. Those powers of concentration could be useful when applied to more enjoyable pursuits. I felt a smile replace my morning scowl as I thought about the dexterousness of her hands and one of my own reached down to twirl one of the stray black curls lingering on her shoulder.

"What the hell do you think you're doing?" Maggie

whirled around and brought the gun back up as if to shoot me with the hot metal.

I backed off, hands upraised to protect myself from her anger. "Whoa, whoa, nothing, nothing! I was just—"

"Fuck off!"

"Hey, that's not fair, I was just—"

"Who cares what you were just doing?" Maggie's brows warned me away from opening my big fat mouth again. I might have ignored the gun, but the brows, I knew better. "You selfish, manipulating shark."

Shark! Says who? "What did I do?" I asked miserably, hands in pockets once more to feign disinterest. I was hoping I wouldn't get a laundry list just then, I was really wondering more about recent memory. I knew too well about the past.

Maggie shot me a glance that said shut up and crouched back down by the engine. For a minute or two she said nothing, but I didn't back off either. "What the hell was that sideshow last night?"

Huh? "What do you mean?"

She turned around to look at me. I'd say we were face to face, but she's more than a bit shorter even when not crouching down. But she didn't look as mad as before, in fact, if I were to put a label to it, I'd say she looked a bit unsettled. "You. Simon. All the folderol in the forest. What kind of jug juice are you pedalling these dimwits?"

So that was it. I sighed. I could argue until the sun went down and Maggie would never come around to the truth. Stubborn, I call it. If I tried to be reasonable, she would dig her heels in and never let it go. But if I gave up immediately, she might just trust me. "You don't believe me, so it isn't going to matter what I tell you." I shrugged as if I didn't care. Truth to tell, I'm not sure I did much. I was getting a little tired of everybody pushing me around.

Maggie glared at me with brows still down, but then turned back to the engine. After a moment in which even I could guess there was very little in the way of real work getting accomplished, she finally said, "You don't mean this stuff is real: other worlds, mind travel?" She didn't look up, just continued poking at wires already neatly in place.

"Would you have believed the Wags before you saw them?"

Maggie tapped at a nut with a spanner for a few dinging moments, before dropping the pretence and looking at me with a healthy dose of suspicion, but also something more. Maybe it was fear, I don't know. "I guess they were a bit of a surprise," she agreed. "But how do you know you're not just making things up when you 'journey' or whatever it is you call it?"

I didn't rise to the bait. "I wasn't sure at first. I thought I was just having weird hallucinations."

"Not unexpected, that."

I smiled. "True enough. What I learned from my guide, though, was true. My own subconscious wasn't smart enough for all that I discovered. I went to the library and had them find stuff for me. It was amazing."

Maggie actually returned my smile a little. "Well, I don't know about all this crazy stuff, but if Simon vouches for it, too, well—I just don't know about these people. Aleria seems... different."

"Nothing like followers to change a person."

That got rid of the smile. "They're doing good work here." Her words were more confident than her tone. "They've saved a lot of green."

"Yup. Doesn't make them less odd."

"No."

It was a relief to have Simon show up, bouncing with energy and a ready smile. "We on the road yet?" He offered a puppy kiss each to the two of us, which left us giggling and wiping our cheeks.

"Ask the one who knows what she's doing," I said, nodding to Maggie.

"We can go," Maggie said as she gently put each tool back into its proper slot. I would always irritate her with that tool box. "What does this one do?" I'd say, pulling a random metal object from the box, then suggesting various lewd purposes to which it might be put. I didn't try that now. Things actually seemed to be going well at the moment. A good time to keep my cake hole closed.

"Well, shall we load up?" Simon finally asked, when Maggie seemed to have things put away like spoons in a rack.

Maggie shrugged. "S'pose. You don't want to hang around?"

Simon looked back and forth between us. "I'm a little fractured by the weirdness, says the man recently recovered from a coma. I'd just as soon hit the road. We can always stop on the way back or some other time, if you don't mind."

"Me?" Maggie looked surprised.

"We were dropping something off for your friend or whatever," I reminded her.

"Done." Considering the way she looked at us, it had probably been done yesterday.

Simon and I knew better than to argue. "Let's go."

You knew it wasn't going to be that easy, right? When we trooped up to sheepishly mention retreat, Aleria was clearly disappointed. In the bright breakfast hall all the shiny faces smiled at us, except Aleria. She sighed and made it clear that she had hoped for a repeat performance that night. We gathered before her feeling like truants before a principal, (well, I did anyway). She sighed, but seemed to give up quickly enough. "Perhaps on the way back…" The words trailed off, but her look was thoughtful rather than defeated. We all nodded our willingness to comply with the possibility then sidled back toward our temporary rooms.

We managed a few desultory goodbyes in which no one kissed me as we lingered on the steps of the complex. I still could not get over the profusion of plants even here and regretted not taking a last look at the indoor forest. A few friendly hugs and vague promises later, we began our way down the steps when we heard an urgent call.

"Wait! Wait!" Aleria was moving along—I can't say running, but stepping swiftly if gracefully, as always—towing someone else in her wake. Simon caught my eye but I didn't know what to think. Maggie squinted. When they arrived at the top step, Aleria's eyes were bright and not just with the effort of locomotion. "I knew I had forgotten something! Can you give Karasu a ride? Her family's in Revere and she had hoped to visit them soon." Breathless behind her was the young Asian woman who had helped care for us last night.

"Must have packed in record time," Simon muttered to me, but Maggie said "Sure, we can. At least as far as Boston. But, yeah, probably even to Revere, if we have time." Belatedly she looked at Simon and dropped her agreeable smile when she saw the clouds forming.

"Can the car carry four?" Simon gave her an out, but he should have known better than to cast aspersions on her mechanical friend.

"Of course it can," Maggie said in surprise. "It's got enough power to get us and all that heavy equipment up the hills here. It's downhill a lot of the way now, too."

There was nothing for it but to welcome Karasu as one of the gang. Aleria just beamed in gratitude, although whether it was to us or to her minion it was hard to tell. Listen to me: minion! Why not just tip your hand in prejudice, eh? But it was too late. We had the interloper aboard whether we wished it or not. At least we could hope she would be pleasant company.

We piled into the little yellow bug with our belongings and the start of a sense of watchfulness. It wasn't just Aleria and her bunch, although the extra passenger weighed on our minds as much as on the car's suspension. The Wags, the Wits—it was beginning to seem like everybody had their eyes on us, so we ought to be returning the favour. Normally I'd put it down to my paranoia, but I could tell Simon was feeling this scrutiny, too. You had to know him really well to see past the pleasant exterior and know when fire lay below and might be ready to explode. It wasn't anywhere near to that yet, of course, but I could feel his watchfulness as much as mine.

Hopes that Karasu would be an amiable travelling companion, as a nineteenth century writer might put it, soon evaporated. Maggie was the first to break the awkward silence as we rolled down the winding lane toward the gate. "What a lovely name you have."

"Oh my gahd," the young woman said with sudden animation and an unbelievably thick Revere accent, "I can't believe you think that. My parents were on this traditionalism kick when my brother and I were born so we were stuck with these names. Can you believe it? Like it's not bad enough living in Revere! I wish we lived in Boston, there are so many better shops there and the parks and people, you know, like more interesting people anyway. I had to get away as much as I could, whenever, you know, just so I didn't have to be home all the time, I mean, really! I begged my parents to let me go to school in Boston but they wouldn't let me until high school and it was just murder, you know. If you had to live with my mother—"

"So how did you come out here?" Simon interjected, deftly dodging between the flying words. "This is a long way from Boston."

Karasu agreed, shaking her head so swiftly and assuredly that I began to worry her head might pop off at any moment. "Isn't it just! I have to get away now and then or I'd just go crazy, stir crazy, you know. Not that everybody isn't great and the food is really good and nourishing you know, healthy and we're all sworn to secrecy about the food and stuff, but you know, can't be too careful. But really, like I was saying it's the best place still, the very best, absolute top drawer for yoga instruction and I want to be a yoga instructor in Boston one day, you know, like have my own studio and have people come to take classes and stuff. I know I'll be a great teacher like Aleria one day, because she really is the best and everybody loves her. She tells me I have moved through the levels so quickly that I can begin teaching really soon…" and on and on she went. I leaned forward to whisper to Simon an offer to change seats but he just laughed.

Seeing no sign of relief, I turned my head to the side and situated myself as best as possible for rest. As the endless monotony of our new companion's monologue steadied into a constant drone, from which I caught only an occasional disjointed phrase, ("he was the very worst" and "well, I just squashed it to bits"), before at last I blessedly slept and all that noise fell away.

I must not have been asleep many minutes when dreams took me back to that strange cave on the mountain. As before I stood before the doubled shadow who was yet flanked by the two barn owls. In my vision the cave seemed warmer and more welcoming, not the jagged slash of night it had been. Its occupants, however, struck me as being just as strange as they had been, more so now that I had had time to digest their presence.

"Welcome again, friend," the voice said to me as I found myself seated upon a comfortable cushion.

"Friend? A word I use with great care," I said, trying very little to hide my irritation. "I still do not understand your apparent magnanimity in offering to help my people. We're hardly the sort of species that would seem a beneficial addition to the universe. In fact, there's a lot to suggest it might be better off without us."

The low chuckle, still doubled, did little to increase my sense of comfort. "We are not gods to choose who thrives and who dies. We merely share the same wish for self-preservation that you do. The Wags are a danger to many. We would wish to protect ourselves—and we can do so better together."

I thought on that. "What about the Wags? Don't they have every right to exist?"

The voice seemed to move closer. "They do, indeed. But must they dwell where they are most noxious? Better they move on to greener pastures, I believe is the term in your tongue."

"Maybe they like it here." Why was I stalling? Surely we all wanted the wretched things gone? Why pussy-foot around? I could make the simplest thing difficult, or so my mother always said. Must be my inner Jane Eyre. "How exactly are they endangering you?"

The voice sighed and in it I could imagine I heard endless years of suffering patience. Had the Wags oppressed them for a longer time than we had suffered? After all, five years wasn't so much, and truth to tell, it had been at first a welcome break from the endless downward spiral of the war. A fresh hell was, after all, fresh. The Wits responded at last, "Do you imagine they show more regard for us than for you? We are all little more than fields to be spoiled, wine to be drunk, food to be squandered. They are very low sorts of creatures."

"I suppose."

"Will you help us, then? Journey here?"

"I suppose," I repeated.

"Very well. We will begin the preparations. Come to us soon."

8

It was nearly evening when we arrived in Worcester. With four in the car there was little chance to make any better time, as much as Maggie might brag about her little powerhouse, we were lucky to have made it so far with relative speed. We had had to stop only twice to clear debris from the ill-used turnpike. Storms had brought down a number of trees and neglect over the years had caused the tarmac to buckle.

It was hard to imagine that the way had once been a vibrant artery across the state to the capital city. Where now Boston lay in quiet solitude, content enough with its internal transportation of electric trams, provoking a sense of insularity from which I'm surprised I, or perhaps even more so, Simon, ever escaped. It's one thing to be the peculiar and neglected child of an unfashionably large family; it's quite another to be the prized son of an elderly lineage. They had never liked our being friends. While we were not quite Laurie and Jo, there had been a strange affinity between our characters just as they had always been a mismatch between our temperaments, but enough of nineteenth century novelistic conventions. Reader, I did not marry him—after all, he was never interested in women for marriage. But the bond between us mattered even more to me now that it had been again tested and found true, and that we shared a new strand of experience—one that was beginning to make me very nervous.

If Boston had succumbed to an elderly hermitage, Worcester had at last come into its own. No longer the modest haven of commuters, and of students who wanted to be out of the city but not too far from home, the rest stop between Boston and Springfield had become a haven for the last vestiges of car culture. Gone were the days of gas-guzzling giants, but there were those who could not abandon the sleek dinosaurs of those days. I was old enough to remember that past, so I didn't turn my nose up, as so many others did, at the small army of recalcitrant hot-rodders who, lacking only one type of fuel, continued their devotion to the gods of steel and chrome. The more gods the better, I say.

While Mademoiselle Ota continued to witter on about the finer points of preparing mung bean sauce while bouncing up and down in her side of the seat, I let my eye wander over the plethora of cars streaming through the new mobile capital, bright shiny steeds of freewheeling life. It was a garish contrast to the empty wasteland of the turnpike with its blasted trunks and stubbly scrub. We had had a night in a green paradise and abandoned it for this desolation row. I think all our hearts sunk a bit deeper as we traversed the way east, regretting perhaps our choice or at least questioning its sagacity. I know I did. The others were silent (except of course for Karasu who seemed to have no OFF button for her lips) but the silence for many hours weighed upon us and the grim determination as we leveraged trunks off the road surely gave us pause. Some impulse drove us forward—more than Mr. Tolliver's final resting place—and the journey wore on.

But the cars that puttered the streets of Worcester restored my spirits. The unnatural hues—or should I say once natural, the charred landscape around us was no indication of colours, I could well remember from childhood if not from our brief sojourn into a verdant world—gave a wild sense of celebration, as if a herd of tropical birds, now glimpsed only on soymilk cans and filtered soy-flavoured water, had descended on this least likely of locations to offer the glamour of a tiki bar to a sleepy northern town. We passed a turquoise car of so ancient an origin that it had fins like a shark emerged from the waves. Parked on a side street I saw a small car that looked more like a toy than a vehicle, but that it had the telltale exhaust pipe that marked all gasoline-powered autos. It was alternately jet black and cherry red, with shiny silver bumpers rimmed with black rubber. It had been carefully restored—or preserved, I suppose. I had heard of the hot-rod culture here, but I had never really seen it for myself. The few times I had been back to the town of my birth I had taken the train and seen little of the downtown where these rare steeds gathered to preen and to mate.

"Look at that one!" Simon called out. I was not the only one captivated. I turned my eyes toward the horizon to see a black monster with eager orange flames painting its side. "It looks like something a buccaneer might drive!" He laughed eagerly and swivelled his head to watch it go by.

"Oh, don't say that," Maggie countered. "Last thing we need is to run into some privateers. They say you'll find them here."

"Arr, Jim-boy," I couldn't help saying.

"Pieces of eight, pieces of eight!" Simon was quick to chime in, his voice strangled to produce tones somewhat in keeping with the squawk of a parrot. It may have annoyed Maggie, but for a moment at least it put a halt to Karasu's endless babble as she stared at the two of us in confusion. Clearly she had not been raised on the classics.

Our little auto pulled up to a berth at the best roadhouse in town, full of laughter and wild looking characters. Bertrand's was a legendary spot. Not that it was famed in song and story—well it might be, but I knew no songs or stories other than it served the most famous, beef-tasting soy burgers there were. Rumour had it, (rumour's not quite story, is it?), that they had some real meat—although the tales carried were that it was not so much beef but the few possums said to dwell yet in the woods of Connecticut. It was all malarkey, no doubt, but the stories persisted because the burgers were so good.

That night—like apparently so many others—the joint was jumping. There were still the old parking lot spaces for service in your car and the service personnel: women in short puffy skirts, men in tight pants and open shirts like toreadors, all on wheels as if they too were autos of some kind, machines delivering food and pleasure to your auto. They swirled and danced with nimble speed, an elaborate ballet of twirling colour, red for the women, black for the men, shiny satin material that caught the glare of headlights and the streetlights and the garish neon of the restaurant itself.

"A big energy suck," Maggie muttered to no one in particular.

True enough but who could be churlish enough to recall one kilowatt from the display before us. After the drab journey of the long day to meet with a second paradise, an artificial one, certainly, but an inspired, created and loved one nonetheless. It was like that long-forgotten sensation, a plunge into clear deep water, a soaking of the senses that thrilled each nerve end with delight. The last gasp of the previous century, a bucketload of dreams never realised or, perhaps, shining for a brief gossamer slip of a moment and then gone—relived and celebrated, but already passed. Revived now, the romantic memories shuffled off the melancholy of loss and lived on as dreams carved in chrome, steel and neon, larger than life as only dreams can be. How had such an Edenic place survived the Purges and the ravages of the Wags? Was it because it was so paltry and provincial, passed and passed over? Better the shade of neglect had held sway to birth this fluorescent faery land. Energy suck, my Aunt Fanny—both of them.

There was no berth open at the spots that ringed the restaurant, so we parked in the hinterlands and abandoned the bug to find our way inside. The lot thrummed with all the renegade energy of Mos Eisley or Casablanca; it was like being plunged into a road romance of the twentieth-century bard himself, he of hot rims, engines and four on the floor. You could tell the tourists from the pros by their plumage, the synthetics from the vintage, or at least highly skilful copies. Simon tugged at my sleeve and pointed: a car hop there, a toreador *en pointe*, a *bona fide* greaser perched on an electric motorbike. Even Karasu gaped—had she never passed through Worcester on her travels from Revere? Maggie grinned. It was a wonderland to feed all her passions—mechanical and physical. Would we ever be able to tear her away? I had to admit it was a lot more than I had expected, a lot more than I had heard, and I was looking forward to whatever might occur with the same old giddy recklessness that used to guide my feet. Harakka had always counselled me to better curb the extremes—why did I only listen to her too late? Between the ascetic and the libertine I had not struck a balance, so the wheel turned once more with the suddenly top-heavy weight. My body was alive, my senses afire. *Why now?* I thought. Why here was plain: what better location. But I had been cold to Aleria's nuanced suggestions. Was my body just running behind?

"Welcome to Bertie's," a cheery hostess greeted us with a Marilyn Manson wig and lips like lacquered cherries. "How many in your party?"

Maggie had to respond because the rest of us were dazzled by the phantasmagoria before us. It wasn't just the tables full of people of every description, many looking as eagerly rubber-necked as we—no, there was a dance floor and upon it every conceivable permutation of mid-twentieth century fashion. What a riot of colour, like some giant had vomited a rainbow in syncopated rhythm. Swirls of dancers eddied in and out, between and through, even up and down as partner threw partner carelessly into the air. Unlike the buoyant caperings last night, there was an edge of hysteria to the movement as if bonds strained near breaking, ready to loose at the right touch.

Touch, that was the key.

Here was a sensual paradise. Not just the food that steamed from every table, bumperloads like in the days of yore when lumberjacks strode the land and pancakes were not dainty fare with syrups, but the people, the plumage, the sinuous shake of their bodies in rhythm; it all conspired to fill the air with such pheromones that the insubstantial seemed filled with solid flesh. The pulse of the music filled my ears and stirred each fibre of my being to a cat-like tension, awaiting food, awaiting prey.

The hostess led us toward a table after some short delay, red heels clacking just audibly in the din, the sway of the hips a nearly convincing counterfeit of gender. We were placed at a small round table that left plenty of space to grope with our eyes among the close-crowded denizens lining the bar, the restaurant, the dance floor.

"I never even knew this was here," Karasu enthused. "I can't believe it! Wait 'til I tell Marta and everyone." Her eyes glittered at the thought of being the bearer of such news and I mourned that Shangri-la should be sullied by herds of beefy tourists from Revere, but it was not my Arcadia to preserve. Perhaps it was the drabs which gave the peacocks such lustre.

"I was here five years ago," Maggie said with an enthusiastic grin. "It wasn't nearly this crazy. Did you see all the cars?" We all assented that it was an auto heaven. Too thrilled to even see our menus yet, the server arrived, took in our shattered confusion and bowed away.

I could see Simon staring toward the bar with preternatural attention and turned my head to see what he could see. A tangle of black-booted youths gathered together in eager conversation. The motorbike riders, I was certain, and at their centre a fetching young thing with starkly blue eyes and straggly black curls and a face of surprising beauty.

"Emon din ki habe Ma, Tara?" I was not certain I had muttered aloud until Simon leaned over to say, "But I saw him first!"

I grinned. "Who sees who first rarely matters. It is who one sees last that matters most."

"And what makes you think he'd be interested in you?"

"Why should he be interested in you?" It was like the old days and suddenly I felt a giddy wave of happiness to have Simon back again. Glory be to all the gods who ever were that he is no longer sleeping like Briar Rose awaiting a kiss. May the heavens preserve all good doctors and nurses and medical staff everywhere. From this unlikely pitcher flowed all the milk of human kindness and I felt drunk upon it.

"Perhaps," Simon whispered in my ear while stealing a glance at the young Adonis, "perhaps he is the kind to share." Had Arcite and Palamon only had such a generous nature, they might have been friends yet and alive to enjoy it. We both turned to regard the treasure. Like a thoroughbred among carthorses he stood, a natural elegance in every movement. They were all dressed alike in a similar fashion—black boots, leather jackets, some even real, black shirts, blue jeans—but he wore his attire with a careless negligence that suggested any costume would fit as well, or as ill. His face featured wide-set eyes that gave him a deer's countenance above the high cheekbones. A Victorian would no doubt say the broad forehead lent him an intelligent look, but I would wait to see whether words would prove it. His lips were a ready feast, feminine in their ripeness, mobile in their action as he sparred with his friends. The hands looked careworn and rough, yet they moved expressively. His frame was fashionably slouched, thin and wiry, tall but not too tall—only a little taller than me. In short, he was perfect, or as near perfect for any faun in this wilderness could be without Pan flute and horns.

"What's with you two?" Maggie broke in irritably.

"Nothing," we chimed in unison, then burst into giggles.

"Christ on a crutch," she muttered, guessing our purpose and scowling. "The more things change…"

"Young lady, such language!" Simon laughed out loud and hid behind his menu as if it were a fan. "I'm shocked, shocked to hear foul words from a mechanic!"

Karasu, who had been blessedly occupied with staring wide-eyed at all and sundry suddenly burst in with a new staccato of noise. "What are you getting? I cannot decide. I know I've heard rumours that their burgers really have beef, but I don't think I can resist trying one and maybe it's really only soy after all. Aleria, don't kill me, but I just have to have one. And what's a malted anyway? Are you having one? I might have to have one just so I can say I did. Have you heard anything like this music before? It's crazy!"

"That's vintage stuff," I said with an air, I hoped, of melancholy expertise. "The kind of thing my parents heard at their parents' knee. Buddy Holly and Stagger Lee, Leslie Gore and Duane Cochran—all the greats." Names half-remembered, but what did they know?

"I can't believe the dancing," Maggie said smiling with genuine admiration. "I don't know when I ever saw such a display. Quite athletic."

"I saw a sign," Karasu piped up. "There's a contest every Saturday night with cash prizes. I bet people come to practice all the time."

"And to check out the competition," Simon said. Our server returned then and we ordered variously according to inclination, only Simon and myself going for cocktails. He got something outlandish with an auto-themed name and its own garish colours when it arrived shortly thereafter, counterfeit fruits gracing the highball glass. I went for a classic which very nearly tasted like real martini. It served in the same way to sharpen the appetite and quicken the pulse. The loping young stranger still lagged at the bar and I was beginning to formulate plans for my opening gambit.

I should have known Simon would be ahead of me. "'Scuse me," he said and popped out of his seat to head toward the bar.

Bastard! I thought, but waited to see what would happen.

After a few moments' conferring with the angelic faun and his friends, Simon returned, the vision in tow. He snagged an unclaimed seat and bid the creature sit between our two chairs. *Clever boy,* I thought. We could see which way the wind blew and prepare shelter accordingly; yes, it would do nicely.

Simon lost no time weaving a web of words about the prize. "This is Brendan, everyone. Brendan, this is everyone. Brendan says he knows the best route to the city that will get us around treefalls and other such hazards. Ought to save us time, eh?"

I leaned in to get a better look of those dark blue eyes. "You live in Boston, Brendan?" Up close his skin was pale as a punk rocker's, his hair pungent with pomade, but not disgustingly so. If I had to guess, I'd say he was about twenty-eight, no more. He must already be done with his compulsory service, I guessed.

He swivelled his head to me and I was pleased he seemed to enjoy the sight, at least enough to smile. Maybe he was only humouring me. There was a bit of a gap in our decades, if I was not a mean bit yet. I decided to let things run their course and see what trotted by. "No," he finally said, having looked his fill, "I live 'round here. But I go up to Boston a lot for the motoring."

"He's a regular out and outer," Simon pronounced him.

"A swell of the first stare," I agreed.

Brendan looked back and forth between us with a quizzical eye, but he was still smiling. One hurdle cleared. How many more to go?

"Never mind them," Maggie said with a huff of impatience, giving us the full weight of her scorn. "They have their own strange language that no one understands. No one."

"We're former conjoined twins," I explained. Karasu stared, her mouth a small 'o'.

"Joined at the elbow. Parted without warning," Simon added with a too-serious look, "Our parents objected to the circus life."

"Yeah, they were strippers."

Brendan laughed out loud and I figured things were going to be just fine. I could feel the smile on my face getting broader and the thoughts in my head steamier.

"Idiots," Maggie uttered and turned to look for the server. I was hoping the food would come soon, because I didn't want to get totally jug-bitten if the night promised the possibility of fun. But I'd already downed my drink and said yes to another by the time the food came. I had to remember to rein in my dissolute tendencies. They were a tad rusty. But a couple of well-mixed faux-martinis gave the table a nice glow.

So did Brendan. He turned out to be not only a knowledgeable traveller, but a quick thinking and all around corky gent. All through dinner, Simon and I were trying to outdo one another at the Nick and Nora chat. Brendan seemed to brighten to the task, although I was no more sure of his interest in either of us than I had been from the first.

But he didn't rejoin his friends. That seemed a positive sign. When I tripped off to the ladies' room, agonised at leaving Simon a chance to pitch the woo with impunity, Maggie followed me to hiss warnings in my ear. "You have no idea what this guy's up to. He could be a free-trader. Do you wanna be mixed up in that?"

I pinched her cheek. I hadn't been crooking the elbow enough to achieve this sense of buoyancy, so it must have been lust. "Don't worry. We'll be careful."

"What about Simon?"

"He'll be careful, too."

"What if he's not wanted?"

"What if I'm not? We're big kids, we'll survive." Somehow though, I was beginning to think I wasn't going to be left out tonight.

"I should just leave you on your asses in the dirt," Maggie said as she walked into a stall and slammed the door behind her. A dishy blonde reapplying some sticky pink lip gloss at the mirror raised her eyebrows at my reflection.

"Girl trouble," I said and let myself into another stall. By the time I came out, Maggie had already sprinted back to the table. So much for uncomfortable silences. She spent the next portion of the meal talking non-stop with Karasu who had quickly felt out of her depth as the plates went spinning and the balls juggling, so to speak. It's not that she was particularly dim, but Karasu lacked that nimbleness of thought that makes someone a delightful partner with whom to sling words over a meal. Brendan, on the other hand, was a delight. He not only recognised many of our verbal touchstones, (his recall of the cheese shop sketch impressed me particularly), but piggybacked on our various flights of fancy with ease. Somehow in the course of that dinner we constructed a world of Wisty-like beauty where the Wags were here simply because they outran a planetary threat of malevolent flatulence in order to find our vile soy-soaked bodies a bland, if safe, fare. Hopeless with laughter, the evening passed with even Maggie defrosting somewhat to join in the giggles. Despite my best efforts to rein in my elbow bending, I was half-sprung by the time we were thinking of settling up and Simon was well and truly foxed. He got things going, but I was going to have to be the one to seal the deal, if sealed it might be.

"So Brendan," I finally said as Maggie was figuring out the bill on her pocket pal, "You must know of a place nearby where we can find room at the inn?"

He turned those blue peepers toward me and grinned. The blue of his eyes was a crystalline clarity that you might expect to find in a mountain stream, half the water frozen, the rest rushing under the crust with liquid speed. Or else it was the gin. "There's a place just around the corner where we all tend to stay. It's nothing fancy." Was it my imagination or did his gaze get a little more probing? His voice did drop a few decibels and maybe half an octave. "It's got a snug little bar. We could have a quiet drink there."

Well, that was easy enough. "Sounds great." My own mouth stretched into a grin, too.

We paid up and he led the way, telling us it was safe to leave the bug in the lot. Maggie frowned at that, but said nothing. We halted long enough to grab our meagre belongings before we trotted over to the hotel. It was indeed unimpressive, but it looked clean enough if not friendly. The woman at the desk might have been anywhere between thirty-five and seventy. Without an excavation party, it would be a challenge to approximate with the cretaceous layer uppermost on her visage. Perhaps it contributed to her ill humour. "Only two rooms," she announced in a clipped voice of uncertain origin.

"Well, that'll do, I think," I answered as suavely as I could manage with a fevered brain. "Maggie—"

"Yeah," Maggie said, shoving me aside. "Let me put this one on my account."

Karasu made some noise about splitting the cost to which Maggie grunted as she signed the guest book. She handed the pen to me.

"Name?" the desk clerk asked.

"Currer Ellis Acton," I said with a completely straight face. Simon, however, got the giggles and couldn't contain himself too well until Brendan pinched his ass, making Simon snort and giggle more until finally subsiding. I shrugged at the woman as if I were perplexed by them, signed away and gave her my account number. Clearly she was not a lover of literature.

"Bar's down here," Brendan said, his voice rich with plummy depths like a good red wine. I fought down the urge to spring on the poor boy as we walked down the dark panelled hallway to the dimly lit bar. He was quite fetching all together. Simon seemed to share my good opinion. It only remained to determine whether those feelings were mutual. Signs looked positive.

We grabbed some cheap drafts and headed to one of the convenient nooks, once again making sure that Brendan somehow ended up in the middle again. I must admit I winced at the flavour of my beer, but I tried to disguise my distaste. There were more important things to consider. "Have you always been into the rod culture?"

Brendan shrugged and licked a bit of beer foam from his lips. "I guess. It became a lot more important when I got out of compulsory. At the time, fighting the Wags seemed important, you know." He gave a rueful smile. "Like a lot of dumb guys, I thought I would be accomplishing something heroic. It's all like that. The war was too stupid to think about, but the Wags, that was more immediate, I guess. Well, you know how that went. You get tired of the sight of blood, especially when it was someone you used to know," he trailed off.

"I just got the call up," Simon said quietly. "I'm supposed to report a week from Monday." Brendan looked at him with surprise, which made Simon chuckle. "I've been in coma for ten years, so I missed the initial calls. I guess they thought I was goldbricking."

"Skiver," I said with a laugh.

"Shirker," added Brendan.

"Malingerer," I said, letting the word roll through my mouth.

"Sluggard," Simon countered.

"Idler!"

"Ne'er-do-well!"

It was like that for some time. Just three friends goofing on one another and a friendly time, a good bosky buzz and a streak of sexual tension ten kilometres wide. I was beginning to feel the downward arc of the buzz, so I thought it best to move things along. With my usual subtlety, I tipped into a momentary lapse of conversation. "Three people, one room, eh?"

"I'm sure we'll be comfortable enough," Brendan said unhelpfully, although he did let his hand stray to my knee.

Simon, eagle-eyed as ever, noticed the movement and said evenly, "I hope I won't be a third wheel."

Brendan turned to him and put his arm around Simon's shoulders companionably. "Don't go running down third wheels. I was always fond of tricycles." A big grin lit his face and showed heretofore unglimpsed dimples, then he simply leaned forward and kissed Simon. It wasn't a full-on serious snog, but it left no doubt as to what we would all be doing tonight.

"Check, please!" I said, getting up.

"We already paid," Simon said, sounding a little dazed but grinning like a fool. We rose almost as one, Brendan lopping arms around both our shoulders, we each holding him by the waist as we rumbled down the hall to find our room. I let go of our treasure and fished the key out of my pocket to let us in. We threw our bags on the floor in a heap and pushed Brendan down on the bed with laughter. He chuckled, but submitted to our taking charge. Simon began with his big black boots, which despite the complicated number of buckles, easily unzipped on the side. I started at the top, helping him shuck off the leather jacket, unbuttoning the black linen shirt. Under it he was pale and nearly hairless, but had some good ink across his chest, a dragon harp. I ran my fingers over the design and he closed his eyes.

"I got that when my mother died." I leaned forward to kiss it while Simon reached up to unbuckle his belt. He tugged off Brendan's trousers and we could see the prize that was ours. We must have seemed like vultures as well fell hungrily upon him, but he didn't seem to mind the frenzy as we worked our way up and down his frame, savouring every bite. It was a while before we finally gave in to the need to remove our own clothes and actually get under some covers, but it was managed without much interruption of service by a little tag team work. Before we retreated to the subterranean round, I noticed more ink on Brendan's back: crow's wings—or maybe raven's, I wasn't sure I could tell the difference. Somehow it seemed just right, though, and I reminded myself to ask about them when time allowed. In the meantime, however, we busied ourselves with finding out how many ways we could wring pleasure from our bodies until we finally collapsed into a grateful slumber, Brendan still snuggled warmly between us.

It was distressing then to suddenly awake around four with an unintelligible nightmare still reverberating through my head. No detail remained to alert me to its purpose, but I was unpleasantly reminded of the darkly violent and vivid dreams I had experienced the week or so before the arrival of the Wags, dreams I had been unable to interpret even with the sage advice of Harakka. It is the peculiar nature of that hour to make you doubt everything you ever believed, everything you've ever accomplished and any reason to go on living. Waking up from a nightmare at that time—even one that has faded too quickly from recall—is a wretched kick in the guts, however delightful the rest of the night might have been. And this was a night I'd definitely nominate for the top ten—no doubt about that. I looked down at Brendan, sleeping with one arm hooked over Simon's chest. Simon was still smiling in his sleep and murmuring something nonsensical. I should have just sunk back down into that welcome embrace, but I had learned to listen to the shrill siren of fear when it coursed through my limbs. It might just be the four o'clock horrors, but I didn't want to take any chances.

I swung my feet out from under the covers, allowing an involuntary chill to ripple across my skin. These two were putting out a lot of body heat and the room felt too cool in contrast. I hopped across the floor to find a shirt—Simon's— and the natural fibre trousers I had got from Aleria's people. I cranked up the heat a little and lay down in front of the air supply unit. I closed my eyes and in very little time, I had stilled my mind enough to journey.

As I leapt into the black onyx temple, my feeling of fear increased. I could not say what it was, certainly nothing tangible. But my body was at once alert and tensed for possible action. As I stepped out into the green sanctuary, I found, through that peculiarity of differences between our worlds, that it was late afternoon and nearly autumnal by the slight chill in the damp air. I looked around me with a weird sense of dislocation. Ahead of me there was an old tree, riddled with a thousand or more insect-eaten holes. Diseased and damaged as it was, the bark had peeled away and landed in desiccated pieces upon lower bushes and limbs, as if clothes discarded. The nakedness of the revealed bleached wood, pockmarked with holes and bearing tracks of sap or water, seemed the flesh of an old lover, deprived of clothes and daring you to look, to see reality as it was and not effaced in some memory of past beauty. I could not recall having ever seen the tree before, but its pale trunk cast upon me a wretched pall that made my heart mourn for its loss. I laid a hand upon its smooth surface and felt the absence of life within.

The sense of foreboding growing within me, I turned and walked toward the river bank, calling out to Harakka. Sometimes it was like this, my calling into the dark of the forest and no answer for some time. The river had provided a convenient meeting place. Once I waited for what had seemed to be two days, although returning to my reality I found I had been gone only four hours. I could not, however, recall it being anything but spring or summer in this world. The nip of fall in the air evoked those melancholy tendencies still associated with that time, mixed as they were with the brilliant leaf colours and the joy of Halloweens celebrated.

There was none of that riot of colour here; the leaves seemed faded but not enriched by the change. I made my way toward the river, jumping at each crackle in the woods, only gradually noticing the absence of bird calls in the trees. It spooked me. I tried to move more quietly, remembering the lessons Harakka had given me, even as I tried to quicken my pace. Stepping out into the glade where the river bent sharply in its passage to caress a jutting rock of grey granite, I was immediately struck by the changes to this comfortingly familiar place.

Floods had swept through, carving new cuts into the banks and settling debris in the crook. The far shore, higher than the near one, showed enormous erosions exposing roots and rocks once concealed. Most distressing, however, was the great grey rock that stood arching toward the river like an ancient sentinel. Many was the time I had stretched out on its surface, warmed by the sun, as Harakka lighted nearby to answer my wandering questions. It was still there, but it seemed as if some deep upheaval had disturbed the very core of the weighty behemoth and it had cracked very nearly in the middle, a fissure opening like a gaping sore on its back. "Harakka?" I cried again as I waded across the shallow bed of the river. "Harakka!"

I felt such a rush of relief and love when I saw that small black and white figure swoop down to the top of the rock that I very nearly swooned with the press of it upon my heart. "Harakka!" I repeated, this speeding my steps to gather the momentum to leap up onto the rock and plunk myself down next to where she had landed.

"You are here, Ro. I was beginning to wonder. You were taken away last time and you were gone so long." Harakka stretched out a wing, shaking it as if to clear it of debris. I resisted the urge to grab her and hug her to me. Birds are so fragile. I had learned that gentle lesson. Even the giant owls that carried me off were delicate creatures—delicate creatures with steel talons, but delicate nonetheless. There was a sudden giddiness that I couldn't suppress, however—maybe I was still a bit tipsy.

"I'm so glad to see you. I had the worst sort of feelings, worries. I woke up in the middle of the night and I had to see you."

"When you were last here, who were the creatures who took you away?" Harakka stared at me with that weird sideways stare that birds have. "They were not of this world."

I shook my head and tried to get comfortable upon the rock. "The owls were maybe from this world, but they were being—what? Manipulated, I guess. These other things were in a cave up in the mountains. They were from another world yet. They said to call them the Wits, but I think they were just goofing on the Wags' name. Their name's probably just as unpronounceable as the Wags'." I was getting excited now, as I thought about having additional allies against the Wags. "They said they could help. They can't quite reach this place, but I might be able to reach theirs with their help. Do you think this is a good thing? I think it might be."

Harakka gave a perfect little shrug with her wings, a move she had copied from me. "It is possible. What were they like?"

I tried to bring the images vividly to mind as Harakka had long ago taught me. "They were voices at first. It was kind of like they rode on the owls and made them larger than they would be normally, so they could carry me to where they were, but without actually going themselves—not that it makes sense, but it was kind of like that. They were shadows then, because it was too disconcerting to talk to nothing, you know?" I looked down at Harakka who was staring at me intently, but who nodded for me to go on. "It was strange to hear them talk, as if it were only in my head."

"How do you hear me?"

I looked at Harakka in surprise. I had never really thought about that. In my mind, I just always said, "Harakka said" or "Harakka told me" but now that I thought about it, her voice was in my head, too.

She opened her beak in that noiseless laugh with which she expressed amusement. "It is how we communicate, too. Or it is how you understand the way we communicate. You hear, we think."

I sighed. Always something new to freak out my mind. What an education I was getting in this old forest. "Well, they did the same thing, then. They—"

"So there were some of them, not just one?"

"Well, there seemed to be two, at least there were two voices that I could hear even though they tried to avoid confusing me, well, it was confusing."

"Did they say anything about where they had come from?"

"Not really. But they were worried about the Wags and they thought working together, we could maybe get rid of them for both our realities."

"Did they say anything about how that would be accomplished?"

The drift of the conversation was beginning to perplex me. "No, but they said it would be possible with some preparation for me to visit their reality as well as here."

"What kinds of preparation?"

"Well, I don't know. They didn't really say. Just that they

were going to make preparations." Even in my own ears I could hear the beginnings of a whine, and took pains to restore my equanimity. "I thought it would be something like how I learned to come here. It sounded like they were really interested and wanted to help. That they needed my help, too." I was realizing that the motivation of pride might be one panel of my wall of defensiveness.

"Perhaps," Harakka said without discernible emotion. Which was not unusual, I reminded myself, although I couldn't help feeling a little irritated.

"What? You don't trust them? How are they any different from you?"

Harakka hopped forward a few steps and fixed me with another stare. "Maybe no different. But one must be cautious when walking between worlds."

"I suppose."

The beady stare was beginning to unnerve me. "You have gained much power. In this world, in your world. Power makes you a target. You have to protect yourself, or better, guard yourself. Power is a magnet. Beings recognise it as a light, seek it out. You need to maintain your boundaries, be alert to draining beasts."

It is to my sorrow that I became irritable, imagining I was more powerful than I was and confident that I knew what I was doing. Power blinds us all, even such miniscule abilities as mine. "I think I know how to take care of myself," I huffed impatiently.

"You have begun that journey, but you will need to progress faster if others are beginning to seek you out. There is much you need to do to shield yourself successfully from those with greater power who wish to appropriate yours."

I would have offered another foolishly arrogant rejoinder, had not a large black cat sort of beast sprung from the shadows to grab Harakka between its teeth and disappear again into the darkness between the trees, leaving me behind shaking and screaming her name helplessly.

9

"Ro, Ro, come back, you're okay, we're here!" Their arms were around me, but it was just too much to suddenly lurch from one world to another. All I could see before me was an endless loop of the big black cat snatching Harakka in its mouth. Not a sound, not a cry, not even an exhalation of breath that I could sense escaped her mouth. Was she waiting for me to save her? How could I save her? Where did the thing go? Where did it take her?

And what the hell was I going to do without her?

I was hardly in this world. I didn't even realise they'd got me in the bed, the two of them patting my head and chafing my hands in some hope of getting me to stop babbling insanely and starting up as if I could run for help somehow. "She's gone, she's gone!" I repeated, even though I must have said it a hundred times already. Now, though, I could see Simon's eyes and began to concentrate on them. "Gone, she's gone."

"Who's gone, Ro?" Simon's forehead creased with wrinkles. How much older he looked in the middle of the night, how much older than all those lost, long years in the unflattering glare of the hospital lights. My poor dear friend, at least I still have you; the thought cheered me some, but still my heart was breaking.

"Harakka! She's gone. A big cat, a monster, came and grabbed her, took her away. She's gone!" I burst into tears which seemed to scare Simon more, although Brendan seemed to find nothing odd in comforting a tearful woman in the middle of the night, although I was betting he was probably angling a way to make a quick skedaddle as soon as the tide began to turn.

"But—how?" Simon hugged me tightly for a quick moment, then looked back into my eyes. "Tell me what happened."

"I was there and talking to her and out of nowhere, this big black cat came and just grabbed her and ran. It was just, like, out of nowhere. Nowhere. I mean, just from the woods, up on the rock—did you see the rock?—by the rock and then it leapt and it had her and ran off back into the woods." I shook my head. "It was all so fast." The words seemed so stupid that they were like sulphur in my mouth. I was worthless, useless and so incredibly stupid. What a waste of my time I had made.

From too many nights like this—albeit for very different reasons—Simon was able to predict my inevitable slide into self-pity and self-flagellation and did his best to distract me. "Did you get a good look at it? Could you tell anything about it? Did you see which way it went?"

I shook my head. It was all a blur. I felt as if my stomach were filled with ball bearings, killing me by the growing weight of my slowness. Hopeless, stupidly hopeless.

"Ro, sleep. We all need sleep." Brendan nodded agreement, patting my hand. "In the morning, we'll be able to think more clearly. We'll come up with a plan." Simon pulled me back under the covers, he and Brendan both snuggling close to offer a kind of animal comfort.

I looked over at the raven-headed young man. "Bet you're wondering 'what the hell?'"

"There are more things in heaven and earth, Horatio," he muttered back at me and, wrapping his arm across my belly, he closed his eyes and was once more asleep.

I thought it would take ages for me to join him in the Land of Nod, but the turmoil of terror and return worked its magic. Suddenly I was blinking awake in the early morning light. Simon was still dreaming, his forearm resting on his forehead, mouth open in a soft snore. Brendan was stirring, so I indulged in a little grope and he awoke with a smile, closing my mouth with a kiss.

"Morning."

"Morning. Still here, eh?"

He shrugged and traced the Little Lulu tattoo on my arm. "I'm not that easy to shuffle off once I stick. Call me intrigued." Brendan kissed Little Lulu, humming her theme song as he explored further, lifting the shirt I had put on in the night. "Tell me more about what happened."

Well, that was increasingly difficult to do as he distracted me, finally making me squeal so much that Simon awoke and we picked up where we had left off the night before. As Simon kissed him fiercely, I took a moment to really stare at this foundling: pale skin, black hair, a lithe body with surprising strength and a great set of tattoos that made exploration all the more fun. There was also that gaping scar in his side that looked like a gunshot wound. So many mysteries to unravel. O, my America, my newfound land, how I am blessed in discovering thee, or however that goes. My heart still ached for Harakka, but I began to understand that it wasn't going to be a simple matter of sending out a search party. I was going to have to find her. But how?

There was a knock at the door, so I left the two of them grappling to see who it was. Of course it was Maggie.

"Are you all going to be ready to go soon?"

"Soonish," I said, at once acutely conscious of how utterly ravished I must look in her eyes. I made a futile attempt to smooth my cowlicks.

"You don't have qualms about anything, do you?" Maggie said with surprising sharpness.

"I can't help being bi," I told her, without much irritation, I think.

"You're not bi, you're just opportunistic."

"I prefer to think of it as flexible." It took me a moment to see why she might be peeved with me. I felt sufficiently abashed to promise, "I'll get us all ready as quick as I can. You going to go get some breakfast?"

She sighed. "I suppose."

I smothered a snappy remark about the great conversation Karasu would supply over breakfast, instead smiling at her back as she walked away. Things are never done when you think they are. I turned back to the bed and the two of them stared at me like puppies caught in mid-tussle. It was as cute as can be.

"I'm going to shower," I said and headed into the bathroom. In the harsh glare of the fluorescent lights I felt the sudden painful reality of middle age upon my face. My eyes, indeed, nothing like the sun, but more like a pale stormlight. They seemed to have grown larger over night. My thin frame was looking particularly angular and awkward, my nondescript hair a tumbled mass of cowlicks, and the Vess greenman on my chest a bit sad. It had been looking increasingly long-faced and morose as my breasts had lost their youthful verve. My brown aureoles stared down in mute embarrassment, as if avoiding my eye. Perhaps it was Simon who attracted Brendan after all. Sigh. *Omnis vanitas*, eh?

As I stared I could hear the sound of wings grow in the back of my mind and I felt myself sway toward the mirror. They were trying to get in. Irritation filled me without warning and I pushed them back out. In my time, when it was my choice. I looked into the mirror as if they were on the other side in some kind of interrogation room. "Not now," I told my reflection. "I'll see you when I'm ready." The sound retreated— or perhaps had never been there. Hey, there's a thought— maybe I'm finally losing what mind I had. Maybe I could quit my job and get disability, then belly up to the oak in the White Horse to drink away my stipend and the rest of my brain cells.

Dreams can be a beautiful thing.

I rubbed myself with antibac, as hard as I could manage, and felt somewhat reinvigorated when I straightened back up (if a little light-headed). It wasn't worth cleaning my hair. I toyed with the idea of shaving my head again, but it hardly seemed worth the bother. Too much time with Aleria's crew. Gets you into an abstemious state of mind—well, in some things, I suppose.

I tagged Brendan who headed into the bathroom next, padding past me with a grin and a quick hug. Simon lay in bed with a similar smile and watched me as I stepped into my tai chi routine. "You should do this, too," I told him, feeling oddly self-conscious. He seemed to think about it, drew on some underwear and stood up on his side of the bed, mimicking my movements as best he could while I tried to correct him. "No, rounder, make the movements flow together seamlessly." He did pretty well, considering.

When Brendan returned, freshly scrubbed, Simon abandoned the effort in order to make his ablutions. Left alone with our new friend, I was overcome with shyness. Without the reinforcement of night and liquor, I felt too naked, even though I was now clothed. Brendan didn't help, lying on the bed watching me as I continued to move through the discipline of the postures. I concentrated on the flow of chi, arcing my arms and feeling the muscles gather and loosen in my legs and back. Yet the whole time I seemed to feel the prick of his eyes upon me. I thought of those crow wings, but somehow I couldn't quite start a conversation then. Gradually the movements of my routine put me into the usual detached relaxation and I forgot him until Simon came out, rubbing his head briskly with a towel. "So you're coming with?" Simon asked apropos of nothing.

"Yup," Brendan said behind me. "You need a guide. I can get you into town faster."

But did we want to get there faster? I asked myself. No matter, we were all silly grins and laughter when we caught up with Maggie and Karasu in the lobby. We were so much caught up in our own entertainment that we failed to notice that everyone else only had eyes for the vid screens on the walls. "What's up?" I asked Maggie.

She gave me one of her patented laser burn looks. "Don't you ever look at your com?"

"I think I turned it off day before yesterday." It would

only have work orders on it anyway, surely. "More Wag folderol?"

"You could say that," a guy in skin-tight PVC top and faux-silk pants said, punctuating his remark with a bark of laughter. "Hope you ain't heading to the city. It's gonna be a bit of work getting there today."

I tried to ignore his singular attire, although Simon was shaking with suppressed laughter, and focused instead on one of the screens where an intrepid reporter was hopping down into the deep troughs ploughed into the ground, presumably — or so it sounded — by a Wag ship. What kind of idiot would do a thing like that?

"Hey, Ro! Isn't that your sister?" Simon was pointing at the screens, which indeed flashed her name at the bottom in various recognisable news fonts.

It's not like I could deny it. There's such a family resemblance that you might suspect my folks of buying in bulk to save on the gingerbread. "Yeah, yeah, whatever." Brendan looked at me with a distinct hint of amusement. It seemed best to move the discussion along. "So what, another Wag's gone down, big whoop."

A fubsey wench standing a little too close to a nearby screen with a miniscule trail of maple-flavoured soy syrup down the front of her stretchy top put her hands on her hips and regarded me with some exasperation. "It is not just one Wag, missy." Missy! "This is about the tenth one since yesterday. Where have you been the last twenty-four?"

"Having mad passionate sex," I told her and then turned back to the screen. It would have been easier to pay attention if someone other than my sister were breaking the story. Local angle — she must have tapped a few favours to get someone to port her up here so quick. Even the network gabsters don't have that much pull alone, however shiny their faces.

"They're acting weird," Karasu decided to fill in. "They've been, like, flying back and forth and conferring with one another, sort of." I really couldn't stand the way her every statement ended in a rising intonation, as if she were asking instead of answering. "No one's sure, but a bunch of them have just suddenly lost power and, you know, crashed. The others seem agitated somewhat." No shit.

"They've been going around shooting things," Maggie added. "St Louis, about a third gone. Manchester, Karachi, a bunch of other places."

Simon stared at my sister as she pointed up to the top of the ridge above her. "Are we going to be able to get through?"

Brendan looked over his shoulder at Simon. He had been looking intently at the background of the images, checking out the lay of the land, I guess. "Do you need to be there today?"

"We have a funeral to attend." Simon looked over at me and then back at Brendan. "It's important."

Brendan looked appropriately sober as he put an arm around Simon's shoulders. "I can get you there. I know ways around this. Won't even take much longer." He looked over at me, then at Maggie, who shrugged, as if it didn't much matter to her. So we hiked up our packs and headed out to the car, which looked all sunny and friendly in the morning light.

"Aren't you worried about leaving your auto here?" I asked Brendan as we three stuffed ourselves in the back seat.

He laughed. "I'm one of four owners, so no—they're not going to miss me. The boys will be quite happy not to have to share, even if it's just parked here for admiration all day. I couldn't afford something like that on my own, even with the government settlement." I raised my eyebrows and he sighed. "Got shot, you know."

"Thought it looked like that. Here?" I asked, touching his side where I'd seen the deep pock-mark last night. Simon returned the earlier gesture, wrapping his arm around Brendan's shoulders.

"I don't recommend it as a money-making scheme," Brendan said with a laugh, but the rest of his face didn't join in the joke. It seemed like a good time to change the subject, so I patted his knee as Maggie got us rolling with a little bit of a whining power surge. Simon kissed his cheek gently and Brendan looked down at the hands in his lap, but there was a hint of a smile on his lips. "We're going to take a little bit of a scenic route when we get past Framingham," he said, raising his voice to be sure Maggie could hear. "We're probably okay until then, although there's a few big holes on the right lane after 10A. Where in town are you going?"

"Mount Auburn cemetery," Simon said.

"In Watertown, sort of," I added.

Brendan nodded. "Okay. I'll get you there." He paused to touch Simon's cheek. "Whose funeral?"

"Mister Tolliver," Simon said. "My cat."

"He actually died a few years ago," I offered. Brendan's raised eyebrows suggested my remarks were not helping. "Oh, he's been cremated."

"Ah."

"More sanitary that way," I said, biting my lip.

"Takes up less space," Brendan added, looking over at Simon.

"Portability is important in a corpse," Simon said, a smile tugging at his cheek. "I can't say how many times I've, uh..."

"Abandoned an oversized corpse? Me too, they can be so bulky and awkward," I agreed.

Brendan jumped in. "Folding could be employed in some cases."

"Not without advance scoring," Simon said with all apparent seriousness. "I can't fold without dotted lines."

"Me either! Otherwise you get random creases and—"

"Your corpse loses all its structural integrity," Brendan finished the thought.

"Is it going to be like this all the way to Boston?" Maggie asked.

Indeed, it was. While Maggie and Karasu entertained one another in the front seat, we gabbed and frisked with one another in the back seat like a bunch of teenagers. Simon told Brendan about his pre-coma life, and I praised his uncanny abilities with images, which led to a joint plan to redesign his hot rod's colour scheme. With reluctance on my part, they even dragged out some stories about my horrifying life as a civil servant and made jokes about the length of my chains. But in the back of my mind, I kept thinking about Harakka, a subject which kept threatening to make me uncomfortably glum. What was I going to do? How could I find her? What would she tell me? I was going to go on being agitated unless I did something about it. For the moment, Brendan and Simon were deep into a conversation on punk rock. I knew from her patient teaching that I should subdue my scattered thoughts and thus retreated into my practiced stillness.

One minute I was with them in the auto's cramped back seat, then slowly I withdrew, hearing their voices yet, but disconnecting from them. Maggie and Karasu chatted about Aleria's training routines, Simon and Brendan about bands from thirty years ago that Simon had seen and Brendan only recently discovered. I felt Harakka's forest close in around me, but she was not to be seen. I sat upon the ground and felt the tears, long held back, begin to flow. "I need you. I can't be without you."

"You're closer than you think."

It was only her voice, but my heart expanded with sudden joy and I opened my eyes to see only the woods and grasses again. I was alone. "Where are you?" But no answer came. I sat there for a few more minutes, but then I let that world go and returned to find Simon and Brendan both watching me. "What?" I wiped the tears off my cheeks roughly.

"Find anything?" Simon asked. He sounded more anxious than he looked, which meant he was trying to hide it from me. Brendan mostly seemed curious, which was less worrisome.

"Only enigma," I said turning to look out the window as if the charred remnants of the National Heritage Corridor retained some fascination.

"You lost someone. I've figured that much out," Brendan said, appearing to choose his words carefully. "I don't understand where you go, though."

I shrugged. "It's all too mad to explain to someone who hasn't been there."

"Even if you have—and I have—it's still wild," Simon said, reaching across Brendan to take my hand in his. I gave it a squeeze. I don't know why I felt so self-conscious. Oh well, yes, I did. Don't want to look like an idjit in front of the new lover. Simple, really. "Ro has access to a world—no, to worlds—that are somehow linked to this one. There're some people in one of them who say they can help us with the Wags. But one of her friends—no, better word? Mentor? She's missing, she's been kidnapped."

"Birdnapped," I said trying not to make my voice quite so gruff. "She's a bird."

"Sounds like crazy stuff," Simon continued, "but we've both been there. Well, at least the one place."

"Not that crazy," Brendan said, squeezing my knee. I noticed again how graceful his hands were in contrast to his leanly muscled arms. He hesitated for a moment, then swallowing, continued. "When I got shot, I dreamed, or whatever, that this big crow came to me and sort of hovered over me, guarding me with its wings. I watched my mate Erik die, and I thought I might die, too. They all said I was really lucky when I finally woke up in the sickbay. The sawbones told me I was just minutes away from dying, but I was never really worried, not really. That crow, I dunno. I mean, I don't... But it saved me."

"That's why the tattoo, right?" I asked

"Debt owed," he said with a jerking nod. "I like to say thanks."

It was group hug time and for once, I didn't feel myself outside things, but very much inside. No words for a while, which was probably just as well. It all needed to sink in, I think. But one thing was clear: Brendan was one of our tribe.

When we got towards Framingham, as Brendan predicted, we had to make a bit of a detour. Autos were backed up so much that a good number of people were simply pulling onto the shoulder and holding impromptu picnics. We couldn't tell if it was due to Wag rubber-necking or some random traffic fatality, but it didn't really matter. We wouldn't be getting through. So off we went onto route 9, gradually angling north at obscure turns here and there until we passed over the turnpike, glimpsing an irregular patchwork of autos and, in the distance, the long furrow that had grabbed headlines that morning.

"Wow," Karasu said. We all echoed the thought. It seemed to easily go on for a mile. There were all manner of flashing lights gathered along it, the largest convergence away to the south. Presumably the ship lay there, the Wag hot rod.

"You ever been curious about the Wag ships?" I asked Brendan, remembering how good it felt to soar as a bird.

He grinned. "Sure, why not? Wonder what they fly on, wonder how fast they can really go. Wonder what it's like to fly like that. Don't you?"

"Not me," Simon said. "I think I'd get sick in something like that, hot-rodding around the galaxy. I'd be weasel-tongued in a minute."

"It would be marvellous to shoot around like that. Off to Paris for the weekend, down to Mumbai for Diwali." I laughed at the thought. "Now, that would be luxury."

We crossed over 128, singing a paean to Saint Jonathan, "with the radio on," although it wasn't. It seemed like no time at all before we were slipping through the crowded streets of Watertown, sneaking up on Mount Auburn, when Simon insisted we pull over at the Stellar Market just before the gates of the cemetery. "I won't be long," he called leaving the four of us to wait. Brendan and I made use of the time with a little extra anthropological exploration, while Maggie and Karasu chatted animatedly about the glories of Bean Town. Maggie hadn't been there in years and noted how much had changed.

Simon returned with two large bags in hand, thrusting them into the car before him. I heard the clink of bottles and smiled. "What extravagance, Mr. Magus," I pretended to scold.

"I have had an inadvertent ten year savings plan, Ms. Parker," Simon retorted, squeezing cheek to cheek with Brendan once more as Maggie backed out of the spot. "I think I deserve to splurge a little on the occasion of my cat's funeral." Rifling through the bag, we saw quite the cornucopia of treats that made my stomach begin to rumble. We had forgotten to eat any breakfast and the sun was well over the yard arm at present.

"You've dropped a good bit of gingerbread today," I said, but Simon only laughed. Brendan was busy inhaling the fresh bread's aroma with a rapturous look on his face. He grinned at me and leaned over to thank Simon appropriately for the bounty. Thus high-spirited we pulled into the drive only to be met by a chained entryway.

"Um, did you check opening hours?" Maggie asked Simon, craning her neck back.

Simon leaned forward, nonplussed. "There must be a bell. It's always been open, 8am to 5pm, 7pm in summer. Always." He looked personally affronted by the locked gate. It was times like these that you could feel his Brahmin blood rise to the top like some kind of sanguine cream. He opened the door and hopped out. Finding no bell, he began to call. "Hello? Hello!" Shrugging at each other, we all got out to join him, peering into the park to look for signs of life.

We heard the crunch of footsteps before the caretaker arrived, his steps echoing in the odd quiet of the place. The initial sense of hope his presence provided, faded with a closer look.

He held a shotgun, probably mid 20C but it could easily have been older. When had I seen such a thing anyway? As if we, too, had been thrown back into a cowboy movie, the five of us obediently raised our hands to the sky.

"What d'ye want?" He didn't lift the gun, but somehow we all felt the weight of its threat. There was no reason to think he was reluctant to use it or that he might find us suitable prey.

Who knew? It was such a barbaric thing to face, none of us could quite believe it.

"We're here for a funeral," Simon finally said, his affronted dignity returning once more.

"No funerals today," the caretaker asserted with a determined shake of his head. His too big glasses magnified the dark eyes and the brows above them. The bald of his head shone in the midday light and the thin flap of hair across the top rose with the slight wind. He had a pipe clenched in his teeth, which moved around as he spoke as if to punctuate the information. And there was the gun, too. I don't think I was the only one for scooting away and returning at dusk. But I wasn't Simon.

"We are here for a funeral," Simon repeated in that tone of voice that had come down through generations of people accustomed to being obeyed. It was compelling. He seldom trotted it out, but when he did, it was best to obey. This man would learn.

The caretaker—I had assigned him that role, but what might he be? Protector, guard?—looked Simon up and down. "Groups require special notification, two weeks in advance."

"We're not a group, we're a handful of mourners with every right to be here."

"Next you'll be telling me you're one of the Cabots—or was it the Lodges?"

"The Eliots on my mother's side and the Brewsters on my father's," Simon said with a full heaping of privileged scorn. "We have cousins who are Lowells, but we don't mix with them anymore." For that matter, Simon didn't mix with much of any of the relatives anymore, but hey, he didn't have to admit to that. He was still a Brewster and an Eliot.

"Whose funeral?" the man said, not quite relenting but clearly somewhat mollified.

"Mr. Tolliver's," Simon said. "My cat."

The man squinted at Simon, then looked at the rest of us. "A cat?"

"Yes." Simon looked coolly serene.

The man exploded into laughter, rescuing his pipe from his mouth and setting the gun to lean against the fence. His face got very red with effort while the rest of us glanced nervously at each other and at Simon, who only smiled in satisfaction. "So, can we come in?"

"Yes, yes, of course. We're only concerned about vandals, you know," the man said as he wiped his head with a seemingly ancient handkerchief. "There aren't any funerals anymore. Everybody's getting frozen these days. A mad fad, I think." He drew a large skeleton key from his trouser pocket and wrestled with the large black lock. With a clank the chains fell and the gate swung open to admit us.

Simon returned to the noblesse oblige. "Thank you, Mr...?"

"Morecambe. Call me Ernest."

"Thank you, Ernest. We appreciate your concern and your duty."

"Never mind. Not much to do lately except shoot at the occasional hooligan. It used to be such a grand park." He looked off across the park behind him and seemed to see the green that no longer spilled across the lawns.

"I remember," I said finally. "We used to come here as kids. We played by the lake and walked through the park all day sometimes. It was so beautiful and peaceful."

Ernest nodded his head, but a kind of sadness came across his face. "Not like that now. But there's still a lot to see. Beautiful things. The lake's dry but the willow's still holding on."

"Is the big tree with the hole in it still there by the side of the lake?" Simon asked.

Ernest nodded. "Just the stump of it, though. Lightning hit it; it fell into the lake bed."

"Could you turn a blind eye to the no picnicking rule?" Simon asked with a warm smile.

"Son, I can turn a blind eye to almost anything these days." Simon grinned and shook his hand. Ernest waved away an attempt to share our bounty, saying "That rich food will give me the gout," so we hopped back in the car and took off on the tour. For Maggie and Brendan both it was a completely new sight. The three of us who had visited many times tried to recapture its glory in a web of words, but the stunted trees and rough hills had the same blasted look as much of the rest of the countryside. Nonetheless, it maintained some of that sense of awe, like the skeleton of a magnificent behemoth. The bleached bones may be all that's visible, but what a creature it was who once lived. The rubble highlighted its absence.

But the monuments! There was still the sphinx and the obelisk, the giant sphere and any number of angels. Everyone oohed and ahhed as appropriate, then we circled back to the lake. Despite the barren landscape, it was like a *madeleine* in tea: *plus ça change, plus c'est la même chose.* I was immediately back on that one perfect day, as if I had buried a crock of gold and come back ugly and old to dig it up and remember. The blasted terrain could not bury the memory of that seemingly topless afternoon. It had been nothing special, just another jaunt to the Mount, but everything had been magical. The sun shone, music of that unknown piper filled the air as if Pan himself had blessed the place. We were indeed held that finger's breadth above the earth, suspended in fleeting magnificence. I looked over at Simon and he too seemed to be holding his breath, remembering, and we clasped arms, embracing, nearly weeping for the children we had been, the world we had known and the long lost years since then. The others could see something passed between us, but wisely left us in silence.

Simon wiped his eyes and turned toward the lake. He put a hand on the ragged stump and smiled. "This is the place." We set down the picnic bags and stood waiting. Simon brought out the little green bag that held Mr. Tolliver's box of ashes and set it down in front of us. "We need to create sacred space," Simon said, holding out a hand toward Maggie next to him. "Hand to hand, we cast the circle." Maggie clasped his hand and turned to Karasu repeating, "Hand to hand we cast the circle." Karasu to me, me to Brendan and back to Simon: the circle was cast. A small gesture, but it changed the feeling of our little group at once. It's not that we became sombre, exactly. Perhaps we became a little more sober, yet we were all smiling gently. Between worlds we were free from time. It was a farewell, but to one who was loved, which warmed the coldness.

After a moment of silent reflection, Simon spoke once more. "We're here to say farewell to Mr. Tolliver, beloved of all who knew him well. May all spirits who dwell in this place make room for his presence. The day I adopted him, he was dedicated to Bast. Great lady, mother of all cats, though his spirit is long departed, I ask that you bless him with your kindness and protection wherever he may be. May something of his goodness alight in this spot. I miss him terribly and it hurts that I could not be there when he passed." Tears were falling down Simon's cheeks—and mine and Maggie's and even Karasu's. Brendan looked sad enough to cry and I could see him give Simon's hand another squeeze. Maggie and I spoke up with stories about Mr. Tolliver—his penchant for striking out unexpectedly from under the couch, for waking hungover visitors by perching on their chests and staring into their faces until they awoke—and soon we were all laughing. Simon dropped hands to reach down for the box, opening it to pull out the plastic bag inside. We all watched as Simon stepped here and there, scattering the ashes, some along the wall now bereft of plants but once overflowing with fronds, some into the well of the jagged stump that once leaned over the tranquil water of the lake, some into the dusty ground at our feet. Little bits of Mr. Tolliver spread across the ground and joined the earth beneath. I said a silent blessing in my heart to that little furry friend.

The bag empty, Simon returned it to the box, then put both back into the little green bag. He looked around the circle at us and smiled, his eyes still rimmed with red. We took hands once more and Simon drew in a deep breath. "Thank you all for gathering here today, my friends here, spirits unseen, creatures from worlds unknown." He looked over at me and I smiled back. "Painful to say goodbye, but without love, life is meaningless. To love is to risk loss, but not to love is to risk a worse fate. Our lives are meetings and partings of all kinds. We hold onto those who sustain us long after they have departed this earthly plane. Wherever you may be, Mr. Tolliver, I hope you are content." We all murmured our assent to the hopeful proposition. "Hand to hand, I open the circle," Simon said as he let go Maggie's hand and we opened the ritual space. "The circle is open," Simon began.

"—but never broken," Maggie and I finished.

"Merry meet and merry part—"

"—and merry meet again!" It was group hug time and a heartfelt sharing. "Cakes and ale time!" I said trying to work the waver out of my voice.

"The hell with that—caviar and champagne time!" Simon corrected.

"Real caviar?!"

Simon sighed. "Real champagne. Faux caviar, but it's supposed to be real good."

"I didn't know you could get caviar from a faux," Brendan deadpanned.

"You have to use a very low stool," I said grabbing him around the waist and smacking a kiss on his cheek.

"And a great deal of persuasion," Simon added as he pulled the jar from the plastic bag. "And crackers—let's not forget the importance of faux wheat crackers."

We spread out the picnic on a horizontal grave stone, raising the first toast to its inhabitants, Thomas and Katherine Newbold. Next, we raised our glasses to Mr. Tolliver and sipped the nectar gratefully. The cold sweet tang of the grapes bit our tongues while the bubbles bounced off our palates. It was a horrible extravagance, but none of would wish it away. The plastic cups were hardly fitting, but any port in a storm had long been our motto. Cut crystal could not have improved that jaunty juice. Grateful for the taste, I could not help adding a final toast as we drained our glasses, "To absent friends."

Brendan put an arm around me as Simon refilled his glass and began to sing "Finnegan's Wake" in a surprisingly strong tenor. We all joined him on the chorus, singing with gusto, although Maggie was more Dubliners and I favoured the Dropkick Murphys:

Whack fol the doh, now dance with your partner,
All 'round the floor, your trotters shake.
Wasn't it the truth I told you:
lots of fun at Finnegan's wake.

Then it was on to the manifold tunes of Saint Shane, vague attempts to dance and a second bottle of champagne. By then Karasu had already set down her glass, but Maggie was persuaded to have a couple more. It wasn't every day we sent off a friend like this. His departure had been much delayed, but it was no less distinguished because of that. Our faces were shining with happiness as well as with wine. I felt as if some small part of the long lost perfect day had returned to touch us with a little of its magic, as if to remind us that there were still days to be treasured, there was still hope for better things. In the damaged landscape of that desolate park, there was yet a thing with feathers ready to arise if we could just coax its wings to flap.

Filled with happy liquids, we fell upon the food, a cornucopia of delicacies including some real fruit from a swanky greenhouse somewhere in Brazil, according to its label. The faux caviar disappointed, but the chocolate pie pleased us all, even Karasu who could not stop talking about it, "Oh my god, I can't believe that I'm eating this but, oh my god, it's so good, I have never had something this good!" While my brain told me the good food at Aleria's was much better and had a longer beneficial effect on my body, I could not help a childish delight in the extravagant treats Simon laid out before us.

When we could eat no more, we moved over to lean against the short curving wall nearby. It was also a crypt, names chiselled into its sides, remembrances of those long gone. We stared at the stumps and skeletons around us and marvelled at the stunted willow's stubborn resistance. The midday sun seemed to shine a little more brightly than it had in weeks as if some stray breeze had cleared some of the omnipresent smog out to sea. It was nearly possible to imagine that the ocean lapped closely by or that the lake still held refreshing waters.

Simon and I sat with Brendan between us once more, but we were all too lazy to do much more than smile seraphically and hold hands. Between the unaccustomed buzz of the champagne and the insistent heat of the hidden sun, I felt myself nodding off into a pleasant doze that promised to restore some of the previous night's leavening of fatigue. I should have known better.

"We were waiting for you," the two owls said as I woke in the dark cave once more. I shook my head to clear my thoughts. It wasn't helping. *Not again, I'm not ready.* As if they could sense my reluctance, the two voices-as-owls moved closer, gazing impassively at my face.

"We need you."

"Yeah, I know," I stalled, trying to think more clearly.

"You need us, too."

"Yeah, I know," I repeated, ever the raconteur.

"We have Harakka," they told me, big eyes fixed upon me. "She's dying."

10

"Dying?" It was as if the ground beneath my feet had suddenly dropped a yard without warning. A heat rose to my face. "What did you do to her?"

"Do not alarm yourself. We did nothing to harm her." The big eyes regarded me with unblinking gazes that were surely meant to be reassuring. They failed miserably in that respect. "She had helped us, we had found a way to affect the creatures troubling your world—"

"Why is she dying, then?" It couldn't just be the champagne that was making me dim.

"We tried to bring her along the same path to our world. She was an advanced creature, we thought she would make a speedier transition, but—"

"You were wrong! What do you mean 'was'?"

"She is dying," they repeated, the twin voices echoing in my brain. "You must come soon. Meet her. Save her."

"And die too?" It seemed like a mug's game all right.

"If you follow the steps, make the transitions," the two voices seemed to be fighting for control, "you will be able to survive, to help us, to help her, to help yourself, your people."

"How do I know any of this is true?"

"Your heart, your mind. They tell you true." The two owls stared expectantly. "When will you come? Will you come?"

"Soon, tonight, somehow. I...will come." Abruptly I withdrew and found myself once more on the sunny dirt of Mount Auburn with my friends asleep, serenely, blissfully ignorant of all that had transpired. I felt tears again upon my cheek, what a day for it. I looked over at Simon and Brendan nodding like sleepy toddlers in peaceful reverie. Words unbidden rose from my fractured heart: *My men, like satyrs grazing on the lawns, shall with their goat-feet dance an antic hay.* But not after today, my morbid thoughts intruded. After today there will be only weeping and gnashing of teeth, I suspect. Typical, Ro, just typical. Faced with a challenge you fold up like a weak folding thing that folds, look at that: I was even at a loss for a metaphor. Sad indeed.

We needed a place, a safe place. I guess that meant another hotel. We were certainly eating up the credit on this little lark. I was supposed to be back at work tomorrow. Ha! Well, I had the days laid by to use. Not sure the boss will approve, but I can invent a sick relative.

Or a dying one. Oh god.

"We have to go," I announced, rising to my feet with a couple of knee snaps punctuating my remarks. Startled eyes met my frantic gaze, still logy with sleep. Brendan reached up to pull me back down beside him, but I resisted.

"What is it, Ro?" Simon asked, stretching with all the luxurious pleasure of a large cat.

"We have to go," I said, trying to smother the tetchy impatience in my voice. It felt like it would strangle me. "We have to go, we have to find someplace to go, some place that's safe. We have to go." Somebody please kill me.

Maggie looked at me with something akin to suspicion. "What is it? Some mystical call from the beyond again?"

"Shut up!" The words were out before I could stop them. "I have to go get Harakka, she's dying. I don't know what it is, I don't care, I don't think I can even do it. I don't know. But who else will?" With surprise, I realised I was crying like a four year old, angry and bellowing. My heart was fluttering as if some kind of bird had been trapped inside my chest and I swayed, nearly falling, sitting down hard on the wall behind me. Like a flash, Brendan and Simon were on each side of me, patting my arms and shoulders in a futile attempt to calm the sudden storm within me, even though I knew it would do no good. There was nothing but a rising sense of panic, a fear that now it was down to me I was as worthless as I always knew, as I always feared.

Ten long years watching Simon in a coma and I did nothing. Yeah, I know, I'm not a doctor, I have no special training to speak of, but shouldn't I have told someone? Shouldn't I at least have mentioned to someone that it might have been my fault, not that it turned out to be my fault, but I sure thought so for a long time. I did nothing. I sat there every Friday. I sat reading my books or talking to the other patients or staring at the vid screen, doing nothing. Wrap me up and send me off to the Wonderful Island of Yam, I am useless.

But I was Harakka's only chance.

That's what it came down to——no one else was going to do anything. If she was going to survive I had to do something. Failure was not an option, it just couldn't be. I had delayed thinking about this so long, it seemed. But I couldn't delay any more. I tried again, strangling my panic so that I didn't sound quite as much like a crazy person. "We have to go somewhere safe. I need to travel to that land once more. I don't know what's going to happen, but I have to do my best, however sad and pathetic that is. Please." They all stared at me. Didn't they know how important it was? I smothered my impatience, kept my foot from tapping.

"We can go to my house," Karasu said, for once not immediately embellishing her simple statement with unnecessary verbiage. I nodded which seemed to release the torrent. "My dad's probably not even there and my mom won't care, she'll probably even be glad. We can use the exercise room. My mom redecorated it a couple of years ago and it's just gorgeous, you'll like it, I swear."

"Let's go," I said, hoping to forestall further effusions. We packed up our belongings and squeezed back inside the car. The brief stint of sunlight with which we had been graced had fled, as if our allotment of luck and happiness had vanished with it. We wound our way back toward the entrance, waving a fond farewell to Mr. Morecambe, who raised his hand in return, the ancient rifle shouldered solemnly as if he might need it all too soon.

I closed my eyes and rested my head against Brendan's shoulder. Simon leaned over and patted my hand. "We'll be there soon, Ro. It will all work out." I squeezed his hand, but I couldn't make myself mouth reassuring words.

The ride across the Hub seemed endless, although we made relatively good time. Maggie was aces when it came to finding those holes in the traffic and standing up to the sparkbuses. They looked like junkies, arms held up to mainline power from the swaying cables overhead, but they all drove like lunatics, cutting into traffic like sharks. Unlike the hinterlands, there were plenty of autos here, the one place you didn't really need a car. Down in the city, the streets were full of pedestrians and pedicabs, but here in Beantown the stubborn old ways remained. You've got to admire a steadfast devotion to history. Part of their rebel status, I guess, the home of the American Rebellion. Simon's forebears would not have been quite so proud of their ancient heritage if there were not that generation of upstarts whose blood fed the Rebel trail. From the gold dome of the Parliamentary house to the gates of Eaton University, the streets were paved with memories of what might have been. A hundred years or so later, the confederation achieved many of the same goals, but imagine how different things might have been if we'd become independent then. To listen to Simon's father, it would have been a wonderland of freedom and intellectual flowering such as the world had never seen since the twelfth century's golden age. But when I look around our disfigured countryside, I cannot imagine that we would not have caused the same devastation in any utopia.

The tangle of streets through Chelsea would have challenged any but a native and Karasu was kept busy directing Maggie's sharp eyes until we found ourselves on Broadway at last. The backseat trio maintained radio silence, our thoughts our own, although Brendan had wrapped his arm around my shoulders as I lolled dazed at his side. I would need to find words soon, but for now silence was golden and the fellowship I knew to be there was enough to keep me from flying into pieces.

Karasu's family's house seemed small and snug. It was bigger than Maggie's little gingerbread house, but much smaller than her suburban veneer had suggested. We were met at the door by her mother, who looked far too young for the role. Not to mention far too arresting: her hair was long and swooped up on her head and knotted loosely, but it was chiefly her eyes that mesmerized. The irises were so dark as to look nearly black and were shaded by a thick curtain of lashes that seemed to be natural not silicon. As she took our hands in turn, I was struck by her graceful movements as if every motion had been considered in terms of achieving the utmost beauty possible. "This is my mom," Karasu said, completely unaware of the effect of her parent, "Suzume." We murmured her name, enchanted.

My fear that she would prove as voluble as her daughter quickly evaporated. Not only was she economic in her speech, but Suzume also lacked the overpowering Revere accent her daughter had acquired. "You're not originally from Revere," I blurted out.

She laughed and shook her head. "My husband and I moved here after we met in grad school. Eaton, well, I was at Eaton. Michael was at M.I.T."

"Which is why he's never home," Karasu broke in. "He's not home now, is he, Mom? He's always working late. It's going to give him hypertension and a heart attack." Karasu continued to mumble irritably. Clearly it was a long standing issue.

Eventually we were able to move into the kitchen and be welcomed with some soup and tea, which seemed the perfect restoration. The simple warmth of the treat was enough to make Karasu's chatter slip into the background. Suzume proved to be as silent as her daughter was loquacious. There was nothing sullen or prim about her quiet. She simply chose her moments. It was refreshing. However, I began to see how it might lead an only child to want to fill that silence with words. It didn't make Karasu's logorrhoea any more welcome, but I decided to try to be more tolerant. Of course, few things are as easy to resolve as to *try* to do something. Lord, what fools we mortals be.

"Mom, we need to use the exercise room. I mean, you know, the temple room," Karasu corrected herself, turning to us. "Mom redecorated. It used to be the exercise room, when I was at home more and doing yoga and Nia and ballet and stuff. It's not that different."

"It smells better," Suzume said, and we all laughed. It seemed to clear some of the tension that had travelled with us from Mount Auburn. We trooped down the hall behind Karasu, for whom the room was nothing special. To the rest of us, however, its bright pine floor and elegant décor were a restorative fresh breath. Suzume had turned a plain room into a simply stunning temple, no longer a room, but a holy place. There was a statue of Kuan Yin, delicate white porcelain, fingers so slender that the lightest touch might threaten their fragility. Hand-lettered scrolls offered koans from the ancient authors and silk flowers brightened the corners, a worthy counterfeit of the real blooms. In the centre of the room, a crescent-shaped zafu waited upon its matching zabuton, the purple of its covering lending an air of artful beauty, as if it were a sculpture rather than a functional item.

"This is a good place." I didn't mean for it to sound like a seal of approval, but to my ears it had that kind of ring. No matter, I was far too exhausted to care anymore what anyone thought of me. Not physically tired, yet there was a kind of fatigue that felt suspiciously akin to depression, but without its weight.

"What do we need to get started?" Simon looked ready to work. It was odd.

"Well," I started already reluctant, ready to drag feet, "We need something to lie on."

"Blankets!" Karasu piped up and turned on her heel to go get some, calling back to us, "Back in a minute. We got lots, it'll be just like a sleep over."

I looked around the room. "We could use those candles to make the circle. Might be a good idea." Maggie and Simon moved to gather up the tea lights. Brendan found a lighter that seemed to work fine. He flicked it off and on. "We need juice. Maybe some food." Everyone was so compliant and agreeable, even Maggie. It was just weird. "What we really need is a drum," I said with some satisfaction, as if I had finally located the Achilles' heel of our little operation. Why was I so mindlessly searching for an excuse for *schadenfreude*? If I were more myself, I'd think of some inspiring words from a great mind of the past, but I was feeling short of stirring catch phrases. Only the absurd came to mind: where's me washboard?

"A what?" It was Karasu, back again with enough blankets to wrap us all like burritos. "A drum? Well, of course! Aleria thought you might need me to drum at some point." She tossed the blankets in a heap and went over to her shoulder bag. Out came a small hand drum painted with the curvy shape of a goddess in azure. She tapped it with a leather-covered beater, smiling up at me. The sound rang out clearly in the room, rich and resonant.

"Wow, where'd you get that?" Brendan was excited for some reason; maybe because it was real leather. It did look pretty old. It sounded amazing, too. What the hell was wrong with me? I'd have been excited about a drum like that, too: one with history, one with presence. I could feel its hum from across the room. Instead I felt like I'd been nabbed by the door while giving myself a five-finger discount. As if I were ten years old. As if I were guilty of something. Why were they all acting so stupid? Didn't they know this was a mess?

"Where's the bathroom?" I asked. It came out all gruff

because I was holding so much in.

Karasu pointed down the hall and I turned without another word, trotting away. Let them wait, let them be safe a while longer. I did need the toilet, but I needed more to wash my face with something, anything, to clean my skin of the stink of fear and craven cowardice. I was afraid to look at my face in the mirror, a fancy cut glass affair, probably old, probably ancient. The small cranes that took flight across the bottom only gave me a feeling of deeper horror at what had happened, what I had let happen. I couldn't help but think it my fault. If I hadn't been so caught up in my own little problems... Yet here I was again, falling into the same old patterns of recrimination and blame for something that had already happened, something that I might just have a chance of fixing, maybe, if I didn't give in to complete despair. How many thousands of times had I played that tune, done in by the itch for the blade or for oblivion. I would give in now but for the beating of wings at my back. Besides, no cutting could release the tightly coiled spring of fear in my guts. Was I more afraid that I would fail, always a likely outcome, I knew, or afraid that I might succeed? No oblivion could erase the thought that I might matter.

But then I would have to admit to just how much I had squandered along the road.

If I had had more courage, more faith in my abilities, I might have been a scholar, might have pursued the life of learning instead of settling for the bureaucratic life. But I quailed. I failed to trust my mind and instead set off on a long binge of hedonistic pleasure-seeking, making a mockery of the master's edict that the road of excess leads to the palace of wisdom. He would not have been fooled into wasting so much of his treasures in vain pursuits. Would it have been different if I had heard the voices earlier, if I too had seen angels and fairies at the bottom of the garden when but a child? For all I know, perhaps I had, perhaps that's what made me so disenchanted with this world, even before GMOification and blasted forests and the inevitable Wags. Why did it take me so long to rediscover the magic that awaited?

And why was my mind so ready to travel down any number of lost corridors rather than think about what lay ahead? Simple really: I'm a coward. I've always been a coward. If I've ever done anything noble or fearless in my life, it was only because I accidentally backed into it, or fell into because I wasn't looking where I was leaping. I couldn't really begin to think about what was going to happen here. I had to think only of Harakka, of her depending upon me, not that I was confident I could save her. Ha! Me save anyone, but I had to try. I couldn't bear to turn my back on her and I knew I wouldn't be able to live with myself if I did. Forget the Wags; I doubt there was anything that could be done about them, despite all the promises of these Wits. No one had ever depended on me for so much. No one would ever believe it; my mother would sigh and change the subject, my sisters would laugh openly. The only one who might just think I had it in me would be my Auntie Dottie, who would cheer anything that would make Gran grumble, but she was ten years in the grave at least.

I dared look in the mirror. I didn't see me. I saw cranes. I saw flocks of them. They sailed across impossibly cerulean heavens, their feathers ruffling with the speed of their passage, all of them trumpeting what sounded like, "hurry, hurry."

Move your ass, Ro. Time's a wastin'.

I took one last look in the mirror. It really wasn't such a bad face. I don't know why I had come to loathe it so much. I felt a twinge of regret, as if after ten years I had failed to get to know a co-worker who was quitting the end of the week, but I said good-bye all the same. Life was uncertain and it was too late to eat dessert. "Be seein' you," I said, giving the island salute.

I walked back down the hall. I wouldn't say I was no longer afraid, but I had decided there was nothing I could really do about it, so I wasn't going to think about being terrified. The others didn't know what they were in for and that was my fault. They had to know. Brendan thought it was some kind of lark. Karasu probably assumed it was just another exercise to master. Maggie thought we were all full of shit. And Simon, I don't know why, but as I looked over at him, he didn't seem to quail in the least. He was ready to go. His trust in me frightened me more than anything. But we had no time for that anymore.

"All right, let's do this," I said, trying to swallow the big lump hesitating in my throat. "But I want you to know that we might not be coming back." I looked around the room to see if they had taken this in. No. I decided to take the unusual precedent of repeating myself. "Listen to me. I want you to know that we stand the very real chance of not coming back."

"We know, Ro," Simon said softly. "We just didn't want to think about it."

I could feel my face flush. "Sorry. But it could take a long time, too. I know we all have places to be, things to do."

"Not me," Maggie said. "I work my own hours. I'm my own boss."

Brendan shrugged. "I'm out of work."

"I'm taking a break anyway," Karasu said with a bouncy grin.

These people, they want to kill me. "What about you, Simon? I know you're not eager for the service, but you have other."

The look on his face stopped me. There was a genuine gravity there, an unaccustomed burden for his features. "Ro, I'm not returning home. I will not be joining the service at their oh, so friendly invitation. The family's got some land up in Nova Scotia, part of an old patrimony. I'm going to go up there. I'm going to stay."

We all stared at him. It was a surprise, no, it was a shock. "Can you get into the Republic, just like that? I thought they were all so picky about who they let in and you had to, you know, well…"

"Like I said, I have a part of a patrimony. I figure if I get over there by boat, I can prove I have a right to be there."

"If they don't shoot you on the way over! Simon, this is crazy." I wasn't even going to pretend to have any patience with this insanity.

Simon only shook his head. "No, my mind's made up. I can always hide out in Kejimkujik if things look dire. What I won't do is serve. I've lost ten years of my life already. I won't sacrifice a minute more to the bloody service and the stupid wars that will never end. Wise up, Ro, you work for them!"

"Not for them, not directly anyway."

Simon waved his hands before me. "It doesn't matter. You do know that it will never end. If it was going to end, it would have ended when the Wags came. But it didn't, they just provided another excuse to keep the money pouring in, to keep the people cowed with fear, to keep the endless thefts of life. I won't do it."

I pulled at my bottom lip for a minute trying to think of something to change his mind. "What will you do without any cafés? Without any galleries? Without any clubs? There's nothing for you to *do*."

"There's curling," Brendan said as light as floating feather, eyebrows cocked invitingly.

"You're not helping," I said, but I was the only one fighting. I turned back to Simon. "You don't even have... a broom," I finished lamely.

Simon hugged me suddenly. "It will be all right, Ro. Let's not worry about it now."

Wasn't that my line? I let him hug me and felt suddenly overwhelmed again. Did I know what I was doing, what we were doing? Oh, shut up. Better to plunge in and throw caution to the sidewalk. "Well, all righty then. We'll have to get started. Ah..." Well, now: there was an awkward moment. Everyone looking at me and expecting the same thing. But someone was going to have to be left behind. More than one. Who? I thought I knew. Was I sure I knew what was best? Better to start with the stage, then with the players. Everybody wants to be number one and no one wants to be a zero, or so said the storyteller. How was it going to be? Evens, odds? Boys, girls? Juniors, Seniors? In the back of my mind the reminder that I didn't know what might happen. The hell with it for me, how long did I want to live anyway? Who was that? Hank Williams? Patsy Cline? Listen to me, babbling away in my own head. At least no one else could hear it, although by the look on their faces, I started to worry I was humming out loud or something.

"I guess, I'm drummer," Karasu finally said as my final syllables hung in the air a bit too long. She picked up the drum and looked at me expectantly. This was as good a time as any to start to feel my way toward the truth.

"It's going to take more than one drummer. You'll be our life line, the thing that can bring us back. When the goddess Inanna stepped into the underworld, she told Ninshubur, her best friend, her confidant, 'Beat the drums to bring me back' and she meant it." I paused and looked at the suddenly serious expressions gathered around me. They were thinking I'd popped a cork. What was this, O'Malley's bar? "All right, never mind that story. It would take days to explain, with diagrams and charts and some kind of illustration. But the drum is our life line; it's what brings us back. You all need to know this," I said, turning away from Karasu who had become my focus. They all needed to know. "The steady beat sends us under. It's hypnotic, like the dancing beats but not changeable."

"We know, Ro, we know. We were all there in the commune," Maggie said fists on her hips.

"It's not a commune," Karasu corrected, pointing her beater at Maggie. "It's a carefully constructed eco-system that also functions as a habitat and a temple. Built according to-"

"I don't care," Maggie shouted, making Karasu duck back. "What else do we need to know?"

"To bring us back," I said with as much patience as I could muster, "three sharp beats and a pause. Here, let me show it." I held out my hands to Karasu who obediently handed over the drum. I felt the hide of the drum pick up and magnify all the tiny sounds of the room. It felt as if even the echo of my heartbeat thrummed against the taut skin. The drum is your friend, my teacher had taught me so long ago; you're pulling the sound out, not beating it in. I raised the beater and brought it down in a bouncing thump. One, two, three, pause and again, and once more. "Then faster, this is our path back to this consciousness," I said continuing the doubled pace.

"When do we stop?" Karasu asked.

"When we're back. All the way back. All of us. Really here and now."

"Otherwise you're lost?"

I could feel myself grimace. "That's the gist of it. Questions?"

"Who's going?"

I didn't really think it would be Simon who asked. I was hoping to figure it out first, or to know when one of them asked. I was sure I would know when they said "me," and I knew that it was wrong. I looked over at Brendan, who was studiously looking away toward an elegant scroll with the kanji for peace, I think it was. It looked like a scarecrow with two faces, which didn't seem much like a way to imagine peace or tranquillity. I had seen it somewhere before, though.

"I'm getting left behind again?" Maggie's voice rose to a sharp squeak. "It never fails!"

"Maggie," I tried to reach out to her, but she spun away like tornado blossoming. Arms folded now, feet stomping, turning our little haven into an echo chamber of vituperative spleen. So much for peace or tranquillity or whatever that was.

"I can't believe you!" Maggie fumed, pointing stubby little index finger my way. *J'accuse* at five foot four. How tall was Dreyfus anyway? "You drag me across the state when I could be making good money, use my car, use me, trot all over hell and back with any random stranger you meet and still when it comes down to choosing sides, *choose someone else*."

"You're going, Maggie." I didn't think I said it loudly

enough to be heard at first, because she just stared at me. "You are. You're going." I smiled. What a dummy.

"You maggot-sucking, slime-livered, brain-sponging wantwit!" Then she turned and burst into tears. I couldn't have been more surprised. My eyes flashed toward Simon, who gave me a curt nod as if to say, go on, make it right. I stepped over toward her and reached to pat her shoulder with some level of reassurance, but she only muttered, "No."

"Maggie—" I was stuck as to how to follow on that opening foray.

"Shut up! You're so stupid, I can't begin to tell you."

"Don't you want to go?" I tried not to sound as lacking in wit as I felt, but I think it was evident in my hesitant tone if nothing else. Blow wild winds and torrents bring, sink me beneath the waves, until my love's tears flow no more.

"Of course I want to go. Of course I want to be there. I didn't think you wanted me there." She was sobbing now and I could feel the cold flush rise up my cheeks. I am an idiot. I ignored her hunched shoulders and turned her gently to face me. Words, words, words. I finally said nothing but wrapped my arms around her. I closed my eyes so I could pretend we were not being seen. How could Maggie not know that she was my life line? Brendan would just have to live with the disappointment. Who knew, after all? Maybe he wasn't going to be disappointed.

Turning to wipe our tears I could see however that he was disappointed, but took pains to disguise it. Maggie sorted, Simon began sharing his experiences to his fellow novice and I turned to the raven-haired beauty. "You know I'm counting on you," I told him, reaching for a lecherous embrace. "You're my incentive to get back."

He smiled at that, a lop-sided grin that still carried the vague weight of not being chosen, the envy of a journey denied. "I'll be expecting you to make it all up to me."

"You will help with the drumming? It could be hours, even days. Karasu can't do it alone. We need to depend on you."

He squared his shoulders and stepped back away from me. "Sir, yes, sir!" He threw me a salute that managed to be both respectful and roguish, then bent forward to plant a kiss on me that I felt to my toenails. "I'll be waiting."

"You better be," Simon added, suddenly standing behind my shoulder. "We have such sights to show you," he said with an ominous laugh, then leaned in for a little sugar himself, squeezing me between them. I had a mad moment of panic. What if we didn't come back? How could they be so light-hearted? Because they don't know: the answer smacked me in the face with accusation. It doesn't matter, I answered myself. It didn't matter. There was so much more to this than I knew. It wasn't just Harakka. The world's seams were sundering. It was the source of the dread I had sensed growing within me, like some gnarled parasite chewing a hole in my soul. All we had were five little people and a drum in a little house in Revere. It couldn't possibly be sufficient. There must be more.

"We need to cast the circle," I said, picking up the soy meal Karasu had retrieved. "Maggie, Simon, in the middle. You two," I nodded at Karasu and Brendan, "keep the beat, watch our bodies. If any of us appears to be in distress, call us back."

"What do you mean 'distress'?" Karasu said, brows furrowed. I had discounted her so much and yet she was willing to do this thing. Flighty as she had always seemed to me, I could see the gravity that now set upon her visage. She was alert, ready to jump into action.

"Well, uh," Hmmm, how to put this. "If we have any kind of trouble breathing or seem to be, uh…" Distressed? What else could I say? Tortured, suffering, afflicted, tormented? "Discomforted. If we are, call us back. We can always start again," I said with what I hoped was admirable calmness. I wasn't at all sure that we would have time to start again, in fact I had no plans to return without Harakka, but they didn't need to know that.

"I'll get in the middle," I said as Maggie and Simon stood

awkwardly in the centre of the room. "Put the blankets down for us to be more comfortable." I walked around them, pouring a stream of soy flour from my hand as I cast the circle around us. "Here we have sacred space, here we have protected space. May all the gods there ever were watch us now and speed our journey and keep us from harm." Vague words yet they filled me with a dangerous spark of hope. Gods once graced this land, this planet and all the others in between here and our destination. Perhaps they were around yet, sitting up to take interest in this foolhardy venture, watching over our timid pilgrimage. "May this circle protect us from all harm and keep us united in our voyage."

I stepped between my two friends and bade them lie down so we could be hip to hip, their heads by my feet. Still sitting up I took one hand each in mine. "Be with me, be safe. We will travel to Harakka's land together. Maggie, don't be afraid."

"I'm not," Maggie protested, but I didn't let her finish.

"Maggie, don't be afraid to take your time. We will wait for you on the other side. If you have trouble making it through, feel for us. Listen to your heart. We are all connected now."

"Enough with the mumbo jumbo already," Simon said.

Maggie snorted.

I ignored him, asking her, "Do you have your mental picture ready?"

"The hole I have to go through? Yeah, the hole that rabbit dug under our garden fence the summer when I was five. I think it was the last animal I saw in the city."

I winced. "They say there are still rats and roaches."

"You seen any? I haven't, and that hole is vivid," she said, chin jutting out with unquestionable defiance.

I nodded. "You ready, Simon?"

He grinned. "A man can die but once. Having nothing, nothing can he lose."

I matched his smile. "I think you're mixing histories."

"All history is mixed. You're delaying, Ro. We're ready."

He lay down and closed his eyes. It was time.

I looked over to Karasu and Brendan. He looked so handsome in the warm afternoon glow. Keep that picture in your back pocket, I told myself, my perfect Gaveston, my Leander. To him I said, "Take pains, be perfect, adieu." I nodded and Karasu started the beat. I lay down. "Let the drumbeat take you." Did I say it aloud or only in my head? Did it matter? Yet I lingered to feel the pale light on my face, to watch the flickering of the candles, and to receive a final benediction from the delicate hands of the statue of Quan Yin from her alcove at the front of the temple. Adieu, adieu, parting is such sweet sorrow, but my eyes closed at last, and with well-trained efficiency, my spirit sprinted for the onyx temple that lay down the tunnel beneath the old maple tree.

I landed with more grace than usual, as if I were somehow more alert, expectant. I stepped out the door and found Simon within minutes. We hugged. He had a big grin plastered across his face: it was still so new to him. I couldn't blame him although a little voice in the back of my head urged, "hurry, hurry." He grabbed a branch of fir and brought it to his nose, inhaling deeply and noisily, then sighing the air out.

"I can't believe how good it smells!" His head swivelled up. "Look at that!"

I lifted my chin, too. A flock of birds flew overhead, geese, squawking noisily as if on freewheeling bender. It was so easy to find wonder here. The plants and trees alone were matchless sculptures of living substance; every leaf different, every branch a miracle. Yet I couldn't help worrying about Maggie as well as Harakka (hurry, hurry) and I knew some kind of useful employment would help. The angle of the sunlight let me know that it was late enough in the day that light and warmth would be needed soon. "Wood," I told Simon, who was looking at a handful of pebbles. "We need wood for a fire."

"Fire?" The very idea, so new, so strange. Wood to burn seemed like such a waste and yet it was everywhere here. We circled the clearing gathering fallen limbs. Simon tried pulling at one much too large and finally, laughing let it go. I put a pile of dead leaves at the centre of the clearing and began to tent the smaller branches around them. Simon watched my progress, finally asking, "How do you start it?"

It was my turn to smile. I held out my hand, one finger pointing away from me. Like a small orange blossom, fire bloomed at its tip. We make our reality, Harakka always told me, but I had never put that skill to practical use. Simon actually goggled at the sight, as if I had become some ancient conjurer. I lit the pile of leaves and the fire crackled heartily at once. "We have to keep a close eye on it," I reminded Simon. "Fire can be a dangerous thing."

"So you remember marshmallows?" His voice sounded strangled. Was it excitement? There was something glittery in his eyes as he stared at the licking flames.

"Yes, and chocolate and graham crackers not made from soy. It wasn't that long ago, really. Or it doesn't feel like it was, but it does." The blaze was mesmerising.

"I hate them," Simon said, choking a little on the words.

"I know."

He moved over to hug me, but we didn't say anything more. I could feel Maggie before she arrived, and turned to look off to the west where she walked, hesitating a little at the edge of the forest, then breaking into a jog toward us.

"Hey, hey! I'm here!" Maggie's eyes shone and I feared the grin creasing her face would reach all the way behind and pop the top of her head off. "I saw birds! And some kind of little furry thing ran in front of me and it wasn't a rat, and there were all kinds of songs in the trees. Why was I so far away? Did you walk here? How did you get the fire started? I'm so hungry!"

"Good to see you, too," Simon laughed, chucking his arms around her in a happy embrace. We listened while Maggie recounted her journey with the occasional breath in between the torrent of words. Gone was her suspicion and doubt. The very smells of this place, the sounds and sticky touch of it all shouted, "This is real." We were there.

"I could feel you," Maggie said after a sudden pause, her eyes meeting mine. "You told me, I know. But I didn't really think..."

"I know."

She stretched her hands out toward the fire, marvelling at its presence. "Now what? How do we help?"

Simon looked at me expectantly, too.

"You tend the fire. It's going to be a long night."

"Wait," Maggie protested, "You're not going to leave us here? We came with you, right? We're here to help."

"Yes, but where I'm going you can't go."

"What you're doing, we can't be any part of," Simon interceded. "Don't go being noble now. If we can help, let us."

"I'm not being noble." I turned and pointed to the mountains, purple in the distance as the sun descended. "I'm going there. Now. I have to get there quick and find Harakka."

"How?" Maggie asked looking a little spooked.

"Like this," I said and leapt up as a raven. I could feel the wind lift my feathers as I flapped my wings to lift me to a low-hanging branch. Why did I ever want to be mere human?

Simon laughed, but I think it was delight. "How many experience points do I need for that?"

"All you need is the will," I said, fancying myself that I sounded a bit like Harakka. "I have to go. Stay here. Be safe. If anything should happen..."

"We'll come get you," Maggie said with that determined tone I knew so well.

"Go back. I don't know that you could even find me where I'm going. Simon, you can find the way back."

"We can find you," he said, putting his hands on his hips. "We're connected."

I looked down at them. So stubborn. "I'll be back. With Harakka. All will be well."

Simon laughed a flat sound. "All shall be well, and all shall be well, and all manner of thing shall be well."

"Would I lie to you?" I called over my shoulder as I took off, wheeling up into the bruised sky that stretched toward the mountains.

11

I flew across the tree tops, enjoying the press of the wind upon my feathers and skin. To be so light, to soar so freely, there was nothing to compare to it. It was a joy that drew some of its force from the knowledge that I had made it happen. Perhaps it was a little too much like a five year old brandishing cookies she had made by mixing ingredients measured out by her parents; I took inordinate pride in my small accomplishment. And the ambitions grew quickly. What about other animals? I could be a trout or a sturgeon.

In such pleasant musings I wasted the time as I flew up to the now familiar cave. I did my best not to think of Harakka and her suffering. Why? Because I was callous? Because I knew it would weaken me? Because I was too frightened to do so? I don't know. Do I have to analyse everything that I do? Do I? God, I'm doing it again.

I landed on the edge of the precipice and returned to my human form, which made me blink into the darkness of the cave as I searched for the Wits. "Hail and well met!" they called to me, their voices, as always, cheery and friendly and not quite right.

"Trubba not," I replied, my voice gruff. It was hard to conceal that I still felt a bit awkward. They were alien beings. Real alien beings: it was weird. It didn't help that now they had decided to assume human shapes, although their outlines seemed unnaturally sketchy. Their skin was pale and bluish, which the nakedness might account for, I supposed. They were aliens, pretending to humans, but they looked like drawings.

And they were naked, amazing how disconcerting naked fake humans could be.

"We have changed our appearance!" the Wits said with a palpable thrill of excitement.

"I see. How... interesting."

Their two heads, one male, one female, tilted at identical angles, more bird-like than expected. I could see now that the two were bound together. It gave me a weird rush of anxiety even as my brain started clicking through the back files. Something about this was familiar. "We thought this would be welcome."

"Uh, thanks, I guess." What to say to that? "I guess you're more like us now."

"We borrowed from one of your travellers. We thought it would please you." They weren't accusing, really. Just trying to figure out my reaction. They had done their research I suppose, so why wasn't I greeting them warmly? In part, because they looked like unfinished animations. The two of them were the same colour from head to foot, including "his" beard and "her" hair. That bluish tinge that looked like some sort of watercolour. That set off a faint bell.

I narrowed my eyes. I'm not sure why. People in books do it all the time when they're trying to concentrate. Maybe the pressure on the eyeballs jumpstarts the brain. Or maybe it just conveys the idea that they are thinking in visible terms. Anything that might coax the faint ringing out of my brain and onto my tongue would be worthwhile. "You say you borrowed from a traveller? One of our people?"

"Yes," they said, brightening considerably. "He had much of the ancient knowledge accessible, facilitated." Huh? "When we visited..."

What? "Wait a minute: *you* visited? Visited us?"

They nodded in creepy unison. "Yes, before, when we first tried to reach your kind. We did not understand this intermediary place, we did not know of its existence. It works so much better for communication."

I tried to smother the laugh that rose up. This was better? How many kinds of crazy were their last attempts to talk to us?

They were just making it up as they went along, too. "You communicated with others?" Didn't I sound like a jealous lover now?

Their look changed. It wasn't quite an emotion as you might recognise it, but the change expressed their dissatisfaction with the outcome at least. "It was unsuccessful. There was an exchange...we learned much of your..." here a nearly imperceptible pause before continuing, "reality grid. No, that is not correct, not according to your system. Mythology. We learned of your mythology."

"Just the one," I asked, already prepared to chuckle when it hit me. Watercolours! "Who was the traveller?"

They gazed at once another, concentrating. "You wish the name? You name things. It is a curious concept."

"We're not connected like you are," I said feeling a touch grumpy and unevolved. "We have to speak out loud and call names. It's no good wanting the toaster if it doesn't have a name."

"We are unclear about your metaphor," they said, turning their concentration on me.

"Never mind that," I said, a hunch forming in my grey matter. "Do you have names?"

They smiled. It almost looked right. "We are Bromion and Oothoon."

"You took names. You took names to make me feel comfortable, right?"

"Yes." The smile threatened to stretch across their pallid faces far enough to draw blood. They had done this to try to reach out to me, to us. They genuinely wanted to communicate with our poor species even though we were a puzzle to them. We had strange ways. We were all separate beings who couldn't even understand each other. They were chained together because they were connected, yet I could only see them as tortured and trapped. All of the sudden I knew them. Not them, rather the characters they had taken, I knew the picture they had seen. It *was* a watercolour. They had met the master himself! I was torn between keen envy and the insatiable desire to know everything.

"I know the traveller! I know him, well, know *of* him. You're from his book, the Daughters of Albion one."

"He is your friend?" They seemed pleased.

"I wish! Jesus! William Blake! He was a genius. Poet, painter, printer, mystic! I admired him greatly, but yeah, he lived a couple of centuries ago. Back in the old country, too." So they believed that this visionary, whose contemporaries had thought him mad, was just a regular guy, a representative type of our kind. I felt the breath leave my body. *Had* Blake just been a regular out and outer until he crossed astral paths with this lot? Was that going to happen to me? Was I going to spend the rest of my days painting these weird visions, trotting too hard and watching my savings dwindle to a nutshell as I tried to convince people these things had really happened to me? It made me shudder.

The pair of them were looking at me with something approaching perplexity. "The traveller is not of your time?"

"He's not even of my country," I said, still goggling a bit. "He's from the homeland not the colonies." Mad as a hatter, too, eventually, I wanted to shout, but I contained myself.

"Time moves differently here." I realised that I no longer noticed the speaking in unison thing, although the two timbres melded harmonically together. Must have been another thing they figured out. Were musical scales different in their world, too? I'd never really thought about things like that. It wasn't like going to Mongolia and tasting new spices. Deep differences. Physical, molecular differences. I knew that if I thought about it for very long it was going to make me wish for a drink. Too late: god, I wanted a drink. "We had thought we found someone close to him, that he had helped introduce us to your people."

"No, I didn't know. He didn't. None of us knew. We didn't know about the Wags either, until they arrived." It didn't matter, did it? I knew what did matter. "Where's

Harakka?"

I wouldn't say they looked sad. I was expecting something terrible maybe, and impressed my thoughts upon their sketchily drawn faces. But something in their faces changed and my heart sank. The voices answered harmonically, "She is below."

"Do you mean she's dead?" No, no, no, no, no.

They shook their heads, the chains between them clanking slightly like an echo of the gesture. "She is below. Where you will go."

Great. "So, which way is that?" I gestured toward the back of the cave. Somewhere in the darkness must be the steps to the great below. Harakka's not dead, but probably dying. They're going to make me as loopy as William Blake. Bug-shit loony, mad as a March hare, as a hatter and all the playing cards. Crazy, hell, don't bother thinking about getting back and losing your mind. The trip was probably going to kill you anyway, I reminded myself. Why worry about what might never happen?

But the two of them did not spring into action. "Perilous is the journey. You should prepare."

"How?"

"You need to strip away the blocks from your perception."

What kind of New-Agey bilge was this? "Look, you want me to meditate, I'll meditate. You want me to chant words of power, I'll do it. But let's get a move on. I don't want my friend to die. I don't want to die either, by the way." Seemed like it was worthwhile spelling that out. I felt better for it. Slightly. Interdimensional aliens from another world across space and times, what were they going to care about a little amoeba like me?

I was beginning to hate that sideways tilt to their heads. So perfectly synchronous that it could not be human. Huh, human, it wasn't even real. All this was a careful illusion for my benefit, which kind of cheesed me off. I hate being the junior partner. "This journey is not physical, although you will perceive it that way. We have to prepare you for each level in

200

which you reach deeper into our consciousness. We did not take sufficient precautions for Harakka's descent. She seemed...ready. Yet..." They didn't bother to finish the thought.

Oh boy. Harakka, who had taught me to travel, to fly, to believe, to change consciousness at will: Not ready? "Um, what do I have to do? This isn't some kind of Olympic event, is it? I'm not really good with wind sprints." Their heads went back to that quizzical angle and I pressed on. "What do I do?"

"To descend you need to remove...encumbrances."

Still opaque: "I don't have a hat to take off," I said trying to squelch the increasing irritability I was feeling rise up like steam from a boiling kettle.

They seemed to feel my shortening temper. "Blocks. Perhaps that may be a better word. You must shift your spirit, your...consciousness."

Ooh, spooky. "And how do you suggest I do that? I have to admit I'm not feeling particularly enlightened at present. If you're such advanced beings, tell me how and skip all this subterfuge."

They favoured me with that sideways look again. It was really beginning to piss me off, but I tried to hold my tongue. Eventually they spoke. "Stories."

"What?"

"Stories. Tell us stories to release the resistance."

"You want bedtime stories? Bedtime for Bonzo?"

They shrugged. In unison, they shrugged. Criminy. "The location will suggest the appropriate story. It will serve to open that point of resistance. You will know. When we touch you, you will know the story to tell. It will be as if a veil drawn will be cast open, glowing. The blockage will be removed."

"All right, I guess."

"This is not your expectation?"

"Huh. No, I thought there would be riddles, maybe. At least riddles."

"Riddles?"

"You know, like what happens when an irresistible force

meets an immovable object?"

"Philosophy, you mean?"

"Nah, tricks." I shrugged. "Same thing, I suppose. It all depends on how you define the rules. Things you might find on a matchbox."

Identical wrinkled brows. They got that down perfectly. "You don't value stories?"

"Well," I said shoving my hands back into my pockets to try to stay my growing sense of impatience, "stories aren't much. Just lies to entertain."

They actually seemed to betray a kind of emotion then. It was horror. "You denigrate the oldest art?"

Why does everyone make me sound unreasonable? "I'm not denigrating art, just storytelling. Don't you use that phrase in your culture? Telling a story? It means lying."

I knew that exasperated look. I had seen it enough in my life. I expected they would explain to me why I was being blockheaded, why I was obtuse and obstinate. But they didn't; they stepped forward and tapped my forehead at the crown. In one motion, I couldn't tell which one had done it. I saw them both move, yet I felt only one finger.

My head filled with an immense white light. When I say my head, I mean my brain sang, my eyes clouded, even my ears seemed to thrum with an unexpected fullness that wasn't quite sound, and although it rang like a gong through my skull, it made no noise. It didn't scare me, exactly, but it set me back on my heels with the sudden force of its power. I nearly swooned because the space around me dropped as if a lift had plunged a couple of extra floors. Then it was as if a mist evaporated and my mouth fell open.

"The Greek philosopher, Alexander of Abonoteichus, once said that all his life he suffered from the vague feeling that he had once inhabited part of a small country with a strange tongue all its own. His memory of that time was dim, shadowed, and the tongue seemed to have slipped from his memory. His parents, however, never mentioned this time abroad from their home. No one seemed to recognise the dislocation. Alexander had been so long in exile that the languages he had learned to speak had become second nature to him and he never thought of himself as a foreigner in his homeland. He was never conscious of difference, never recognising the loss that had occurred or the patrimony lost. Yet now and then he would turn a corner and hear someone who spoke in that long lost tongue, laugh with relief and joy, then greet them as friend and countryman. In that moment, he knew all he had lost, and in finding his fellow, all that had been restored to him.

"This is the way we find our clans, the way we forge our identities. We all have come from lost countries and our tribes are only discovered when we hear the words spoken in our secret, forgotten tongues. But we know, unconsciously, that our long-parted comrades are out there and we yearn eagerly to encounter those familiar sounds. The language is not one of mere words, however, but one of a touching, spirit to spirit, the recognition of the kindred soul. Find your people in this world and pull them close. It is the task before us all." With that, my mouth shut up once more and my eyes opened.

"What the hell was that?" I asked, blinking at the Wits. They had changed into more golden selves and were grinning at me like a couple of drunken maroons. I kept blinking because the cave had changed as well. I think the light that dazzled me came from the two of them, but that didn't explain the altered terrain behind them. Rather than the craggy darkness that had been the entryway of the owls, there was now a much smoother surface with stalactites dripping down like frozen streams which looked vaguely like caramel and toffee. I felt as if I had been transported into a confectionary. I finally stopped my goggling long enough to realise that the Wits were talking again.

"...a kind of blockage." They finished and smiled expectantly in tandem.

I guess they were waiting for me to speak. "Uh, huh?"

Wow, of all the gin joints in all the towns in all the worlds, they never would have expected something quite that dumb surely. My mind had been filled with…what? Various thingummybobs and oojimaflips that didn't really mean anything, or had there had been some thought there? What did I know of Alexander of Abonnynonny hey hey? It was as if something profound had finally dawned on me, but it slipped away as quickly as it had arrived like a drunken revelation. Weird to find yourself spouting words that you didn't think, or did I? But the thoughts slithered away leaving me with a bereft absence. It was worse than nothing. It was such a feeling of deflation. That's how I felt when the Wits looked at me with such disappointment. Something had happened and I had failed to understand its significance or even recall what I had said, or they had said back. Well, when all else fails, ask: "Could you repeat that?"

They looked at each other and then, I did not doubt, repeated the information verbatim. "This is how it works. You release information with the story told, you free the paths that had been closed. When you discharged that tale, it cleared a kind of blockage." Once more the expectant look reached out from their shining faces.

It seemed too simple.

"I tell a story and whoosh, we reach the next level." I looked around. It seemed to fit the location. Was that what they were really telling me?

They seemed almost to chuckle at that, but they nodded. "We help."

"You help tell the story?"

"We help release the block by choosing the story." I remembered the touch to my forehead and the blinding white light. "Ah. So, one down?" How many to go? Upper or lower, as one might ask of cheeks? From the look of things, I guessed we were descending. There was a weird residual effect of the event, like a fuzzy hangover kind of feeling that made my head feel muzzy and my tongue thick. All the muscles in my body seemed a little loose and about two seconds behind normal speed. I felt like an echo of myself with ten percent lost resolution in sound and picture.

"Perfectly normal for your species," the Wits disconcertingly said. I noticed even as I was squelching my thought of irritation that the attempt to give them names had not settled in my head. I think I had finally accepted that they were just not human, however much they might try to comfort me with appearance.

"Don't you know it's rude to read people's thoughts," I finally said. My obstinate mind added a few rude sobriquets to the end of that statement.

"There's no time," they said in return. Their voices were calm, but the urgency came across nonetheless. "Can you prepare for the next descent?"

My mouth felt as if I had swallowed some kind of downy creature. An irrational panic seized me. Was this what had done in Harakka? No, no, I told myself crossly, failing not failed, dying perhaps, I was more certain minute by minute, but not dead. Somehow that seemed the key straw to clutch at and clutch it I did. Damn the hangover, psychic or not, let's push on and show what I'm made of: "All right."

I didn't even get a moment to regroup. They reached out for me, this time a swift touch to my forehead, between my eyebrows. This time I saw them, I saw them both touch me as one. It made no sense physically. But I knew the place they activated, this location, one Harakka had taught me. This was the centre, the third eye, the leading point: Insight. Was there a kind of physiognomy to what they were doing? All of these thoughts rushed at once, yet before they could do more than bullet through my brain, I was overcome with a dark shade, a light of darkness it seemed that shone on me, which couldn't help but seem wrong, illogical, but eerily accurate. It blinded my senses like the white light had done and suffused my brain, my vision, my hearing with a deep indigo glow. A sudden sense of calm descended upon me, quite unlike the joy I had felt with the white lights. Was it joy I had felt? I only realised that name for it as my senses were bombarded with the new light. It was an accident, only an accident, and something monstrous laughed from behind my eyes.

From the depths of my brain, came a bolt of insight. Not for me, not for Harakka, but for the Wags. Of all things, how very strange to focus on them. Yet all at once I could see them and I understood exactly what they were doing. They *were* just kids, just hot-rodding. It was just a hormone-fuelled (or whatever their equivalent was) tear for them, a real wild weekend. They weren't going to leave until they were forced out, forced by the bronze to leave, and the bronze weren't up to the job, or forced by a lack of fuel or wherewithal to head home again to the bosom of their parents, (if bosom was the right word for their jellified selves). If we had the technology, but of course, we didn't. Curse the economies that made improvements in rocket travel take a back seat to corn production! It won't feed the poor, I recall an MP garbling, his fat finger distended in haranguing accusation. We couldn't herd them off with helicopters and Buddy Holly-killing turboprops. Contemplating our powerlessness, I was filled with inertia, until a new insight broke in.

"What do you see?" The Wits were coaxing me. What did I see? I saw the long line, the trajectory from which they had come, the land, the orb, the planet. So far, so very far, yet no time at all to them. Wait, was it the Wags or the Wits whose trail I followed? I couldn't tell anymore. There was so much we did not know, so much of which we were ignorant! I turned toward the Wits to try to capture this fleeting feeling, to harness the awareness that had ricocheted into my brain, but they were fading, I was slipping away from them, from the cave where they beckoned to me. It had become transparent and I was passing through, passing through skies, stars, nights, days, and still they called, "What do you see?"

I closed that great open eye and tried to concentrate. "I see the pathways of the night, of the trail through the stars." For the moment, I could still see it and them, as long as my eyes were closed, or the eye, as it were. Where was I going? What could I see? Where could I go?

"Whose trail?" Their voices seemed gently reproving. I had forgotten something important. But it didn't matter: instead, the master's words were running through my head: "Every morn and every night, some are born to sweet delight. Some are born to sweet delight, some are born to endless night." Here it was, his vision filling my eyes, all three of them, I realised, and I could not believe the joy of it, the sheer exhilaration of that magnificent grasp he had to comprehend the truly endless night. It stretched before me, luminous darkness with spirals of light freckling the void, a sweet delight. All of it lay before me, behind me, above and below me; I was the traveller who stepped in the master's tracks. This shadow world, these shadow worlds, I corrected myself, were not a patch on the infinite stretch of the truth. So tiny, so tiny. Every night and every morn and all mine now, all mine to touch, to stretch through.

I tried to rein in my thoughts, but I was seeing across galaxies, further than the last Explorer had done, to nebulae I'd never dreamed on, strange irregular colourful sprawls that exploded like fireworks in the distant black. I wanted more. The hunger awakened was becoming insatiable. The road of excess leads to the palace of wisdom, those were his words, the words of the master. He must have known, he must have been reaching back across these centuries to tell me. I knew his words for a reason. I had been born to be a tiger burning bright across the galaxies of the night.

"What do you see?" The Wits urged once more, an edge of something approaching concern creeping into their tones. "Where have you gone?"

I looked around me and I had no idea. All I could tell was that it was all the same despite the multitudes of difference that sparkled before me. Here or there, it was one, all one. I was one with it. What did it matter where I was? I am everywhere,

everywhere is in me. It was better than the night kitchen, better than the drugs, better than anything I had ever experienced. Let it never end I sighed, as I had sighed to innumerable lovers over the years, let it never end. Let this floating go on and new delights fill my eyes, my ears, my fingers' grasp. There was no breath, but smell was never my best sense. Could I taste it, I wondered, and stuck out my tongue to discover.

"Where are your wings?"

Wings? Had I wings? Is that how I got here? That's right, I had been a bird. I knew a bird. Harakka. The word came to me and with it a sense of calmness, a pause in my outward journey. I flailed and considered where I was. Where did I need to be? Harakka, that's right. She needed me. I needed to find her. Something should be connecting us, but I couldn't sense it. But I could hear the Wits. "Where am I?"

"Close by," the Wits encouraged me. "Come to us. Hear the sound of our voices."

It seemed simple enough and I flapped my wings, speeding at once through the stars of the endless night back toward the cave I had left, returning faster than I had left across the impossible distance. Although it felt as if the winds were hastening by me as if I were on a rollercoaster, there was no fear, only the exhilarating pound of my heart as the wonders passed through my head, before my eyes. I was a fireball, I was a comet, I had glories in my tail. The rush of speed made my temples hammer loudly but I was beyond pain. I did not breathe and a voice in my head said, wonder at that, but the whoosh of the journey distracted my ears who heeded not that warning knell. The descent made me giddy with a permeating thrill that filled my body wings to toes. I pelted through the sky, through the mountains. When at last I returned to the cave, I landed with a final flourish of speed, feeling quite pleased with my careful descent and well-controlled landing. I folded my wings up and settled on the cave floor. I was less surprised this time to see that it looked different. All seemed to be in order. It was cooler and damper, sure, darker despite the soft blue glow of the Wits. Unlike the radiant glow of gold, this was a subdued colour. I was certain, more or less, that it was the next level. Of course, of course, I thought. And all shall be well, and all shall be well and all manner of things shall be well. Something of the elation remained, animating my every fibre.

It is a measure of my ignorant smugness that it never occurred to me that I had come so close to fatally failing. The relieved looks of the Wits should have been enough for me to guess it. But I was too wrapped up in my success to notice that I was just barely tripping on the edge of rescued oblivion. It took me some time to notice. Too much time, as it turned out.

"That was magnificent!" I crowed, my wings folded demurely. "I saw galaxies, saw worlds unknown, saw the ends of the planets, these planets anyway. Ends, beginnings, it's all the same, eh? What amazing universes there are out there. He was right: some were born to endless night! I could see further than Ray Milland. Really! I can't wait to go back."

"We don't doubt it, but what have you brought back?"

"Brought back?" In the time it took to pronounce the words, everything shifted. I could feel chill brush against the back of my neck. What? What had I? What had I brought back? From where? Should I go back? My mind quickly offered. I was eager to say yes, eager to venture out once more into that infinitude. I spread my wings, then stopped puzzled. It wasn't, as I thought initially, a query about stopping at the galactic gift shop.

There was something inside me.

I could feel it running. My heart raced. My vision doubled, cleared and then blurred once more. "What's happening?" It was running through my skin, up and down. Panic seized me. Wings evaporated, hands began to grope blindly. "What is it? Make it go away!" My flesh rippled, revolting from the glacial sensation of whatever slipped along my limbs, doubling back, crawling ever faster as my hands chased after, scratching with a growing frenzy of fear. "Make it stop! Make it stop!"

"We cannot," the Wits said, faces impassive and seemingly

incurious. Did they know what it was? Had they caused it? Just because I didn't listen to them? Is this what happened to Harakka? Did they stand by while she fought against something uncanny crawling under her feathered hide? Panic pounded in my eyes, tangible and bright like an alarm. The Wits were unmoved. "You must release it."

What the fuck?! "It's under my skin," I snarled back at them, knowing they did not care. The ripple of its presence moved up and down my torso, seeking an opening, that was all I could imagine. Bile rose and I clutched at my throat. The thing seemed to be heading there. It paused and began to sort of rotate, shiver and shake. There was a rumble like a rocket getting ready to take off and the thought of it pushed me beyond the edge of panic into the rich crunchy middle of it. My fingers tore at my neck. Suddenly they found purchase and I pulled, no longer concerned about what it might mean, not fearing any kind of self-immolation as much as the horrid touch of that thing inside me. Let it be gone, out, away.

I ripped the flesh apart at my throat, heedless of the cost, only wanting that itch under my skin to depart, the alien presence ejected from the confines of my body, out, out damn spot. I convulsed and out it came through the rip in my neck, a small creature of multiple limbs and a scurrying motion that seemed as surprised to be here as I was to see it. I quelled the urge to crush it under my heel. I clasped my hands around my neck to find the rupture healing itself, the jagged ends painful and moist, but returning to wholeness. Looking down, I saw the creature and blanched. As repulsed as I was to have the thing under my skin, I felt pity for it once it was released. What alien world had it staggered into? It skittered across the floor of the cave. Did the movement suggest panic, or was it only my sudden empathy. The appendages called to mind some kind of insect or bug, but more complex. What was that mythical creature that still lived in some parts of the desert, or so it had been reported? With pincers and a curly tail, poisonous or so it was rumoured. Some are born to endless night indeed: here was one who belonged there.

"What is it?"

You'd think that would be me, but it was the Wits. What is it, indeed? If a monster, a tiny one, a pitiful one, size is relative. Under my skin it was huge, under my scrutiny, less so. What is it? From my journey to the stars I had brought it back. A wave of remembrance hit me like vertigo. Sweet delight and endless night! But what had grown under my skin? Is this joy that I feel? No, not as I look at the feeble creature skulking across the uneven terrain at our feet. "Ignorance, fear…" Suddenly I realised just how far I had gone, how little held me in this journey to the stars. The Wits had a slim tether on me all the way, but where was my own? I might have been lost out there. I might not have come back. Would that have been terrible? Perhaps not, I thought, remembering the joy. Perhaps yes, my thoughts countered, remembering my friends. I closed my eyes and tugged at the thread linking me: still there, still holding. A reassuring ripple returned to me; they were still binding my spirit to theirs, and the joy of that connection flooded my head.

I fell to the floor. Belated shock, I suppose. Here I had been afraid of ending up as loony as Blake, but had no fear of plunging to the ends of the universes, dying alone and freezing. Freezing? Why freezing? There was no sensation of temperature at all. With a shiver I understood. Cold was aloneness. Damn my impulsive heedless plunge into any experience than caught my fancy, here it was again, but the stakes higher than any before. I had nearly pitched headlong into death a couple dozen times in my ignorant youth, but never into such oblivion while in my right mind. The skittering creature extended a hesitant leg toward my prone face, curiously reaching toward my pallid visage. Unbeckoned the words wove through my brain, "on a pallid bust of Pallas." Who was that blackbird?

"Is this my *bête noir*?" I contemplated aloud. The Wits did not speak, staring curiously at the two of us crawling on the floor of the cave. "I have not named my fears. Harakka taught me to name the fears before any journey. It is important to know what controls you and holds you back." The creature edged closer, its spindly legs waving with tentative movements. Friend or foe, friend or foe?

"Speak friend and enter." It moved closer. One black limb stretched out to touch my neck where the jagged scar had been palpable to my fingers. I looked into its shiny black surface. I couldn't see anything that looked like eyes. The curse of our species is that we rely so much on our eyes, such easily hoodwinked organs. A face or a vase? We could never be sure. The obsidian shell gleamed in the soft blue light. Its leg pawed at my throat. How deep in the mountain were we now? The silence was profound, oppressive. The Wits were a part of it. They were no help now. With a shock, I realised that they did not breathe.

I let my eyes return to the creature before me. I was not conscious of making the decision, but I reached for my throat, tore open the scar again and let the little monster crawl back inside me. The tiny legs tickled a little, and I nearly gave in to the urge to vomit up the presence in my gullet, but the sensation passed as it descended. I could feel each click of its limbs as I sat up. It crawled deeper and deeper inside me, but as it did so, the movements grew finer and smaller and then all at once I could not feel it as it slipped somewhere into my solar plexus.

I looked up at the Wits. "What just happened?"

They actually grinned at me. "You tell us."

"You're joking, right?" Here's the deal, I made a monster and then I let it get back inside me. I had no clue. Claggers and hammers, it was a crazy thing that made no earthly sense.

"'Earthly' is a very limiting conception, *ne c'est pas?*"

"Hey, don't speak French to me," I grumbled, but I was feeling awfully good, all things considered. You try ripping your own throat open to swallow some kind of uncanny creature from beyond the stars, see how you feel. By all rights, I should be rather rough having more or less taken it on the chin so directly. Yet I could feel tendrils of that lost joy return and plump my veins with a thrumming sense of hope. So near to failure, but I pulled it out at the last minute. *Don't get cocky, Ro,* I hastily cautioned myself, catching the four eyes of the Wits.

I was more than a little shocked to see that our surroundings had changed again. The light was no longer the soft blue it had been, but very much a greenish hue. Not going to be flattering this light, I couldn't help thinking. The walls were a kind of pink granite, veined richly with black seams and the light, such as it was, seemed to catch the glint of crystals as the Wits shifted position, coming closer once again.

"Are you prepared for the next descent?" they asked in the irritating unison.

"No, no, no I am not ready," I said at once, tipping back away from them. I wasn't even standing up for one thing. "Hey, traumatized here," I added, my feelings of joy evaporating in an instant.

"But there is no time," they reminded me, and I could see Harakka in my mind's eye struggling weakly on a cave floor somewhere else. I could almost hear what she was saying but the Wits stepped in and repeated, "There is no time. You must continue the descent."

"I'm not ready." I didn't care how cross I sounded. I wasn't ready. This was a lot to ask of some stupid human who had barely begun to fix the shambles of her life in the last couple of years. I just wasn't this strong. I didn't have it in me. I was inordinately proud of dealing with the monster thingee, but come on! "Don't I get to rest up? Contemplate my progress? Eat lunch. Or tea, whatever time it is. I need to rest."

"There is so little time. You must hurry."

"No, absolutely not," I said, getting up on my feet and folding my arms with what I imagined to be decisiveness. "I cannot."

But it was too late. The Wits leaned in and although I dodged away, they touched me with their single pointy indexer right at my breastbone. For a second we all froze. I blinked.

They stared. Maybe nothing was going to happen.

Then all at once I sensed it happen. A weight sprang into my chest. It was as if my heart had literally turned to stone. The burden of it dragged me down. I slumped on the floor. "What's happening?" I gasped, the tonnage of it crushing my lungs aside.

"Your heart seems to have turned to stone," the Wits said, their even tone lacking any sense of surprise, although I rather hoped it was not what they had expected for me.

What fresh hell is this? I wondered, trying desperate to draw breath. I should have stayed in the endless night.

12

"You're not going to help me, are you?" I asked needlessly. The Wits watched me gasping on the floor of the cave. Their expressions, identical, of course, exuded complete disinterest, or so it seemed to me. They had been concerned enough when I had flung myself across galaxies, hadn't they? But here gasping for air in front of them, they could not have cared less.

"We cannot," was all they said.

Insufficient, I thought. *That is insufficient.* Here I am with my heart on the floor and all they can say is "We cannot." How was I so sure it was stone? How the hell was I going to blinker my way out of this one? It's another one of these infernal tests! What the hell? How many were there going to be? What is the point of all this?

"Removing blocks," the Wits murmured without the slightest sound of appreciation from me. "We do not inflict these upon you, dear friend."

Friend, they called me; funny way of showing it.

"You choose the tale to tell."

"Tale," I gasped, "This isn't a tale: it's a heart attack, from the inside!" Where else, the back of my mind chattered, but it didn't matter. They were unmoved. As far as I could tell, anyway. Why had I been so sure that they were concerned while I was hurtling across the galaxies? Had I imposed such a tone on their words, their voices? Was there any truth to the concern, or its lack? Gaah, who knew? I might be creating this whole scene from my addled brain, over-tired and filled with any number of dodgy substances. It could all be a dream. Yes, yes—that was the most likely answer of all, wasn't it?

Why then did my heart seem fit to burst with the

unbearable weight of itself? I had to think of something or I was going to suffocate. What a horrible way to die. Not to mention ignominious, lonely and embarrassing, no, let's not mention that. I looked up at the Wits, observing me. Damn their watercoloury hides. Another test, yes, yes, did you get it? Yeah, I got it. How was I supposed to rescue myself this time? This wasn't some metaphorical rite of passage; this was physical trauma!

I rolled there on the floor a minute more, wondering where all this was leading. How could a simple organ have become so heavy? Was this all in my mind, too? Yes, of course, you moron. How to get out of it, then? Well, that was the sixty-four hundred dollar question, *ne c'est pas*? Terence, this was really stupid stuff and I didn't like it.

Concentrate, I told myself as I huffed against the damp cave floor. There had to be some way out of this or it wouldn't be a test. I was not going to admit that there might be some way that my species might not be capable of finding. It was a distinct possibility, but I wasn't going to acknowledge it. I had to believe that there was a way for me to survive this. Marshalling all my powers, I tried desperately to calm my thoughts and my feverish body. *No, don't try desperately,* I scolded myself. *Breathe. Okay, not deeply, it's not possible with a heart of stone, but shallow and slow. Keep the panic under control. You've dealt with worse, when... when?!* the panicky part of my noggin shrieked suddenly. *Minutes ago, so shut the hell up, you worm gargling, pusillanimous ick*, I returned with as measured a tone as I could muster. It was all in my head anyway. *Calm, calm, calm, calm.* It had seemed useless, but I was beginning to concentrate. All those years of drug-free practice were finally paying off in a tangible way. Hallelujah, I suppose.

Okay, Ro, think about it. What is this but a literalisation of your usual state? I mean, look at it, I thought, somewhat disappointed. *That's you in a nutshell, heart of stone. Have you ever cared about anyone but your own selfish self?*

I love Simon, I amended immediately.

You put Simon in a coma!

Did not, I argued against my worse half. *You know that's not true.* But it feels true, I knew. I was a louse. I used, I abused, I ignored; look at poor Maggie. Was it possible to not notice that she had been in love with me? Possible for me.

And what about Brendan? the insidious voice interrogated further. *What is he but a prop to your ego?*

No, no, he's more than that, I swear.

But the voice in my head was adamant. *You're using him, like you've used everyone in your life. Heartless, cruel, spiteful, you have never given of your heart. No wonder it's turned to stone.*

Well, I wasn't going to take that kind of sentimental trash from my subconscious. I have given my heart any number of times, sometimes only for a second or two, sure, but no less completely for that. Can I help it if no one wanted it? Or inevitably not for very long. I'm just not the loveable type. I had learned to conserve value.

What about Maggie? the merciless voice said. Talk about your towns without pity. Like a bird on wire, if I could remember what that looked like, I had tried in my way to be free of all entanglements for some time. *O tempora, o mores*, it wasn't my fault. It was the music, it was the dance, it was the way she gave me that glance. I didn't know that she fell in love; it was just one of those things, a long simmering attraction that was never meant to come to anything. The last of my wild years, days, hours, so close it might have been missed. It was the two volume novel all over again, and not my fault if the sky grew dim and the sun turned some sort of brown if not black. She deserved better.

You knew, the nagging tone persisted.

The stone felt heavier than ever, a boulder, a brick, a binding too tight.

*I did **not** know,* I insisted. *It just got to be a habit, a comfortable place to go. Not love, never that. We both knew it was just a silly phase we had to be going through at the time. Missing Simon, missing the warmth of his presence, the gradual acknowledgement* *that he might not come back. We were grieving, it wasn't love!*

But didn't you mutter one night, locked in her sweet embrace…

Never! I swear.

But didn't you want to do so?

This conversation was not helping. If anything, my heart seemed to be even heavier as I sank to the floor in deepening pain. I had to get my mind off this mountain-ramming path. A snatch of lyric filled my head as if in response: "I've had oranges and lozenges, porridges and sausages." I clutched it like a life raft and let the mantra fill my skull. Repeated *ad infinitum* it drove that disapproving voice, which I suddenly realised sounded very much like my third grade teacher's, right out of my consciousness and into my socks where it was swiftly muffled.

All right, stone: what beat stone? Not scissors or paper. I glanced up above me. The Wits were unchanged, still gawping at my flailing efforts. The stalactites drew my gaze, though. Long pointy accusing fingers, or a solution? Water, that was the answer: water beat stone, it took a long time, sure, and I didn't have much of it, (even now my heart seemed to be slowing, each breath was a laboured inhalation), but water had to be the answer. I could do a lot, but could I summon a flood? Without killing us all? There had to be another way.

All at once, it was simple. How to melt a heart of stone?: tears. I was going to have to come up with those, which presented a bit of a problem. Could I really make myself weep? Without a sad sentimental movie or music? Could I conjure the goddess Bette or even Saint Harry's wistful croon? No, what I needed, as the man himself might say, was something true. As soon as the word hit my brain, I knew. A litany came to mind at once: Simon's ten lost years, Maggie's broken heart, Harakka, Mister Tolliver, my lost years of waste and abandon, all the lost trees, plants, clean water, dead birds, so many dead birds littering every street and yard, the Wags and their mindless eating of anyone who crossed their path, and oh, the war dead! Countless people, men, women and children of every age, chewed up by the machinery of war and fed into the prisons to await death, whether by the Wags or to be murdered by each other, raped, abused, abandoned and neglected. There weren't enough tears in the world for all the wretchedness, and at last I remembered the line I had forgot in the master's poem: "Every night and every morn, some to misery are born." Too many now in the desolate blast that is this world. When would she shrug us off, as Saint George was wont to say? Maybe that's what the Wags were here to do.

Only gradually did I become aware that the cave had changed once again. I would say that my heart grew lighter, but sorrow weighed heavily yet, figuratively now, rather than literally, and I knew that my selfishness had manufactured this block. When I refused to look outside myself, Harakka had tried so hard to teach me, the world always seemed small and pitiful. I had begun to see the world with her eyes as a place of wonder, but the times I lived in, *o tempora, o mores*, called more convincingly for horror. Had it been less so in other times? Think of Pompeii, think of the Great Fire of London, the sacking of Troy, or the destruction of the Great Buddhas. There were horrors a-plenty in any age.

"Your kind are slow to progress," the Wits said softly.

Their words brought fresh tears, but I understood the need to witness the failures, to note the torturous progress, if progress it could be called, that we struggled toward. I had, however, given up asking "why me?" At least there was that.

I heaved to a sitting position, the change bringing a dizzy absence to my head. I felt infinitely weaker than before, my limbs trembling with the effort of rising. I wanted to believe it was just the effect of my heart being under siege, yet the enervation seemed systemic. Maybe I needed a rest. Looking up at the Wits and their expressionless mien, I doubted that would be possible. The changed colours around me seemed to indicate a positive passage to the next level, but there was likely to be no respite for me, I knew. I stared at the momentarily immobile Wits. What were they really? Had they come to help? Had they come to help themselves? Did it really matter? Would we get out of this? What did they truly want?

"The same as you," they said softly in the echoing confines of the small chamber, as the yellow pulse glowed weakly, as if the gentle tone could ameliorate their intrusive presence in my mind. "To protect our kind, to find our way to a better life, to share what we know and learn what we do not."

"What can we teach you?" It was not false modesty.

"So much that we have forgotten: The confines of flesh and its vulnerability, the distance between spirits individuated, the ability to communicate without touching, with abstractions. There is such beauty in your species' tongues."

Good lord, they sounded almost envious. "Do you not speak? At all?"

They made a sound much like a sigh, and in its sound I could hear a hint of the music they could make. "Our tones are much like your music, although of far greater variety than that of which you are capable," they explained without a trace of smugness, though I could consider it earned. "We communicate instantly. But the choices and mistakes made in your communications, different tongues, regional differences, tone as well as timing. It is…an exquisite art."

Yay for humanity; inefficient but charming.

"Do you wish to see us as we really are?" the Wits quizzed me, as if the question were somehow related. I guess this was all part of getting to know you.

"Um, sure." Why the hell not? In for a penny, in for another antiquated coin of the past.

I had no idea.

One minute they were still the sketchy Blake characters, and all at once they were not. What were they? Words fail me. Oh, mumbles. If I had a thousand heads each with a thousand mouths which each had a thousand tongues, I could not begin to tell the thousandth part of what they were. It was fortunate that I was only sitting up, as I doubled over in pain immediately. It was not really a physical sensation as the heart had been, but rather a fundamental revulsion at what could not be. They stood naked. Naked? Without flesh, can one be naked, my panicking brain reasoned all too logically yet edged with an escalating hysteria, before me, revealing a truth that I had been glad to have hidden.

The Wags were no preparation for this unveiling. Strange as their physiognomy had been to us, they were still flesh that presumably had some kind of blood or other fluids running through those pudgy bodies. Lord knows, they were squidgy enough to suggest all kinds of effluvia. This was another ballpark, another galaxy, another concept altogether that my mind could not quite grasp. Instead my gut clenched in very real pain as the sickly yellow glow of the cave seemed to mock me. Why hadn't the first few "tests" had this kind of physical effect? Was I growing weaker? That gave me something else to worry about, surely, but not enough to take my eyes off the Wits and the strange vision they provided.

The weirdest thing was all the while I could hear (or was it feel?) them comforting me, as if apologetic for the way I was perceiving them. Poor benighted lesser species! We offer to show you the wonders of the worlds and this is how you react? Clutching your abdomen like a frail patient in the last stages of cirrhosis? Blake had returned and made great mad paintings and crafted wild unfathomable poems, all human, all metaphor for the uncanny sights he had seen, (did he see this much? The grouchy part of my mind doubted it). But what did I do? Yowl and moan like a cat pegging out from a painful wasting illness. It was hardly dignified, some rational part of my brain continued to narrate, hardly spoke well for the species. I was letting the side down, no doubt.

But what was there to do? Think, think! Well, the last test was definitely physical, hitting me right in my heart; weren't they all really? Was I just noticing the results more now, maybe because I was flagging? What about this one? Slamming into my gut, my solar plexus, what's there? Stomach? Liver, gall bladder: these were the waste removers. What on earth did that have to do with this revelation before me? But there had to be some kind of connection, surely? The heart thing worked, it was a physical metaphor. Revulsion and revelation linked somehow here.

I had to look again, to really see the Wits, or whatever they really were called. It amused them to use that word, that was all. Their real name, if they had one, surely must be as unfathomable to my little head as their sight was to my eyes. I steeled myself for the jarring sight, but I was overwhelmed yet again by the shock of seeing them once more. What was I seeing that made my belly seize up and roil? It was no good; almost before I knew it I was heaving up my guts on the floor of the cave. I hardly thought there was anything there to displace. Stale champagne flavoured the spewing stream. It came from another lifetime, another world. I wiped the muck from my gob and turned my orbs back to the Wits. Blurring my sight a little helped, and I tried to concentrate on the sound that the Wits produced.

It wasn't music precisely, but it had the power of it, the flow and, most importantly, the ability to soothe the savage breast, or liver, or gall bladder, whatever it was that was making the sight in my vision become nausea and vertigo there in my belly. The Wits, they were one, such as it was. No, not even one, but united. No, whole. That was it. They had masqueraded as two, but they were one, and if there had been a hundred of them, they would still be one. I could bear the sight more now that I understood that. I began to grasp our species' separation, the unfathomable gulf that lay between each of our kind. How unconnected we were. How marvellous it must feel to be so linked, to be one. A shift in the tune of the Wits' threnody seemed to jog a piece of my mind. What had Harakka said over and over? We were all one, our apparent separations part of the detritus that formed the illusion of suffering. How had I forgotten that? Oh, I don't know, perhaps it was the shock of meeting these wild aliens who tried to communicate with my pathetic dinosaur brain by fixing cosmic revelations to physical locations on my body.

The nausea seemed to be passing. Although I had closed my eyes once again, in fatigue more than anything else, I could see the Wits yet before them, lingering like a burn on my retinas. But they were less revolting now, were they changing again? Or was it just the cave itself? Yes, that was part of it. I blinked my eyes open again and blessedly, they were gone, no, not gone. I could hear them in my head. But they were sparing me the sight of their true selves, for which I was eminently grateful. My mind could take only so much expansion at once and I had pushed past my limit a few levels ago. How many has it been? How near to the end might I be?

I was lying on the uneven surface of the cave floor, barely able to lift my arms, no matter how much the voices of the Wits urged me on. The orange glow surrounding me and seeping behind my closed lids seemed to be healthy and energising, but I had a wild thought that I was past resurrection. If Harakka had been unable to survive... *no, no, don't think about that...* what could a pathetic soul like me, a mental half-pint, a spiritual cripple, accomplish? I just wanted to lie there and let my consciousness slip away even if it meant forever.

Inevitably came another touch from the Wits. My eyes were closed, so I had no idea whether they had physically touched me or how, and I didn't care in the least. I was giving up and the fate of the world hanging on my shoulders or the lives of my friends depending upon my success was not enough to make me lift my head from this rough surface and care. It was all very easy to think my planet needed me, yet quite another to do anything about it the way I was feeling.

But then I heard music. Not the ethereal music of the spheres that the Wits had massaged into my brain with their silken tendrils of thought, but real music. Saint Dusty, in fact: it stirred the cloud of memories before I knew it. Why here, why now, that song so loaded with that irrepressible charge of my first time? He hadn't been the son of a preacher man, but that long lithe body had been the initial one pressed into my flesh in that singly indelible way, so that those opening notes of her song, playing coincidentally in a nearby room, carried the weight of it forever after. Wherever I was when I heard that husky cadence, a part of me stopped and swayed with the memory. Faded over time, romanticised at moments, sardonically stripped of its power at others, the charge lay there nonetheless ingrained. Evoked at unexpected moments, and what could be more unexpected than lying in an imagined cave in another world with unearthly beings? It sparked the memory which lived in my flesh, that first penetration by another, the original melding skin to skin, the total fundamental surrender to another's flesh.

Then I noticed that the Wits had taken up human form again, although they were translucent, almost ghostly as they headed toward me. They floated on the air. I rolled on my side to see what they were up to, feeling more disoriented by the sudden shift from gut-clenching nausea to what? It wasn't just the momentary blip of Saint Dusty filling my head. A profound charge of sensual pleasure ricocheted through my limbs. My body stirred despite the fatigue. What were they up to? The Wits did not retain their latest shape for long; instead they surrounded me, evoking tangibility if not a fixed form.

Then they touched me. This was not the psychic contact the pair had made me feel before, not the impression of touching, the approximation, but a pressing of flesh so much like the real thing as to be indistinguishable. Although the first impact came low on my belly, it spread quickly across my skin, moving like roving hands and rushing fingers but much more quickly, more comprehensively, enfolding the whole of my body in a warm embrace that made me gasp with surprise and, yes, pleasure. It was a familiar feeling, a welcome one after the tribulations of this seemingly endless journey downward, and I acquiesced at once to its seductive pull. I told myself I was too weak to do anything else, but I was past caring.

The touch was thorough, though at first tentative, as if they were learning the way of flesh, its resistance, its resilience.

They were quick studies. I didn't even open my eyes to see what they looked like now. It was not possible that they could be the reassuring humanoid shapes they had been at first, one male, one female, I realised belatedly. From head to toe I was caressed. The Wits explored my skin with curiosity, seeking differences, sensitivities. It didn't take long for me to climax pleasurably, coming with a strange helpless power despite the fatigue that wracked my limbs. My involuntary cry seemed to pause and refocus their ministrations, as if the positive results had redirected their experiments. If it sounds coldly calculating, there was nonetheless an effect more potent than any I had met before. The singularity of their concentration was phenomenal. Their touch fluctuated between feather-light and rough. I undulated, gasping. Hardly a trial, I thought; it seemed that perhaps this was a reward for passing the other tests and I gave in without a thought, knotting into raptures despite the bone-weariness of my limbs. Had I once a lover this comprehensive I would have been faithful to the ends of the universe, crawling after them through firestorm or glacial pit regardless of any other consideration, if only they would ply me with such unending bliss.

Or so I thought for a time, as I arched and sighed and cried aloud, as I reached ever higher ecstasies. I found myself again breathless, but without the panic that had come before when my heart had been attacked. My skin prickled with the thrill of it all. This could go on eternally I thought, a wicked grin no doubt plastered across my lips. There, no, there, ah, there. Every centre of pleasure invoked, examined, stroked. I could keep this up forever, surely. But as the Wits explored the further realms of fleshly experience, I began to realise I was being depleted and not just of fluids, although I was already overcome with a powerful thirst. The raptures were depriving me of my senses and of the memory of what I had been doing. I had had a purpose here which I tried to recall between pinnacles of increasing frenzy.

I began to fight against the tide of endless stimulation. It wasn't that they were pitching the gammon at me, I think they meant well. They were exploring, too. The Wits had expressed their desire to know more of flesh. They had learned quickly and exquisitely, I could attest to that. But I had a purpose here. I was beginning to understand that it was my passivity as much as anything else that was at issue here. Indulging like a fat tick, content to bleed dry any host I latched onto, it was selfish. What was I? Dido, Queen of Cabbage? No, I needed to respond. I needed to reciprocate. Could I return their ministrations? Could I pleasure those who weren't even flesh? How did this all work anyway? I wasn't even sure how to begin. But I had to try, so I opened my eyes expecting to see their bodies once more and was a bit disconcerted to see nothing but air. Almost in the same instant, their touch evaporated.

There ought to have been a sense of accomplishment in seeing the cave change once more, the light shifting from a warm orange to a brilliant red, yet I retained only the gnawing sense of depletion. While there was a suspicion of coming closer to the end of my descent, I had begun to realise that at the end of it I could only be falling into the open arms of Ereshkigal. I had come knowing death was a distinct possibility, but now the dull reality of it seemed inescapable. I had slipped down through that prism of colours from the cool to the hot. What's hotter than red? Had I reached the bottom? I had started with the head and ended with bloody red. It had to be the last stop on my downbound train. The fundamental level, the animal realm.

I shook my weary head and gazed around the cave. It was simple, smooth and completely Wit-free. Strange that they had deserted me now. Perhaps they had given up. I could understand. My limbs seemed too heavy and weak to move, but I struggled to sit up at least. The red glow of the walls made my eyes ache and it was hard to adjust to seeing more than the outlines of things. I crawled across the floor and tried to steady myself, to rise with the help of the wall. My legs were shaky. All the pleasure of just moments ago had drained from my flesh, leaving an empty echo behind. My skin still pulsed.

I blinked my eyes, willing them to improve my sight as I glanced around the space. It was all smooth bare walls, not a stalactite to be seen. Empty, except over in the darkened bend there appeared to be a small lump of rags, carelessly tossed to the floor by some previous traveller. I squinted trying to make sense of the contrast of dark and light. No, not dark and light, black and white.

Black and white? With a sob I stumbled forward, landing hard on my knees, uncaring of the ragged pain, mindless of anything but the need to make my way across to see if it were true, to see if it were possible, to see if she were dead. "Harakka," I mumbled. "Harakka!" I lifted the impossibly light pile of feathers to my chest in a desperate hug. "Harakka."

Deep within her chest, there was the slightest murmur of a heart beating yet. Birds are so hard to hold, so delicate, so tiny under the camouflage of feathers. I shrank from crushing her fragile pinions, but I had to have her as close to me as possible. "How could you leave me, how could you sacrifice yourself for this fool's errand? Harakka, I've failed, I'm failing."

"I am no sacrifice." The words were barely audible yet there was a fierceness in her reply.

My spirit surged with hope even as I sensed the effort it had cost her. A fluttering, like wings but miniscule, trembled through her body. "Harakka!" I held her close, risking damage and sobbing. I knew she was dead but I could feel a strange sensation at the same moment, as if she had passed through the wall of my chest into my heart itself. An answering call in my breast assured me it was so. Why not? I made my own reality, did I not? Harakka was a part of me, always had been, and now, always would be. Despite the despair I felt at her death, there was a respondent elation, too, at being forever joined. We could never be parted again.

Almost at once, however, my joy faded to sorrow. I was failing, if not in my journey, then in my health. It was as if I were melting and all my strength were bleeding out onto the subterranean floor. Was I dying? I had tried to prepare for this inevitability, yet on the brink, I resisted. *I carry Harakka within me*, I thought, *I cannot let her pass from this world and all others*. I had to dig my mystic heels in and fight the dissolution. If I could just hang on.

With that thought, the Wits returned. If they had ever been gone; perhaps I simply had not been able to sense them any longer in my weakened state until now. I couldn't see them however, but I could hear them. Their voices or sounds were comforting, but resigned, too. "We cannot help you survive here. We have done all we can. You should release your spirits and be at peace."

Spirits! They knew. "Why?" Why what? I don't know. Why allow me to come this far only to fail? Why lead me here to this final spot only to be reunited in our collapse? Why couldn't they help me? Why couldn't they save us?

Why was I asking?

They were unfathomable beings from another reality. They had no obligation to help me, no ties to us but a common aim. It was useless, a last ditch effort. "I can't save us, Harakka," I said, maybe not even aloud.

Yet she answered, "All will be well."

Well, that's all right then, I thought as I sank once more to the floor. *That's just peachy*.

"Good-bye, thank you, peace to your kind."

At least they were polite. "Thanks? Did you learn anything from all this?" From our deaths, from our suffering?

"Perhaps. We thank you. We shall endeavour to employ our findings to purpose."

Yeah, right. So long, thanks for all the fish sticks, oh wait, we didn't have any.

"Be at peace."

And with that they were gone. I wasn't sure how I could tell, but they were gone, and we were alone, befogged and lying on the floor of a cave, far from anyone and anywhere.

"I'm sorry, Harakka. I must be such a disappointment to you."

"Child, you have come so far in such a short time." Although it came from within me, her voice comforted me exceedingly. "You have succeeded beyond all expectations."

"But we failed. We're in the suds, for sure."

"There is always hope." Her voice was unnervingly calm.

I was too tired to fight against her faithfulness. What did it matter anyway; whatever the story, at least I wasn't going to die alone in this pit. "Harakka, if we are going to die down here, I'm glad we're together. You made my life so much better."

"Has it been worth it?"

Why did it seem that she was grinning at me from somewhere within my breast. I sighed and let my eyes close. "I've seen sights I would never have seen on my own, met beings from other worlds, and smelled fresh flowers in a forest. Yeah, I guess it was worth it."

"Well, in that case, before you die, you might want to tell your friends. Did you keep your link to the ones left behind?"

Was it a feathered thing rising once more in my heart? Hope might rise, but I wasn't sure I could. Yet with practiced discipline I reached my senses out for the threads that bound me to Simon and Maggie. I could feel the threads. However, I could not quite follow them up and out of the endless depths. "I can't do it." Everything was beginning to take on the swirly sense of starlit night.

"You must try." Her voice seemed to come from outside me again, either that or I was beginning to lose all structural integrity myself.

I made an attempt to gather the threads and pull them toward me, what seemed to be me, or had been me. I was no longer sure. I couldn't really feel anything in my hands. I tried to conjure up a vision of Simon's sardonic grin and Maggie's wrinkled brow and their visages swam in front of me before dissipating, too, like reflections in a stone-struck pool. The waves rippled out and washed upon my skull. My head filled up with nonsense again, not cabbages and sausages this time, but something about having lain down in lovely muck, happy till I woke again to luck, or was it duck? Truck? Fuck? Poetry was stupid stuff; every word has to be right.

I was certain I was remembering it wrong. It was just one thread of the carpet of me unravelling, loosening and unknitting itself. I was coming undone. Stuff I had once known was getting lost; it always had, hadn't it? Was I ever able to remember one thing as it really happened, as it was really written? Did it matter? Everything was swirling. Like a galaxy spinning its arms out wide and dissipating. Look at all the stars swing off the ends like glitter across the universe. *Is this dying?* I thought. Harakka's voice did not immediately respond. Was I losing her as well? I felt half-sprung, as if I had a bottle of rioja inside me on a hot summer day, melting, even blistering in the hot sun.

"Don't let go." Was that Harakka's words in my ears, my heart, my head? What was there to hold on to? I reached out for the limits of my flesh. The cold floor of the cave greeted my searching senses. Its chill was creeping into my limbs. The meat of me lay still. The Wits had been right, there was nothing left to do but die. Yet my mind put up a feeble resistance to the thought, aided by Harakka's words. I had been left here to rot like a bad veal cutlet, past the sell-by date, or not passing inspection, substandard, not prime, not even worth salting. How much we hide from ourselves the truth of our meat, the simple fact of these tenuous folds.

As the Master said, we are all at the mercy of the old woman upon the rock who gathers up the lovers' groans and the martyr's sighs in her cup of gold to give us life, to strike her fingers down our every nerve, to fling us into the world's embrace. I was born of solid fire. And so I burned myself until I chanced to find the place and the ones who bound me down for their delight and I burned them instead. It took Harakka's careful teaching to bank that flame and turn it to something warm, though none of that mattered any more. The Sun Moon

Stars all shrink away now and I was left with this black cavern, its emptiness, nothing to eat or drink, nothing to restore the decaying flesh. Sweet sleep come to me, I have no need of this frowning night.

"Don't let go. Remember!"

The voice returned. It no longer mattered to whom it belonged, only that I try to make some sense of it. Yet the sounds that struck my ears, (my heart? My brain?), no longer received the same comprehension. Don't let go, don't let what go? Don't let go what? The coat, the hope, the life? What can I hold onto here? I do not sleep in beams of light; all is darkness here. What was flesh will fade, the meat putrefy and each atom, each little galaxy, become undone, slow and spin wider, each circuit farther apart, until the centre does not hold. Infinity holds me in the palm of its hand, beckoning me to join its endless hours. Was this once a leg, that a spleen? Never mind, it works to become part of the whole, to break down into the component parts, to be what it had been before it became me, a child yowling in a late night storm, born to endless night and sorrowing morn, to sweet delight and the world's poor scorn.

Wasn't that what the Wits had taught? They were all one. Could I not be as well? To become one, I must come undone.

"Don't let go."

The words echoed again. I must still have ears to hear, a mind to think. Was this life yet? I could not conceive of my body as it had been, seeing only an elongated pooling morass, like some Dali painting. It was the natural order of things, dissipation, undoing, return return return to the mother who gave us birth. There was something more, though, too. What had it been?

"Remember!"

Remember? Remember what? The body I had been, the life I had lived, the reasons we had come to this distant world within a world? Did any of it matter now? Remember life: the smell of the trees, the heat of the sun, the rippling laughter of a shady brook, but these were all from Harakka's world, not

231

mine. They were as much a part of my mind as the thoughts buzzing through it now like dreamy damselflies. If the spirit I am went anywhere, they were going with me. They were more real than the vegetable universe into which I was born. The Master was right as usual. Better this shadow world than the last gasp dying twilit land I had left behind, hours or days or weeks ago. Time was different here.

"Remember!"

Again, that word; remember what? That all this was one, no more real and every bit as changeable as shadows? If my spirit, our spirits, released, it would all fade, all fade away. What remains? Memories? Do they visit us in our final hour to show what we have done or left undone? I tried to conjure up my friends again, my body was even less present than before, but I was freed from its fatigue as well and found it possible to see them clearly now. Simon deep in concentration over his drawing table. Maggie tinkering over an engine, fingers blackened and smudges on her freckled cheek. With a surprise I suddenly remembered my beautiful Brendan and Karasu far away in Charlestown, drumming yet. Could I really hear them? Was the beat still echoing across time and space? Was it only my heart striking a few last thuds before it ran down to silence. Good-bye, good-bye, parting is such sweet sorrow, that I shall say good-bye until I find surcease of sorrow, sorrow for my lost loved ones. Good-bye, good-night.

Even the effort of thinking had become too much and I lay in simple animal exhaustion, sensing the failing rise and fall of my chest, the dogged expansion of my lungs as I stubbornly hung on, refusing to let go of this body, this life, this home. And Harakka, I could not let go of her. I knew if I let go, she would be gone forever. I might be dead, but I wasn't willing to be parted from my friend.

So there in a cave in a distant world I waited. I waited to feel my body decay. Already the myriad processes were winding down, the bacteria within taking hold, spreading, eating away the staggering cells that lost their purpose, forgot their work and shuddered to silent idleness. It would all come down to gases, I realised with the ghost of a grin. My morbidified flesh would break down into component chemicals forming noxious gases that would gradually escape through the various apertures that would gradually appear in my corpse. Death by body fart, you can't beat that.

And just to show the comic horror of life, I realised I was drawing flies. Down here in the hidden bowls of a distant world, the vermin of the skies could find me. Two big bugs buzzed around me, looking for a place of purchase. Go on, feast away, there's plenty for everyone.

One big insect flew right up to my nose and stared into my closing eyes. Yes, yes, nearly dead, go ahead, I thought. Tuck in, the food's still warm. But it only sat there and buzzed, its translucent wings droning a nagging tone that disrupted my peaceful capitulation to unbeing.

The other flew to my lips. I could feel it walking back and forth as if assessing the welcome it might find in that cavern within this cavern. If you fly in, I won't fight you, I tried to tell the little fly. Go on, it's all yours. I felt something hit my tongue. Prepared for revulsion, I was surprise to taste sweetness. I was surprised to taste anything at all, figuring I was long past it. Ambrosia: who knew death's kiss would be so delightful? The savour spread like a ripple of pleasure through my skin and bones. I was treated to one last ecstatic burst before oblivion.

"Get up, you lazy slattern," Simon's voice buzzed from the bridge of my nose. "We have things to do."

13

"Yeah," Maggie added, now perched on my chin. "Look lively, you mangy slapper."

"What the hell?" I blinked and tried to focus on the bug sitting on my nose, while Maggie tickled around my chin.

"Well, you won't believe this," Simon buzzed from his perch on my nose, "well, you would, mind you, thousands wouldn't, but a turtle told us we needed to help you." With a little bounce, he flew up in the air, tiny wings beating furiously. "I have something for you, too." He zipped around to my mouth and settled down near where Maggie's minuscule feet were pacing back and forth.

I could sense the tiny little legs settle on the edge of my lips and then something dropped into my mouth with a startling and almost salty sensation. I swallowed. All at once it was as if trumpets were blaring in my bloodstream or confetti and fireworks exploding through my head. Like an electric jolt, the energy shot through my limbs, reanimating them as if they had wills of their own. I wouldn't have said that I regained the will to live, but I had certainly restored the possibility. "I'm not dead, am I?"

The bug that was Simon laughed, a squeaky little sound. "I don't think so, but maybe you were. The turtle said that you were dying and could really use our help."

"Are you sure it was a turtle and not a tortoise?"

"Well," Simon said with a grin, "she *taught us*."

"Go eat your beautiful soup."

"I never know what the hell you two are talking about," Maggie said. I couldn't see her, but I tried to picture itty bitty fists resting on her miniature hips in a perfect picture of irritation. "We were exploring the forest around where you left us, really cool stuff, I can't believe you didn't tell us about this place, by the way, you selfish stoat."

I grinned. Things must be all right if Maggie was getting angry with me.

"It seemed like ages, by the way, and we were getting hungry, but then this tortoise came by and said we had a friend in trouble."

"Which was odd enough," Simon said, droning somewhere near my left temple. "I don't know that I have ever seen a turtle outside a zoo back in the day. I've never seen one speak. Or heard one speak, I suppose I ought to say."

"Anyway," Maggie cut in, her aggravation with Simon growing, "it knew all about you and where you were and everything. It pointed us to the mountain but we knew we'd never get there. We couldn't turn into a bird like you."

"But you could turn into flies or bugs or whatever it is that you are?" I tried to sit up. I was feeling almost human again. Maggie and Simon buzzed before me, hanging in the air. "Gnats?"

"That was the tortoise, er, turtle. She turned us into this, but that was after she brought us to the mountain." Maggie zoomed up in the air in lazy circles.

"Who knew turtles could move so fast?" Simon continued. "One minute we're down in the forest, the next zoom! we're on top of a mountain. But we had to sneak in, so that no one could see us. And she gave us the gifts."

"Gifts?" I rubbed the back of my neck which felt stiff. I felt stiff all over, come to think of it. This art of dying was strenuous stuff.

"Yeah," Simon said buzzing louder now and looking rather like a bee. "Water of life."

"And food of life. You wouldn't be here without it." Maggie was turning into a wasp now. I didn't want to tell her what kinds of irony I saw in that. But there was something bothering me nonetheless.

"What did you give for them?"

"They were gifts," Simon said, yellow striped and rotund now. "They were given to us."

"Gifts of power," I said feeling a bit impatient that they knew nothing of this land, but that was my fault wasn't it? I had just abandoned them as babes in the woods.

"She did say something," Maggie said as she zipped around the cave faster and faster. "That we should help restore the balance. That was it, right, Simon?"

"Yeah, sounds right." He wasn't really listening, just flying around buzzing high and low. In a way, I could understand. When I first flew, it was all I could do. Now that I was regaining strength, however, I knew things were dire. Which balance had to be restored? And how? And by whom?

"I think I can walk now," I said at last, gingerly lifting myself to stand. "Maybe we should think about leaving here."

Maggie and Simon said OK in unison. They looked at me expectantly, or so I imagined from their attitudes. It was kind of hard to read the expressions of insects. "Um, could you maybe go back to your normal shapes? It's a bit disconcerting to keep watching you, uh, change."

"Hey, this is as far as I've got," Simon said with some irritation. "I've been trying and I don't know how."

"Me neither," Maggie chimed in. "We're not going to be stuck like this, are we?"

"No, no," I reassured them, although I was wondering myself whether they would be locked into those shapes until we returned to our own blazing world, so very far away.

"How do you change?" Simon asked. "I've been changing into different bugs OK. Shouldn't it be easy to change back into me?"

"Yup," I said, sounding like such an expert. I tried to cast my mind back to my first days as a shape-shifting novice. "The first thing is to relax. No, don't give me that look, Maggie." The two of them landed on the floor of the cave, although Maggie seemed to express irritation in her buzz. "Close your eyes, all hundred and thirty of them or whatever, and concentrate. How does it feel to be you? Think of all the details that make you, the shape of your arms, legs, the profile of your face, the contours of your body..."

And like that, they were back in their familiar shapes albeit sitting on the floor and blinking at one another and me. Simon broke into a grin right away and leaped up to hug me. "You did it, Ro, you did it!"

"You did it yourselves."

Maggie grinned despite herself and after a moment, joined in the hug, even giving me a little kiss on the cheek, which I tried not to make too much of, but I kissed her back with relief. It was good to see them again. "And now let's get back home."

"How?"

"How did you get to me?"

"We followed the silver threads you left us."

'Well, now you can follow me." My words, as usual, were more confident than my thoughts, but it seemed reasonable enough. I laid my hand on my chest. I could not hear her voice, but I knew Harakka was in there. She would help me. "Up this way," I said with conviction, "I know a short cut." My friends followed without a word and I turned my every thought to our exodus. Surely it was getting brighter up ahead. No matter, the way was shorter now than when I had come down. It had to be the way out, I was making this reality. I was in control here; it was my world after all. My steps felt lighter, whatever that water of life stuff was, it was good. The cave grew brighter. The entrance was just up ahead.

Then I saw the owls. For a moment I thought the Wits had returned, which made me nervous as well as a little relieved. I don't know how I knew, though, that they were different, but they were. Ye gods, what now? The Goons?

"Uh..." That was the total sum of my witty banter for them.

"Do you know them?" Simon whispered.

"The one cannot leave," the owls said in unison, but

somehow not the same unison as the Wits. For some reason it made me want to break out in laughter that I recognised as hysterical.

"Which one?" Maggie said, a defensive tone leaping to her voice and a stubborn frown to her lips. They didn't know who they were messing with, I thought with satisfaction. God, I love my friends.

The Goons pointed at me, no, I realised a heartbeat later, they were pointing into me. Harakka: she could not leave. Maggie and Simon, of course, didn't know that. The two of them both looked at me with something approaching panic.

"She's part of me now," I said as evenly as possible. "And I have to go, my planet needs me." Maggie and Simon just stared at me. I'd have to explain later.

"The balance must be maintained," the two predators intoned together. "The one is part of this plane now and cannot be reclaimed."

"The balance can be adjusted," I said, stubborn to the end. "I cannot remain; the balance would be displaced by that as well, *ne c'est pas*?" That'll toast their biscuits.

The Goons shifted a little, considering I hoped. "The balance must be maintained."

"Then I'll have to give you another." The words were out before I knew it, before I had any idea what they might mean. But I knew all along, didn't I? This is what the Wits were trying to show me, teach me, help me understand. "A trade! I can give you another."

"One of these?" The Goons looked a little too greedily at Maggie and Simon.

"Absolutely not! They were loyal to me, they rescued me, they brought me back from death. I will never part with them. You'll have to come with us to claim your soul." Yeah, let's cross that bridge when we come to it, I thought, wishing they would not immediately call my bluff or I would have to reveal I had nothing but Canterbury tales.

"Let us go, then."

"You'll have to carry my friends," I said with sudden inspiration. Why not? I knew they were going to be crashing soon after all they had been through. My suggestion was met with dazed looks by the two of them. The owls, however, simply spread their wings and stretched out their feet for my pals' shoulders. Simon yelped and Maggie reached up to swat at the birds, but I tried to comfort them. "It's all right, they won't hurt you," I said although even I winced at the firm grip of those talons. They hung in the air outside the cave's broad entrance, waiting. I closed my eyes and reached inside for Harakka's reassuring presence and I stepped off the cliff into the air.

"Hey," Simon said, "it's her, I mean, it's she. Harakka!" Maggie just stared.

"We are one now," I tried to explain as I flapped beside them. "I didn't have time to explain before." It seemed odd to look down and see the white on my belly, but I flew as sure and as strongly as when I had been a raven. "That's the imbalance they're talking about."

"What, you're, you've got her...inside you?" Maggie's voice sounded strained and small. It may have been the flight over the pines. Suddenly it came back to me how much she hated heights, how she wouldn't even stand near the window in my office.

I flew closer to where her legs dangled helplessly and tried to speak soothingly. "Yeah, Harakka died...sort of. Her body died, but she's part of me."

"Does that officially make you a split personality?" Simon asked. He was holding onto the ankles of the owl that carried him, forging some kind of control over the event I guess.

"No," I laughed. "We're joined together. It's hard to explain. But it's a great comfort."

The flight to the meadow where the temple lay seemed shorter than usual. Perhaps the Goons were in a rush. Despite all I had been through, I felt glorious. It must have been the food and water of life. Amazing stuff, I knew I owed a debt to this land for the help it had offered me. *I will return to feed you*, I promised. I had a feeling there would be others to join me. The unexpected mode of travel may have cowed my pals a little, but they were already beginning to recover their sense of wonder at this extraordinary land, even more glorious when its riches were glimpsed from above.

But they had a jarring landing when we arrived near the temple; the owls let go of them a few feet above ground while they were still moving fairly swiftly. Maggie tumbled across the ground, rolling like a hedgehog, while Simon landed with a heavy grunt, offering up, "Thanks a bunch!" as he lifted himself up. The impassive Goons stood at the ready, as if waiting for me to open the temple to them. Harakka had taught me about the power of liminal places. "Move with care," her voice came to me now.

"Enter here under my command," I said, trying to find the right solemn tone and the specific words that might protect my friends, my world. The Goons seemed to acquiesce, bowing as they passed me to enter the oak door of the temple. Maggie and Simon looked at me with something approaching worry, so I just grinned and shooed them in. "You're gonna have to trust me on this," I said with a bravado I didn't really feel.

It was good to be back in the cool onyx interior. Years might have passed; the temple seemed so long away from my touch. I laid my hands on the walls, adjusting myself to its energies once more. *This is all new for you, isn't it*, I asked Harakka. *You've never seen this sacred place.*

But I would know it immediately, she answered. *It is your place.*

I smiled, eyes closed. This room filled me with such confidence and strength. An idea had been forming in the back of my mind, which I was certain was going to work, if I could manage everyone around me. I looked up. Maggie was examining the floor of the temple, while Simon rested his face on the smooth black wall. The Goons stood stiffly in the middle of the floor, waiting. Or so I imagined: they weren't quite tapping their talons on the floor, but everything in their demeanour spoke of taut readiness. But I wasn't going anywhere until we were ready. I closed my eyes again and reached out with my senses. There! I heard it clearly now: the drums.

The sound filled me with such joy. How long had it been? It was hard to gauge. Was it years or days or only hours? There was no way to be certain. But the beat remained steady and beckoning. It was time to go home. "Follow me."

We climbed to the top and emerged in what appeared to be pre-dawn light. A very dishevelled-looking pair greeted us. Karasu knelt on the floor, eyes closed, yet beating steadily on her drum. Brendan sat cross-legged, mallet in his left hand, head bobbing along with each strike. They both blinked upon our sudden return, owls in tow. We all sat up and at first they leaned back in surprise, then thrust the drums aside and sprang up to greet us. Brendan wrapped me in a hug so tight I could hardly breathe. He only loosed me to clap his lips onto mine in a kiss that nearly made me swoon. "Welcome back," he said, when at last he released me. Keeping hold of my hand, he made next for Simon, planting a kiss of equal ferocity on his ready lips. I swayed a little with a great silly grin on my face, watching Maggie and Karasu dance in each other's arms. Inarticulate sounds of pleasure and greeting exploded all around me, but the silence of the Goons cut through it all. They were observing the scene but seeing something very different than I.

"Which one?" they asked me in predictable unison. Everyone looked at them in surprise. It wasn't just the fact of owls talking. Their peremptory tone made it clear they expected to be obeyed. But I wasn't having any of that.

"You will not have either of my friends. They brought us back with drums. They kept the faith, the lifeline between worlds. You will not have either of them."

Karasu and Brendan were perplexed, but looked somewhat mollified by my words. Maggie just looked steamed.

Simon looked over at me and somehow that look unsettled me. It was an expectant look, not like he was waiting for me to explain myself as I had been expected to do hundreds of times. No, he was waiting for me to lead. For a moment, I faltered. Then Harakka's voice rose inside me, warning there was no time for this vacillation.

"We have work to do. I know everyone's tired," I said, trying to look encouraging even as I saw the clear signs of fatigue on all their faces, "but we need to do one more impossible thing before breakfast."

"What are we going to do?" Simon appeared ready to join in, bless his heart. What a fool to follow a fooler. Yeah, shut up, I know, Harakka. It will work. I think. The Goons were looking at me too; did I only imagine it was through narrowed eyes of suspicion? Maggie seemed to be withholding judgment, but I was pretty sure she was going to be willing. Karasu and Brendan just looked exhausted, but there was no time to worry about that.

"We need to find a volunteer for the Goons," I said, rubbing my hands together briskly as I had seen people do in films countless times. It seemed to convey serious purpose. I did want to convey serious purpose, but the result just seemed to be confusion and quizzical looks. Oh, that's right. "These guys, the owls. They're the Goons. They want someone to come back with them, you see."

"Where?" Brendan asked.

I didn't like the speculative look in his beautiful blue eyes. "Not you, my dear. Where they would take you, you wouldn't come back. We need to find someone who doesn't plan to return." Or can't. Yeah, that's the deal. "I have a plan."

"A cunning plan?" Maggie surprised me with that old line.

"So cunning…" I started, but I was stumped for a good response.

Simon filled in quickly, "that it could steal your wallet, buy you drinks and dinner, and still leave you with the check at the end of the night."

"That's a cunning plan," Brendan agreed sagely, before we all cracked up, The Goons excepted. They continued to stare intensely at me, as if that would somehow speed up the process.

"We have to go down to the bay. Grab the drums and whatever we've got to drink, blankets, candles, um..." What else?

"Why the bay?" Karasu asked.

"It's the nearest open space we have." I just hoped it would work. It was a measure of my friends and all the madness we had been through in the last few days that they set about doing exactly what I asked without further questions. I marvelled that a week earlier, it would not have been the case.

Things have changed, Harakka murmured within me.

Indeed, indeed, I agreed. *Now, what else, what else?*

You need nothing, Harakka reminded me, *nothing but your will and the power your friends can give you.*

"All right, ready? Let's go!"

What a ragtag little bunch! We looked as if we were heading for a lacklustre picnic or perhaps a desultory game of some unrecognisable kind, with two strange pets in tow. The owls didn't half draw attention. Maybe someone would think we were Hogwarts fans. *They'll think I'm a Putney supporter, eh?* I told Harakka.

Just be glad it's early, she said. *With luck we'll see only drunks and bin men.*

Or no one at all, as the case happened to be, at least not until we got down to the shore. Then it was only a pair of middle-aged men in cloth caps, sitting on an overturned barrel and sharing what looked to be the last beer of many for the evening. Their eyes seemed particularly drawn to the owls, however, and not to us.

"Owls are generally said to be nocturnal creatures," the taller one ventured to tell us as we sauntered past with as little ostentation as was possible for a cluster of people on the way to invoke spirit-walking of major proportions.

"They come out at night, you mean," the shorter one clarified. "To hunt, I suppose."

"Indeed," the first continued, unperturbed by our steadfast ignoring of their conversation. "Their eyesight is a good deal keener than ours and allows them to see miniscule creatures even in the dark of night."

"But it's light out now."

"Course it is. That's why the owls need seeing eye persons to lead them around."

"Oh."

I couldn't help grinning as we walked out of earshot. Soon enough they would move along, I hoped. We didn't want to draw any attention or let other people get in the way. When we seemed far enough and not too deep into the muck of the once proud bay, I stopped and considered the location. It would have to do. *Pity we don't have wellies*, Harakka sighed.

"This is it?" Simon said, lifting one foot fastidiously from the mud. "So, what the hell are we doing here?"

Sooner or later someone was bound to ask, I guess. I tried to relax, so I could sound confident and persuasive. "We're going to bring a volunteer here for the Goons."

"Who are the Goons?" Brendan asked. There was just a touch of aggravation in his voice which made me wince slightly, but it was well-earned after all. How long had he been drumming without sleep? I shall make it up to him with as much enthusiasm as I can muster, I promised. After a bit of sleep myself, I bet I would be able to muster whole regiments of enthusiasm, I thought looking at his gorgeous form.

You are feeling chipper, Harakka said archly.

Nothing like the food and water of life itself to pick up your spirits, better than lobster thermidor and fine sham-pag-nee.

"Well, the Goons are guardians from another reality. They have to restore balance in that world because I have upset it." Yes, yes, take the blame, it's the easiest way. "I brought

Harakka back with me, which I ought not to have done, but I couldn't help it. So now we have to restore the balance by sending someone in her place."

"Brought her back?" Karasu ventured to say.

"Inside her," Maggie explained all too briefly.

"She ate her?!"

"No, no, no!" Simon was just about killing himself laughing, as I tried to dissuade Karasu of that peculiar notion. I thought I could hear Harakka laughing, too. "It's hard to explain, but our spirits melded at her bodily death. She dwells within me. I can hear her." Simon stopped laughing then and gave me an unnervingly penetrating look. And that was the first time I stopped to think what this all sounded like. *Don't give in to that*, Harakka said.

But for a moment I teetered on the edge. Admit it, it all sounded complete bugshit crazy. I have dragged all these people across costly miles of roads and to strangely distant worlds and through harrowing experiences for what might be nothing more than voices in my head. I may have snapped my cap. I was a cuckoo not a magpie, deranged, demented, disordered, dicked in the nob and ready for sectioning.

If it's all in your head, Harakka said evenly, *then no harm done, eh? What you're about to do will result in nothing but an inoffensive waste of their time. You throw your arms around a little, make strange pronouncements, meditate for a bit, and rely on the strength of your friends to keep you from any real harm.*

"Ro?"

I looked around trying to quell the sudden panic. There was a part of me that wondered where this doubt sprang from so abruptly. That part of me, however, did not doubt.

"Ro?" They were all looking at me now, plainly worried, which was not helpful.

What was the worst that could happen? Harakka was right. *Let's do this*, I thought, *and devils take the hindmost*. "Come, let us march against the powers of heaven," I said with a mad grin at Simon. "Ah friends, what shall we do? Carry me to war against the Wags." The predictable watermelon cantaloupe hubbub began, but I raised my hands to silence them. "Okay, not war exactly, but the effect should be the same in the end. We're setting a bear trap, and as the woman said, you don't need to catch 'em all, just one big fat one."

"Ro, are you insane?" Maggie asked without rancour but with plenty of concern. I marvelled again at her bright pretty face and how much I would miss it if this all went tails up.

"No, not insane, though I trust you to doubt it. Indulge me for a few and if nothing happens, I'll go along quietly to wherever you want to commit me. Deal?"

After looking at one another for a few seconds, they murmured assent and returned their gazes to me.

"What we're going to do is get a substitute for these guys." I jerked my head to indicate the owls, who still stood by silently watchful. "If we're lucky, there will be repercussions of a beneficial sort for the rest of us." And if we're not lucky, we're dead. Consequently, I was kind of leaning toward the whole Ro is crazy camp at present. But fortune favours the bold, right? Isn't that what Lucian said? Or was it Alexander of Sammy Sosa?

"So, what exactly are we going to do?" Simon said, looking a bit sceptical yet.

"Strike up the drums, march courageously, Fortune herself sits upon our crusts," Blank looks all around; serves me right trying to be literary. "Send me under, send me out to fetch one to bring back."

"One what?" Maggie looked frankly sceptical.

"A Wag, of course." Had I not been clear? Clear as the mud of this bay, no doubt. "That's the substitute."

"How—?" Simon started, but then suddenly stopped. "How can we help?"

"This means more drumming, doesn't it," Brendan said with overly dramatic weariness. Nonetheless, he picked up his drum and looked expectantly at me.

"Yup, but we have to be quick about it," I said, hearing

Harakka's urging in my ears. "I'll cast a quick circle and be on my way. I need all of you to hold onto me and bring me back." And to watch out when I do, because I won't be alone, argh. *I can't tell them that*, I warned Harakka.

They will know, she assured me. *They're catching on to all this quickly. Is this how it's going to be from now on?* Oh yeah, hell yeah, which one of us said that? Didn't matter, there was work to be done.

I grabbed Brendan's free hand next to me. "Hand to hand, I cast this circle."

He smiled at me, then when I nodded he understood, dropped the drum and picked up Maggie's hand, repeating, "Hand to hand, I cast this circle." Maggie followed suit, joining hands with Karasu, Karasu with Simon. Simon gave me a look and tentatively reached for the first of the Goons, repeating our mantra.

The Goons could not have been more surprised, but after a moment's hesitation, the one on the right lifted its wing and took awkward hold of Simon's hand. "Hand to hand…"

"To wing!" giggled Karasu and we all laughed.

"Hand to hand, I cast this circle," the Goon stubbornly repeated, taking up the wing of its partner, who repeated the steps and held its white feathers out to me. *Look at those eyes*, Harakka said somewhere inside me, *the wisdom of ages lies within them*. I found it too much to gaze into them, however, and flushed, feeling somehow graceless and gauche as I grasped its soft and surprisingly heavy wing. I could feel the charge though that assured me the casting worked.

"The circle is cast. We are between the worlds, standing at the gateway. Here we are protected, here I can move between states of being. I will be travelling not to another world, but across this one. I need you all to hold onto me, to help me return."

"This is like before, right?" Simon's brows showed his concern although his voice remained assured.

"Kind of." Yeesh, how to explain something that I didn't

really understand myself. "I will be connected to you all again with the same silver threads. All of you." I looked over at the Goons. I don't know why exactly I had cast them as some kind of adversaries, but I needed them and that amazing otherworldly power most of all. They were so impassive, though, that I didn't feel as if they would have any conviction about maintaining that contact with me. "Keep the circle around me, I need the protection. I'm going to ask you for a steady drum beat to give me wings, but it shouldn't take me long to be on my way. What I don't know is how long it will take me to get back. Simon and Maggie know how to check the lines; they saved my ass on the last journey." I shared a big gnashing grin with the two of them. God, I love my friends. "If all goes well, I'll be coming back with a Wag.

"Needless to say," then why am I saying it, I corrected myself, "this will be dangerous. Be careful, protect yourselves even at the risk of letting go of me. One way or another this has to work."

"Whoa, whoa, wait a minute," Simon said. "You didn't tell us what we were signing on for here. I'm all for getting a substitute, but not at the price of you."

"No way," Brendan added, less articulate but every bit as indignant.

"Guys," I tried to soothe them. "It will be all right."

"How do we know that?" Maggie broke in. "We just got done rescuing you from some insane mountain and we had to turn into bugs to do it and now you're saying that was all for nothing? Forget it, Ro, we're not risking it."

"So I should just give up? C'mon, *mes amis*, this is Saint Crispin's day for us. We have to come through, it's not just for us, it's for our little planet. I'm really not good at noble, but it's hill of beans time, you know."

"What the hell are you blathering about?" Simon said, his irritation plain. "What makes you think this will have the slightest impact on the world-wide infestation of these hot-rodding aliens? You're getting delusions of grandeur, kiddo."

"You're going to have to trust me on this."

"How many times have we heard that," Maggie said, arms folded and jaw set. "And every time it's the same disaster."

"What about this last time?" I thought I had a winner there. "Everything was fine."

I thought Maggie was going to lose her eyeballs, they hopped out so much with her indignation. "You nearly *died*! You call that 'fine'? You lost Harakka, we nearly lost you, and now we're stuck with this debt to pay that we don't really want to have to pay. Fine?"

"Maggie, it doesn't matter. We few, we happy few, we band of sisters and brothers and birds, we're all that might be able to pull this rapidly depleting planet back from the edge of disaster and chaos."

"You sure it's not too late already?" Simon said, but he was smiling.

"It may be. If so, well then, the fiends seize it, I'll end my days as an unrepentant elbow-crooker and give it up as a bad job. But there's a chance that it's not too late and this little thing may be just enough to tip the balance back in favour of our world. I just need your help while I make one more little trip."

"I'm in," Brendan said, striking his drum for emphasis. "I don't understand half of what happened here, but you'd have to be stupid to ignore what we've seen." His eyes seemed to blaze a kind of defiant fire that dared anyone to disagree. "Well, hell, if you think you can do it, Ro, I'm here."

I looked over at Maggie. She shrugged and then, to my surprise, laughed out loud. "Fucking hell, Ro. I should never believe you. If you screw this up, you'll be on carburettor duty for the rest of my life. Even if you're dead."

"Carburettor, uh, that's some kind of mechanical thing, right?" I grinned. "What about you, Karasu? You have every reason to doubt and you don't even know us that well."

She shrugged. "I've seen more than you think. Aleria has trained us well. I will do whatever is needed to save the planet. I believe."

Despite myself, I was impressed with this pint-sized warrior woman. As much as her way of speaking irritated me, I started to recognise the steel beneath the surface. "Thank you." I looked at the Goons, who continued to stare at me in their inscrutable way. I wouldn't deign to ask them a thing. They were only waiting after all, but they would have to help if they wanted their prize.

"Let the circle expand as far as it needs to do. Keep the beat steady and stay connected. And if there's trouble, save yourselves." The words came out with a cavalier grace but I was beginning to realise that the chances were awfully good. *I don't know what I'm doing, Harakka.*

All explorers feel their way along, she hushed me, *follow your gut.*

I lay down as they began to beat the drums, a little ragged at first but quickly gaining power as they found their groove. *Here we go,* I thought, perhaps needlessly, but Harakka answered, *it's going to be all right.*

Same old drill. I cleared my mind and headed for the tree that led to my temple. Once within the familiar black walls, I stopped and gathered myself. I jumped when Harakka spoke, because the voice came from outside me. "How shall we proceed, my dear?"

"Wha?" Now there was an unintelligible syllable.

"What did you expect? You carry me within in your waking world, but you can do whatever you wish here."

Huh. "When we move to another realm will you be inside or out? Just trying to keep track of things."

Harakka chuckled. "It will all depend upon you."

"Not what I want to hear right now." I sighed. When did I become an adult? "At least we're still together."

"Shall we go?"

I was delaying, she knew. "How will I know where to go? It's not like finding your world. I knew where that was."

"Picture where you want to go and just open the right door."

"It sounds so simple when you say it." But I knew it was. "I love you, Harakka. I'm so grateful you're still here with me."

"I'm grateful you kept me with you," she said with that weird bird cackle. "And I love you, too, Ro, as any fule kno."

I looked down at her in surprise. "I'm rubbing off on you, aren't I? This is disturbing."

"The lyf so short, the craft so long to lerne."

"All right, I'm going, I'm going." I drew in a deep breath, let it out as a sigh, and stepped up to the right door.

At once we were plunged into darkness and beset by a fetid odour. There was a kind of clanking noise and a grinding sound, as if some kind of machinery had not been adequately oiled before use. I fell to my knees and stumbled forward, groping for some purchase in the dark. I felt an edge that might be a door and tapped at it to no avail. I worked my way back up to my feet and let my fingers run along the edge of the joining until I found something that seemed to be a latch. I looked back into the darkness but could not see Harakka's white feathers gleam. *Fortune favours the bold*, I thought once more, and pressed on the latch. With a swish and a little grinding, the door whisked open and there it was: the cockpit.

I was on a Wag ship.

I couldn't tell if he, she? it? was more surprised than I was, but at least I had sort of planned to be here, so I had the drop on s/he. The one big eye blinked slowly at me and the jellied body squelched around to facilitate that movement. I couldn't stop staring at the horn on its head, which seemed, up close, to look more like an appendage than a tusky bone of some kind. Well, who had seen one this close and lived to tell, not that I was assuming I would.

However, I had at least a momentary respite because the Wag turned its attention back to flying the ship. The apparent control panel looked like a system of different coloured lights under a smooth transparent surface, well, transparent originally but now covered with various kinds of slimy trails that could just be effluvia from the Wag's body, or else spillage from various snacks. As I looked around the cabin, I started to guess the latter, because there was detritus everywhere. It was a real sty, there were even fast food wrappers littering the floor, jammed under the sort of chair, I guess, that it sat upon, a kind of hammock that seemed to be encrusted with ick.

Well, slob or no slob, I was going to have to make the final jump into that gelatinous mass. *Let's do it*, Harakka said, inside my head once more. *Now why do you have to sound like the end of a war film*, I scolded her, but I closed my eyes and jumped.

14

It wasn't at all what I expected—not that I'm sure what it was I had expected. The second leap took me within the creature, which was a very strange place indeed. Mind you, this comes from someone once trapped in death's limbo at the bottom of a mountain talking to a couple of owls, but trust me, being inside the mind and body of a Wag was something else entirely.

I had ridden along with other creatures before. Harakka had taught me how to do it. The first time, I hitched a ride with a hare. It was exhilarating to bounce along with its balletic hops. Naturally the second trip had to be with a tortoise, feeling the comforting weight of its home, the power of those claws and jaws. I'd been little more than a hitchhiker then, a thrill rider taking vicarious pleasure from the peculiarity of the experience. I had had no purpose.

Inside the skin of the Wag—was this gelatinous ooze skin, really?—I had to seize control and lead this ship back to the bay. How to do it? It was overwhelming enough just to be inside another mortal, let alone one so completely different from me, from us. Its thoughts, its feelings were so new. I struggled to maintain my own identity even as I invaded the Wag's interior. The animals I had hijacked did not seem to notice my presence, or so it had seemed. Would the Wag?

I tried to divine its true self, ignoring the distraction of a language I could not comprehend. It was difficult, no, not difficult, bloody impossible! *Relax, relax* – was that Harakka or me – focus on something you can do. Look through its eyes, er, eye. I peered forward and looked out to see the window and the control board, or whatever it might be on a ship like this. The Wag was touching something on the board that made the ship dip precipitously at a nearly forty-five degree angle and I saw another ship swoop dangerously closely right underneath us.

Great: they were playing their normal game of chicken, probably over some crowded urban centre, too. I tried to lean forward to see out the windscreen and found the Wag was going along with this inclination. In the back of my mind was the hope that having held the image of a Wag in mind as I set out, that I would simply go to the closest one. I'd hate to find myself in, say, Barcelona – especially since the ex-president's massacre and the explosions – but after looking fruitlessly at blasted mountains and clustered villages, I spotted something that made my heart leap with relief. It was the Old Man – or what was left of him since a Wag ship back in those first confusing days clipped off most of his profile.

All right, we were in New Hampshire. At the speeds this thing could fly, we could be back to the bay in minutes. All I needed to do was to get this Wag to fly in the right direction. So far, so good – the Wag had leaned down to give me a good view. Maybe it wouldn't be all that difficult to get it to bend to my will and fly back to Boston. On such foolish assumptions as these have whole nations fallen beneath the heels of conquerors.

I had no more than invoked that thought than I realised that something was amiss. Although I was concentrating on influencing the Wag to lean the ship more southerly, I began to sense a resistance and a growing noise. What the hell? I barely had time to express the thought before I understood what the noise was: the Wag knew I was there, or at least that there was someone interfering and it was babbling excitedly to its mates.

Listen to me: babble! A species so advanced as to make our notions of interstellar travel seem like cosmic pull-toys in space, here I was making fun of the way they spoke. But I couldn't quite put aside the picture of these adolescent thrill-seekers I had gleaned from my encounter in the depths of the mountain, so I maintained an indelible desire to smack down their destructive exuberance that had left our planet in ruins, fear and mutated warfare. No doubt our idiot species would find ways to keep the latter going, but I could at least cut down on the immediate scale of it if I were successful.

But success was not a given. The Wag was resisting and others seemed to be drawing near. Could it tell where I was? Could it even conceive of how I was infiltrating its phocine form? *Harakka, what do we do? Forge ahead, yes, forge ahead.* I concentrated on trying to persuade the Wag to fly toward the bay, focusing every intent on getting the ship moving on the right course. Initially it seemed to work. I could see the terrain arc beneath us as we shifted in a generally southern direction. In fact, in minutes I glimpsed what looked like Lake Winnipesaukee – at least what was left of it, a mud-strewn pit of refuse and baked brick wetlands – and a cheer rose to my ethereal lips.

It was quickly quashed by the Wag's frenzied response, ripping the ship's orbit back into the opposite route. Grimly determined, I redoubled my efforts and managed to swing the ship back around. I knew I needed to distract the pilot, too, so I changed tactics. The first inspiration came from childhood – exactly the ways I distracted my sisters.

I yelled. I went "la la la la la!" I sang the Banana Splits theme song. I repeated the words to the most jangling poetry that I knew, out of order, half-remembered. The Wag was trembling with anger. At least it was paying less attention to the way the ship flew. It was convenient to have two personalities with me, one to distract and one to direct.

Another sound intruded into my consciousness gradually. It was the garbled eructation that surely came from the other Wags, a kind of inter-ship communication. They knew something was up. This was a problem, surely? Can I throw them off the trail? Probably not. Have to concentrate. Wait – all I needed to do was shut off the communication link. Was it mechanical? Or were they conversing directly head to head? I couldn't really tell.

"Maggie!" I reached for the silver thread that linked us, although I was beginning to feel like Durga with eighteen arms. As soon as the thought took form, of course, the extra limbs sprouted. I'll think about that tomorrow, I hastily promised myself and reached for all the threads. "Maggie, Simon, Brendan, Karasu! We need to block the transmissions between the Wags."

"We hear you, Ro, we'll do it if we can," Simon answered, sounding a little doubtful.

"Listen, do you hear their burbling?" I tried to make sure the sounds were humming along the silver chords, like primitive electricity. "Go Phil Spector on their asses, make a huge wall of sound that saturates the airwaves between them." I don't know what I thought would happen, but I was suddenly blown back by the force of the chatter that ensued. Like a flock of garrulous seagulls my friends unleashed such a cacophony that even I was momentarily nonplussed, forgetting exactly what I had been doing.

I only hoped it would produce the same effect on the Wags. Certainly mine was disturbed by yet another assault overwhelming its hedonistic fun. It jumped up – what a sight! Its manifold layers jiggled intensely with the effort, and a screeching erupted that was quite unlike its previous emissions. It sounded, for all the world, like a child's temper tantrum, which I suppose it was. It careered around the cockpit, striking out impotently with its noodley appendages and gaping with its stomach mouth. We kept up the verbal assault and I maintained the influence upon the navigation that was bringing us to the coastline now and heading the ship toward the bay. C'mon, c'mon, I begged the Wag, the ship, my friends, the universe, the Wits, the Goons, and Durga for good measure – this has just got to work.

I wanted to crow when I saw the bay open up ahead of me, but I figured it would be fatal to lose a moment's concentration. Instead I took a firmer grip on the Wag's consciousness with my multiple arms. The being seemed shocked to find itself in a kind of mental embrace, which limited its already circumscribed movements. It fought like a five-year old too tired for bed. Such screeching! I had never heard anything like it, and while the sounds were all inside my head, (my head! my projected head, I suppose), they were none the less effective for all that. How I longed for ear plugs. *Harakka, how can we stand this?* I wondered. *It's not for much longer,* she soothed. *Focus, focus.*

I had one thought: *down, down, down.* Set the ship down, there by the edge of the poisoned water, into the muck, not too near my friends, but not too far away either. What did the Wag think? Whuuhorrrragh, I heard. What did it mean? I wasn't sure, but I was going to ignore it anyway because all that mattered was setting that ship down exactly where I wanted it.

But the Wag was onto me. With a shriek of annoyance – amazing it seemed to feel no sense of danger at all, just insurmountable irritation with my attempts at interference. It tried to wrest control of the ship back from me. I wasn't sure if the other Wags were in the proximity, but I had to chance it.

"Everyone," I yelled back to my friends, "Pull hard, pull us toward the shore. Just grab hold of anything you can sense along the wires, jerk it hard and get us down." I was unprepared again for the force of their compliance. All at once the ship was rolling ass over tit through the air, plummeting toward the bay. I had horrible images of ploughing right into the mud, suffocating under that primeval ooze. The Wag seemed to be worrying about the same thing all of the sudden, whipping its appendages into action, slapping at the control board as if it were some insane Whack-a-mole carny game. With a jerk the ship righted itself but the ground was coming up at us with precipitous speed. I could not hear the expected squeal of brakes, but our downward descent was slowing rapidly although perhaps not hastily enough to forestall impact. If this creature were to splatter across the windscreen of this vehicle, would I be killed too – and Harakka as well? Had I survived the magic mountain because I was anchored in another reality, or because my friends revived me from actual death? Would the Wag be killed by the impact or did they have more resilience than our fragile fleshly forms? I imagined a splat and reconstitution as quick as a tennis ball. Oh Webster, you were so right, here we are about to be struck and bandied as may be—all this and so much more babbled in my head as I let the short seconds elapse in a paroxysm of confused panic. Some mystic traveller I was.

The impact, when it came, was both worse than and different from what I expected. In the rubious dawn light the ship met the rancid surface of the bay and wedged decisively into the mud. We were all splatted against the now-useless window which proved surprisingly painful for something I was experiencing only ethereally. I suppose the positive side of a gelatinous body is that there are few breakable structures, nonetheless the massive dislocation of flesh across the unforgiving window was sorely resplendent in its dolorousness. It hurt like hell.

Consequently, we were all reeling as the Wag picked itself up from the darkened glass and staggered to the hatch. I was trying to shake the agonizing swirl from my noggin and I could feel Harakka doing the same. So much for the joyride—I had not known just how vulnerable one could be while hitching these rides. But the job wasn't done yet. As the Wag lurched forward, I tried to re-establish our control. At first I could do little more than gain a sense of equilibrium as the creature itself did, but I reached out for the strings that bound me to my friends and sensed their worry. I was quick to send reassurance, "We're fine, fine," but also knew they needed to be braced for another round of tug-o-war.

"When we get outside, drag us toward the circle, but not inside it," I explained, hoping they would remember that all important detail. "And don't leave the circle, whatever you do!" God, my head was reeling still from the impact. I could almost see the cartoon birdies and stars swirling around my noggin. Did the Wag feel this way as well? I could hear it muttering under its breath, (did they breathe? How did their anatomy work anyway?), but it didn't immediately call for help or signal to its pals.

Getting to the hatch proved to be more of an ordeal that I expected. Wags are not made for locomotion. Massive plops of jelly are not aerodynamic. So we waddled to the hatch where the Wag made a number of complicated swiping motions at another kind of control panel, plunged a kind of object into its gob. Was it a breathing apparatus? Weapon? Music player? What would the Wags' hit parade sound like: I'm just a jellyroll for your love? Put your gelatinous appendage on my shoulder? *How hard did you hit your head,* Harakka asked at last. Can you get a virtual concussion?

At last with a nigh on silent whoosh, the hatch opened to allow fetid water and slime to crest up over the opening, making the Wag moan in what was surely irritation. Who wants swamp juice all over their shiny hot rod? It blorped its way out of the machine, then turned as if to survey the extent of the damage. I almost expected the Wag to put its arms on its approximation of hips, but apparently that gesture is unique to our species. Would it call to its mates for assistance—or some kind of Wag AA roadside service? We might not have much time, so I grabbed hold with some of my Durga-esque hands and yanked on the silver threads with the others.

I wasn't prepared for the sudden yelping motion as we flew backwards toward the circle. The Wag, too, was hit unawares and made a confused grunt as we schoonered across the surface of the brackish bay. As we were dragged toward my friends, I could see the Wag's ship dipped into the waters like a discarded dinner plate. Nothing makes high-tech machinery look as foolish as being knee-deep in the oldest elements. On this planet anyway, gravity was the ultimate arm-biter. Water, while scarce and largely polluted still had massive force when it chose to employ it. Hello, Boston.

The Wag was howling now, though whether with pain or merely frustration, it was hard to tell. I was sure it was itching to eat somebody to make it feel all hunky-dory once more, so I fervently hoped my friends remembered that key point of the circle's safety. Maybe I was selling the Wag short—maybe it bore us no malice, perhaps it only thought of us as primitive food on the hoof. "Can you believe it?" one Wag might say to another, "They walk right up to be eaten. So docile." Did it still think that with one of the cattle in its head? Did it even recognise me to be part of the same species? The Wits were able to communicate with me easily—was it because they wanted to do so? The Wag didn't seem to get across the language barrier and I certainly couldn't seem to manage it either. I almost missed the cool precision of the Wits.

Well, I did say almost.

We were skidding across the mud shore now, just yards away from the circle. The Wag had twisted its head around to see where it was headed, so I could see where my prone body lay at the centre of the ring. Everyone was leaning in, concentrating on pulling this lumpy form into their midst. For a second I seized on the image: my friends, my amazing friends. Look at them all. Simon, who days ago was deep in a coma; Maggie, who days ago would believe none of this; Brendan, who days ago didn't even know me, let alone trust me to plonk him down in the middle of alien shenanigans and travels to other worlds—and Karasu? Well, I barely knew her at all, but I had absolute faith in her abilities, not for me or even for my friends, but because she believed in something bigger than any one of us, or all of us together. Damn, I was lucky.

The Wag was trying vainly to slow its hurtling toward this group, snatching at the ground with whatever it could muster. I could sense a definite whiff of fear, probably something it had not been accustomed to experiencing on our planet where they had ridden rough-shod for so long, (*what does that phrase mean?* I idiotically quizzed Harakka, expecting no answer, though she telegraphed a quick *tell you later—concentrate!*).

With a jerk, our forward momentum suddenly halted. The Wag blinked at the circle of humans and made several protesting sounds, but it didn't seem to want to make a break for it or immediately charge into action and start chowing down. It seemed like the right time to make my move. Leaving another's body was as ticklish as jumping into it in the first place. You didn't want to take more with you than what you brought in the first place.

In a trice I was back in my own body, barely touching down in the temple at all, experiencing it mostly as a flutter of Harakka's wings as we crossed through. I sat up only to get hit with a double whammy of nausea and light-headedness. Guess I was carrying the virtual concussion with me. But I had to shake it off. "Stay inside the circle, guys!" I reminded them, although everyone seemed braced and alert. Simon gave me a solemn nod but Maggie just kept her eyes fixed on the Wag.

I turned to the Goons. "There you go, wrapped up with a bow."

They stared at me.

"Your substitute!" How could they not understand? They looked at each other. I looked at them. We looked at the Wag, who looked back at us from its one eye. Any minute now it looked like it was going to make a break for it. Well, when I say break, I suppose I meant that it would rumble off in its gelatinous way back toward its ship – or worse, call its mates for help, which seemed both a distinct possibility and the worst possible outcome. "Take it!" I urged the Goons, but still they stood dumbly. Were they looking for a handhold? Giftwrap?

"Ro, what the hell?" Simon seemed to share my irritation, either that or it was proving contagious. "Why won't they take it?"

I was wondering that myself. "Hey, we went to a lot of trouble to get you this substitute. Why aren't you taking it?"

At last the Goons, responded. "This one is very different."

True enough. "You said a substitute. You weren't specific about the kind. One living being for another, eh?"

They seemed to dither. "You are asking us to accept a very limited sort of creature in the place of one with many skills and abilities."

"It will learn new skills and er, abilities with your help."

"It will not," they responded with granite implacability. "It comes to us as it is. It becomes part of our reality."

The Wag looked at the Goons as if it was beginning to realise that they held its fate in their claws. It began to struggle against the bonds that held it. I flashed the circle with a quick pleading look, and everyone snapped back into action. "I think you've got me all wrong. I am offering you a rare and special creature here." Under my eyelashes I sneaked a look at Simon. I saw the grin flit across his face. He knew.

"These are the creatures that brought our world to its knees," he offered, tag-teaming with me just like the stupid old days, when we talked ourselves out of jams with free-traders and zombie runners. "They took over the planet."

"We have been at their mercy for years now," I added, turning on the note of pleading that once worked with my parents, but only up until the age of five. It still worked with my boss, though. "They form a vast network of ruthless killers and sadistic overlords." The ruthless creature in question muttered on, no doubt figuring that we were selling it out.

"We are helpless before them," Maggie added. "Take this one, understand it, absorb it—whatever it is you do."

"Right," I said, picking up her thread, "this individual is a piece of the whole. They are part of a collective mind that you will be able to assimilate."

"It's far more than what we have removed," Simon suggested winningly.

The Goons looked more carefully at the Wag, which mirrored their doubtful looks.

"Look at the sophistication of that ship!" I thought that was a rather good point myself. "It provides ample evidence of the advanced nature of their culture and their knowledgeability." Never mind that they were like teens in their folks' cars, motoring around the 'verse without the slightest idea of what lay under the hood, so to speak. I suddenly understood that was why they were crashing and burning. They really had no idea how the things ran, and the ships were beginning to break down. All we had to do was wait— and hope none of them drove the intergalactic equivalent of a Honda, or the wait would be an interminably long one. But if we could speed things up—all the better.

For their part, the Goons seemed to be considering it. They didn't harrumph and confer, but they did incline their heads a little closer together. Simon and Maggie continued to offer helpful suggestions about the superior nature of the Wags ("their eating habits alone show wonderful efficiency and advanced motor development!"). The Wag seemed to have figured out that it was in a tight spot and was bugling for its mates. The plaintive sound of its cries made me wonder if it weren't being ignored.

Nonetheless, it seemed that the Goons had decided in favour of the trade. "We accept," they said simply, and before I could draw two breaths, they had moved to flank the surprised looking Wag, taken its viscous appendages in their wings and were gone. There wasn't even a puff of smoke.

We all stood for a minute or so, blinking at each other in the pale dawn. My head still ached, but I felt a sense of relief that grew with each moment. It worked! It damned well worked! I saw my lopsided grin reflected in the faces around me. With a whoop I ran and embraced Simon and dragged in Maggie and then we were all in a big knot, laughing hysterically and jumping up and down. "Let the circle be open!" I yelled to no one in particular, or maybe just to Harakka.

"You did it!" Brendan laughed, his face flushed an excited pink.

"*We* did it," I corrected, but gave him a bear hug anyway, followed up by a very warm kiss.

Simon elbowed his way in and stole those lips from mine. I was grabbed by Maggie who planted a happy kiss on me, too. I hugged her fiercely. "I'm sorry for everything," I whispered in her elfish ear.

"No, you're not," she laughed.

Karasu, not apart from us and yet separate, was the first to say, "Sirens."

We lifted up our heads like a herd of caribou (or so the natural history channel lied to me). Sure enough, sirens were coming. It was a newsworthy sight, the downed Wag ship. We had to motor or we were going to have some explaining to do. God, my sister might even show up.

"We can go back to my house," Karasu said, gathering up her drum and the blanket she'd brought. "We can figure out what to do now. I think we have a good chance of fighting the Wags now with all you've learned."

Maggie nodded, grabbing her things as well, but Simon stopped me from doing the same. He looked rather gravely at me and at Brendan. "I'm not going."

"What do you mean?" Maggie demanded.

"I'm not going," Simon repeated. "I'm getting drafted, remember? I'm not going back. I never planned to go back."

"What—where are you going to go?" I asked as if I didn't know.

"The summer place." Of course, the old family shack—a twenty room mansion with acres of land on the temperate shore of an island.

Nova Scotia!

"Whoa, kiddo—are you planning to do a runner?"

"Yes," Simon said, arms folded, mind made up. "I already looked into it. The protocols with the commonwealth have been suspended since the beginning of the war. They won't send me back if I can get in."

"Curse their independent Canadian hides," I said with a laugh. "Never could follow the rules of the mother land. You know you may lose all your assets and credits."

Simon laughed, but there was something harsh in the laugh. "Nothing like ten years in a coma to make you lose all attachment to funds."

"Guys," Maggie said, "They're getting closer."

"You ever been to Nova Scotia?" I asked Brendan.

"Nope."

"You got room for two more?"

Simon laughed at me.

"Ro, don't be an idiot," Maggie said grabbing my arm.

"What are you going to do?" I asked her.

"I'm going back to Aleria's. I'm..." She paused and looked at me a tad defiantly. "I'm going to stay there and work with them. There's nothing for me back home either." It was to her credit that she didn't sound bitter.

I wrapped my arms around her and squeezed. "I think that's wonderful." But I was a little surprised to see tears on her cheek when she drew back. "We can work together on the rest of the Wags. I got an idea."

There were lights as well as sirens now, shattering the early light with garish bloody gases of crimson. We could hear the screeches as the various vehicles sought the nearest possible parking to the shore.

"How are you going to get there?" Maggie asked Simon, hastily wiping her cheek.

"Up to Portland, over to Yarmouth. We can find a bushie willing to fly us over, I bet. There were always some willing to do anything for the right amount of cash. I ought to have enough money to get us all over there."

"Sounds like the beginning of a beautiful friendship," I said with a grateful smile.

"We have to go," Karasu said, pointing at the approaching phalanx. "They'll be here in a minute."

The three of us hugged Maggie and Karasu. "We'll write, we'll call," I promised. Then we took to our heels and ran toward the north shore as the press crawled over the muddy shingle. They went straight for the ship, many of them wading out to peer into the still-open hatch. As we blended into the gathering knot of onlookers, I saw a couple of the more astute types flag down Maggie and Karasu, who shrugged to show their complete ignorance of the goings-on. *Be safe, Maggie May*, I sent the thought out to her, knowing she wouldn't hear but feeling better for it anyway. It was the right thing to do, Harakka agreed.

"You sure you want to go to Canada and break the law," I asked Brendan. In the early light he looked younger and even more beautiful with those perfectly blue and somewhat asymmetrical eyes and that nose that twisted just a little to the left. Gorgeous, just gorgeous.

He smiled and slung his arms around the two of us. "Sure, why not? If I don't like it, I can sneak back. I got a lot of sneaky training, you know, the army and all."

"Pity we couldn't fly the Wag ship," Simon said with a touch of wistfulness.

"This is just like the end of *Casablanca*," I told him as we turned and started hoofing it toward Charlestown.

"No, it isn't," Simon said. "If it were, you'd be on the plane and I'd be walking away with Claude Rains."

"You ever been bit by a dead Wag?" Brendan asked.

"Have you seen the sirens of Titan," I said, not wanting to be left out all together.

"No," the two said in unison, "but I've heard them wail."

"It's going to be a long walk to Portsmouth," I said, pretending to be cranky. Brendan took that as a cue to sing the words to the tune of "Tipperary" and Simon put his arm around my waist as we walked side by side. "There's no place like home."

"Home is where the heart is," Simon said, his eyes on Brendan's profile.

"Harakka says keep watching the skies," I said, feeling a momentary chill.

"Does she think we can get rid of the Wags?"

"Well, we can help them to depart sooner than they would have."

"But there's nothing worse out there, right?" Simon smiled, watching Brendan walk backwards, still singing. I shook my head, despite what Harakka murmured in my heart. "Good. For a minute there, I thought we might be in trouble."

About the Author

K. A. Laity is the author of the novels *Owl Stretching*, *Pelzmantel*, *The Mangrove Legacy*, *Chastity Flame* and the collections *Unquiet Dreams* and *Unikirja*, as well as other stories, plays and essays. Her stories tend to slip across genres and categories, but all display a lively intelligence and humour. Myths and fairy tales influence much of her writing. The short stories in *Unikirja* found their inspiration from *The Kalevala, Kanteletar*, and other Finnish myths and legends: the stories won Laity the 2005 Eureka Short Story Fellowship and a 2006 Finlandia Foundation grant.

Dr. Laity teaches medieval literature, film, digital humanities and popular culture at the College of Saint Rose in New York, though she was at NUI Galway as a Fulbright scholar for the 2011-2 academic year.

Laity grew up in Michigan, where you are never more than six miles from a lake or river. Her hometown is Lansing, but she spent a lot of time at the family cabin in Kaleva, as well in the glorious forests, rivers and lakes of the various state parks. She's lived in many places and loves to travel, spending a lot of time in the British Isles. A stick insect at the Butterfly World Project has been named in her honour (can't top that!).

Lightning Source UK Ltd.
Milton Keynes UK
UKOW02f0212040814

236264UK00002B/14/P